Soul Betrayer

Ubiquity Book 2

Allyson Lindt

Chapter One

Michael thought this would get easier. The first time he was forced to tear a foreign power from another angel, to banish her to the worst fate any agent could suffer, regret threatened to consume him.

These days, *seek* was status quo, but *destroy* still left an aching pit in his chest. He hated sentencing the beings of heaven and hell—his colleagues—to an eternity of non-existence.

With luck, this time no one would have to die. If he lingered on it too long, guilt would paralyze him with indecision.

Lights flickered in the hotel hallway, as if mocking his hope, and a faint breeze from the air conditioner rushed over him. He paused in front of the room Abaddon gave him the number for, and extended his ethereal reach enough to feel, but not so much he would register on his target's radar.

Jagged edges of aura pushed back, slicing his senses. This was the place.

The red glow of an LED stared back at him from the electronic lock. A single shock from his finger, nothing to leave burns or traces, and he could short-circuit the device. This was something he loved about technology—destroying it was so much more subtle than blowing a hole through a door.

He wanted to give this guy the benefit of the doubt, though. No reason to barge in unannounced. He knocked.

Since he started hunting, he'd torn the extraneous power and the very essence from several angels, but this was his first demon. Not that there was much difference. They were created in separate places, but in the end, *demon* and *angel* were simply labels. Maybe being named in hell would make Azazel more pliable. Not that Michael believed it. All agents started as nondescript sources of power that appeared either in heaven or hell. A cherub served until one of the original angels—himself, Gabriel, or Lucifer—gave it a name.

A name granted purpose, made the cherub a demon or angel, and allowed then to assume a physical form.

The door swung open. Azazel's aura flickered and danced in spikes of light, bleeding into the dimly light hallway, as if the power inside him didn't know who was in control. That explained the jagged sensation Azazel radiated. The demon had an extraneous cherub. For reasons yet to be discovered, a century or two back cherubs started appearing on earth. They couldn't survive without a physical form, and survival instinct drove them to inhabit the first they came across. Sometimes human, other times an inanimate object. Recently, agents discovered merging with one meant extra power. Judging by the electricity show Azazel emitted, sharing his brain with another entity was wreaking havoc on his psyche.

"The great and mighty Michael." Azazel leaned against the doorframe, boredom in his tone. "So it's true."

This looked more cliché with each passing moment, down to the cheesy script. If Ronnie were here, she'd have a sarcastic retort. Her name added an ache of longing to the pit of disappointment growing inside. He extended his energy through the room and surrounding area. Nothing big or obvious, simply a blanket to hide their activity from passersby and keep Azazel from phasing someplace else.

"Azazel, you are in violation of the agents' code of conduct. You've taken another life, in order to further your needs. Surrender the cherub now, and you'll be granted absolution. Refuse, and your existence ends this evening."

Michael wasn't fond of the memorized monologue. When he helped innocents integrate, he played things by ear. After the first few *Seek and Destroy* missions, when he realized none of his colleagues would yield, he came up with the speech. It kept things simple.

"Who says they're lives?" Azazel asked.

Michael swallowed a sigh. "This isn't a philosophical discussion about what defines life. Cherubs are sentient, not energy drinks. You don't get to pluck one out of existence because you need a little pick-me-up."

Azazel furrowed his brow, as if considering the words, then his posture shifted, back going rigid and fists clenching. "I guess we'll have to agree to disagree."

Michael's shield wobbled, tugging at him from the inside like someone trying to yank off a bandage. Azazel flickered then solidified again. He was stuck. Perfect. Michael reached for his arm. Once contact was made, Michael would absorb the foreign entity, send it back to heaven, return Azazel's energy to hell, and destroy the name that granted him distinction.

In the milliseconds it took Michael to summon his strength, laughter clattered down the hallway. A family rounded the corner. Mother and father in their early twenties, daughter four years old. The stats flowed through Michael in a blink, as any mortal's information did.

To the family's eyes, the two men standing in the hallway would look like they were having a calm conversation. It was part of Michael's shield. If anything seemed amiss, it would vanish from their thoughts by the time they reached their room.

Knowing that didn't stop Michael from hesitating. They were innocent. Another thing he knew without question.

The tugging adhesive feeling shattered, and Michael stumbled from the recoil, as his energy wall crumbled and fled back into him.

"Hello." The girl waved at them.

"Hi there, darlin'." Azazel crouched to her eye level. "You havin' a good evening?" He could have phased from the building, and no one would have been wiser. Why did he engage instead?

Tension tightened every muscle in Michael's body. Keeping people safe—ensuring lives weren't ended—was his primary goal.

Discretion was paramount as well. The world didn't need to think heaven and hell saw earth as an open battlefield. The media devoured stories about exploding balls of flame crashing into city buildings. That was thanks to Ariel, the first angel Michael went through this process with. Since her destruction, he'd prevented any more public act-of-God-like displays.

Mom grabbed the girl's hand. "Come on, honey. Pizza's getting cold."

Michael felt the sparks race across his skin at the same time he saw Azazel's aura flare. The instinct to protect humanity at all costs took over, and Michael flung out a new blockade of energy, shielding the family and fogging their minds at the same instant Azazel brought a crack of lightning crashing through the four stories above them, through the floor, and to the ground twenty feet below.

A gaping, smoldering hole stood where Azazel had been an instant earlier. The stench of burning wood and melting synthetic carpet singed Michael's sinuses, and smoke rose into the now-visible sky.

The girl screamed, terrified at the sight, and her mother joined in.

Michael wanted to comfort them. He itched to sooth the distressed family, or better yet, shift their world so it had never happened. Memory fogging worked for glitches—things people would rather ignore. A five-foot crater running through a hotel? That couldn't be masked.

Their fear and panic were tangible, permeating his skin, drilling into him thanks to inherent empathy. It left the foul taste of chalk in his mouth, and ached in his joints. The wide eyes they turned on him sparked with distrust. An almost tangible bubble of *back the fuck off* radiated from the family. He cast an invisible platform over the hole on every floor, so no one would fall in. It would dissolve in about an hour, and as long as no one tripped or stumbled into it, they'd never know. However, he'd risk reports of people walking on air to keep anyone from getting hurt.

He hated to step away instead of reach out to the family, but his options were limited. Blinking out of site to move to a new location wasn't possible here. Their eyes were wide open right now, and he wouldn't be able to make them forget anything they saw. As he strode for the stairs, irritation and frustration mounting, he pulled his cell phone from his pocket and dialed 911. "Yes. I'd like to report a freak act of God." He gave them the address.

The moment he entered the stairwell, he phased to his ethereal form and vanished from the mortal plane. It had taken him months to track down Azazel, and now the bastard was gone again, leaving destruction and terror in his wake.

I could reach out to Ronnie. See if Ubiquity has anything on him. Michael growled at the errant thought, and the surge of longing that mingled with his frustration. He didn't understand why he still missed her, but giving into the impulse to see her again wouldn't further his cause.

This was going to be a long decade.

* * * *

Ronnie gave Izzy a tight hug. "I'm glad you're doing better," she said and stepped back. Izrafel was a fallen angel who had gotten caught in the crossfire when Ariel, one of Ronnie's colleagues, made a bid for more power, and destroyed half the city in the process.

Some angels and demons chose to fall and become mortal because they no longer believed in what they did. Izzy was one of those who had decided he'd grown as much as he could ethereally, and opted for mortality as a chance to become more.

The foot traffic outside the corner coffee shop parted around them, people going about their day. She nodded at Holden, the man standing next to him.

She didn't want to admit it, but she was a little jealous of Holden having caught Izzy's eye. Sure, she had Irdu, who was incredible. She missed Michael, as much as she was trying to get over him.

But Izzy was sweet. And sexy. And smart—which was like extra sexy on top of it all. It was a good thing demons and angels didn't believe in things like monogamy, or Ronnie would think she was getting greedy. "And it was nice to meet you. I hate to cut and run, but…"

Izzy gave her fingers another squeeze before letting go. "I never thought I'd see the day that a lost, amnesiac demon would become a corporate drone."

"I'm not a drone." She focused on the teasing banter, and not the way Holden rarely took his eyes off her. The afternoon heat beating down on her exposed shoulder blades was pleasant. His gaze? A lot more blistering and uncomfortable. She wanted to think the heavy stare was because he knew she lusted after his boyfriend. It probably wasn't. "I'm more like a queen bee."

"Right. Tuesday night?" Izzy asked.

"I'll be there." She waved over her shoulder as she strolled away. She could have phased back to work, but she wanted to take her time returning. That, and Holden might not be so easily compelled to forget her blinking out of sight. If he was a prophet, and had the ability to see a demon or angel's aura, he'd witnessed enough weird shit in his life that he'd remember someone vanishing in front of him.

The moment she rounded the corner, she dialed a familiar number.

"How'd it go?" Lucifer asked.

"Next time do your own dirty work." She liked Lucifer. In a past life she'd loved him. It meant she was a sucker for his requests, and he knew it.

"That good, huh?"

The memory of Holden's attention sent chills down her spine. "Creepy bastard wouldn't stop staring at me. An entire meal, and I'm supposed to pretend I don't notice?"

"So he either knows what you are, or he's worried you're trying to steal is boyfriend."

Busted. "I should have just asked him." Ronnie rolled her eyes. "*Hey. Are you glued to the fact I glow, or are you just jealous of the way your guy watches me when I'm in a skirt?* I'm not doing this again."

"You mentioned that." His voice came from next to her, instead of through her phone. "This isn't about me."

She glanced sideways to confirm he'd fallen into step beside her, and then she pocketed her phone. "Yeah, yeah. Greater good and all that bullshit. Even if it weren't for the whole gawking-boyfriend thing, I don't like lying to Izzy."

"You've mentioned that too. You'd rather tell him the man he loves is using him to get insider information?"

"I'd rather not tell him anything, but—"

"My point."

God. He was so infuriating sometimes. It figured one of her closest allies, the only person she could talk to about this situation, was Lucifer. Arbitrator for humans and agents alike. She'd love to talk to Irdu about it, but she'd been sworn to secrecy. She hated lying to her boyfriend. "You know that's not what I mean. I'd rather he know the truth, and if that's the reality of the thing…"

"Don't blow this for sentiment. Who do you have watching him?"

"Tia, but that's not the point." Tiamet was a demon Ronnie had worked with when she was in retrieval. Tia loved office gossip, and—like most demons—good ice cream. She wasn't powerful, but she made it up in enthusiasm. She was also Ronnie's boyfriend's sister. Not that anyone could know—demons weren't supposed to have siblings.

Izzy's safety was always a concern, but more now because until a few months ago, he hosted a cherub. It had been stripped from him, leaving him more mortal than he was used to. He didn't understand the limits of his human body yet.

Ronnie might feel better about the whole thing if she knew whom to be worried about. As a conglomeration of Metatron, an original angel who Gabriel tried to destroy thousands of years ago, and Uriel, the cherub Lucifer named and tried to use to bring Metatron back to life, Ronnie had both of their memories. But the few thousand year gap between one vanishing off the radar and the other popping into existence meant she didn't know who the power players were in heaven and hell. It wasn't as if there were a company roster somewhere that said *these agents might be mentally unstable, and lusting after power.*

Lucifer and Ronnie passed a candy shop, and she watched the taffy maker spinning in the window, until it was too awkward to walk and study the hypnotic rhythm at the same time. The place had the best homemade caramel.

"If you think I'm wrong about Holden, why haven't you said anything to Izzy yet?" Lucifer asked.

Because she wasn't *certain.* Admitting that doubt made her feel weak somehow.

"Exactly." His tone implied he knew what she was thinking.

Arrogant ass. "If it's not true, I'm not going to break Izzy's heart over it. He's happy with this Holden guy." Besides, if it was true—if Holden was involved in a string of agent disappearances—Izzy was her and Lucifer's way to get to him. And Izzy was a lot more likely to play the doting-boyfriend role if he was actually a doting boyfriend.

"It'll all work out. I promise." A smooth assurance bled into Lucifer's tone. "We've got at least a day until the apocalypse." And with that, he vanished.

"*That's not funny,*" she shouted at the empty air.

"It's not supposed to be." His voice whispered in her ear, though he was nowhere to be seen.

A few people turned to stare at her, and a couple others crossed the street. She didn't care. Ever since she figured out how to merge the two voices in her head into one, she was secure in her sanity. Having the memories of two separate individuals might be disconcerting, but it didn't make her nuts.

She was tempted to turn around now, go back to Izzy, and pull him aside for a serious conversation. She'd been on the receiving end of Lucifer's *it's for your own good* deceptions. After he named her Uriel, and stuck Metatron in her head, he lied to her for months about why she heard voices, hoping things would just work themselves out. She figured it out eventually, but things would have gone a lot faster if she had the truth up front.

This was different. Angels and demons were disappearing from Ubiquity and around the world, and Holden could have the answers to why. Lucifer didn't want to spook him. He and Ronnie didn't want to be wrong, and they did want to find their people before Holden and his friends had a chance to—

She wasn't sure what the consequences would be. But humans kidnapping agents? Finding a way to restrain them without getting their asses kicked? That couldn't be good.

If Michael were here, she'd have someone with a little more worldly experience to bounce her thoughts off. She bit the inside of her cheek, hoping the external pain would scrub his name from her mind. It didn't work. Loneliness hammered against her ribs, begging her to seek out one of the few beings who tied her past to her present.

It was his decision to leave though, and she refused to chase after an angel who would rather be a ghost than feel anything outside of duty.

She did have someone she could talk to, though. Even if she couldn't tell Irdu everything, she could speak in generic terms. *Which means more lying.* Maybe she'd just pop into his office and say *Hello* instead.

All it took was a thought *Ubiquity*, and she stood outside his ajar office door. She nudged it open a few more inches and poked her head in to see him engrossed in his work.

As an Incubus, most people saw him as whatever they considered attractive. For her, that was his natural appearance. Kool Aid red hair, tall, wiry frame, and piercing amber eyes.

"Do you have a minute?" She asked.

He looked up, startled, and a wicked grin crept in. "I might have as many as two or three if you want to cuddle after."

Ronnie laughed as she stepped into his office and closed the door behind her. She and Irdu were still finding their footing in their relationship, but it was almost guaranteed he'd put a smile on her face.

He hadn't always been a demon. Once upon a time he was mortal, and a cherub found him. Unlike any other mortal that happened to, Lucifer happened on him, and made him a full-fledged incubus. Irdu had negotiated the same deal for his sister, Tia, to save her life. In return, he did Lucifer's bidding and kept the secret of his origins.

Ronnie wasn't even supposed to know, but Irdu's telling her had helped save her sanity. Then again, a lot of what they did for each other—sex and otherwise—helped keep the two of them sane.

Irdu was in front of her in a blink, tangling his fingers in her hair and nipping at her lips. "You're exactly what I was looking for," he murmured against her neck.

"On your computer? You're not going to find me there." Another twinge of guilt nudged her at another secret she was keeping from him. This one not so big, just a bit more embarrassing.

"Good thing you showed up then. I might have wasted an entire afternoon."

She hooked her fingers at the base of his neck and pressed into him. "I think management prefers you call it *work* rather than wasted time."

"Fuck management." He dragged his fingers up her leg. "Starting with you. Only question is, on the desk or against the window?"

She hadn't come here for sex, but it was certainly better than thinking. "It's the middle of the day. Agents are going to see if you press me against the glass."

"Window it is." He gripped her hips and spun her away from the door.

Her phone chimed with the ringtone she used for office numbers.

"Ignore them." Irdu dug his fingers into her skin. "You're in a meeting."

He made a compelling argument. Normally her body didn't hold onto injury. He had a gift as an incubus for leaving the most delicious sting behind when he wanted.

His desk phone rang.

"Don't they know we're trying to have a moment?" She buried her head against his chest with a groan.

The ringing stopped, and then both phones went off at the same time.

Irdu sighed and let her go. He pressed the *Speaker* button on his phone. "Yeah."

"Don't suppose you have our wonderfully charming COO in your office." Samael's voice sounded hollow.

"Nope. Haven't seen her," Irdu said, gaze locked on Ronnie the entire time.

Fraternization wasn't against Ubiquity rules— agents liked fucking too much to enforce a policy like that. But Ronnie and Irdu were one of the few relationships that had lasted longer than it took to contaminate the janitor's closet.

Samael sighed heavily. "Sure. If you do see her, tell her we're being investigated by the Securities and Exchange Commission."

The SEC. But they investigated financial issues. Things that would cause harm to investors, cases like that. What did they want with Ubiquity?

Ronnie grabbed the receiver, taking the phone off *Speaker*. "Is that a new kind of cryptic code phrase? The clock strikes two at midnight." She kept her tone light, despite the spike of nervousness that ran through.

Unlike some of her colleagues, who had filed their sense of humor in a rusty old cabinet somewhere, under *Open Never,* Sammy would appreciate the joke. Way back when, before humanity was much of anything, before Lucifer fell, Samael and Lucifer were lovers. So were Metatron and Lucifer. Ronnie had a complicated past with the demon, but she also had a good idea of who he was.

"Perfect timing. How did you know I was looking for you? I need you on damage control," he said.

Or maybe he wouldn't like the teasing. This must be bad. "I'll be back in my office soon." She didn't take orders, from him or technically from anyone. When Uriel and Metatron merged, becoming her, it made her one of the four most powerful servants of heaven and hell, and an original angel. She only answered to a single higher power. But Ubiquity, humanity's largest search engine, was a public-facing company, and she was that public face.

She stole another kiss from Irdu, after he made her promise they'd pick things up after work, and less than a second later, she stood in her own office. She placed a series of calls, asking PR to write her statement for her final approval, and Art to be ready to film her webcast and push it to every site they needed, ensuring the news trended before the SEC press statement spread far and wide.

Getting all those ducks in a row in a matter of minutes wasn't a trick of heaven; Ubiquity had good tech. There were advantages to being responsible for what people saw when they searched for things.

Six months ago, this was Gabriel's job. Before he tried to destroy Metatron for a second time and let his megalomania shine through. She'd temporary relieved him of his power as thanks. If she could wish the work back on him without giving him any other authority, she'd do it in a heartbeat. Talk about the ultimate punishment. Knowing him, he'd enjoy it

Half an hour later, she sat in Video, in front of the camera, speech half-committed to memory and scrolling on the teleprompter, in case she needed the reminder. The same text would be released when her footage was.

She flowed smoothly through the talking points. "Ubiquity International, Incorporated, was informed today that the Securities and Exchange Commission has received complaints from our investors about our offerings." She kept her smile fixed in place as she talked, wishing she could weave some kind of magic voodoo on the camera to make this all go away. Who reported them, anyway? She wasn't aware of any complaints.

"Rest assured, these allegations are false, and we'll be lending any support to the SEC that they request." Something like this could tie up their assets for months. Being an earth-based business, they needed money to operate, the same as anyone else. Normally, they were liquid enough it wasn't an issue.

On the surface, Ubiquity was the world's largest search engine. Under the covers, it existed to find rogue cherubs, extract them from their human hosts, and return them to heaven or hell before their lack of knowledge could cause someone harm. With the recent turmoil surrounding Ari and Gabe, and the revelation angels and demons were stealing cherubs, Ubiquity needed to ramp up new development on algorithms specific to tiny portions of the population. That meant they needed more hardware and the cash to pay for it.

"As always, Ubiquity has the answers you're searching for. Reach out to our PR department using the contact information in the comments, and we'd love to speak with you." She paused after the last sentence, keeping her expression and posture pleasant, waiting for the *all clear*.

"And… we're done." One of the lower demons stepped from behind the camera. He gave Ronnie a thumbs-up. "Looking good, boss. Editing is on hand, and I'll have the final in your box in half an hour for approval."

"Thanks." She let her frozen grin slide away and worked her jaw a few times to get the feeling back in her cheeks. It was going to be a long week.

Chapter Two

Izzy dropped into a sitting position on the rooftop, not caring when the concrete bit into his bare legs. A trickle of sweat slid down his back and his breath came in short gasps. Every inch of him ached from the morning workout, and he was okay with that.

It was a foreign feeling, dealing with something as simple as the pain of pushing past his limits doing sit-ups and crunches. After almost three thousand years of the immortality which came from being an angel, and another hundred or so living off borrowed power after he fell, he was adjusting to being mortal.

He was okay with that, too.

"Hey, handsome." Holden's familiar baritone made him smile. Strong fingers rested on Izzy's shoulders, and Holden kneaded along his upper back. "You're working too hard."

A breeze drifted through the air, cooling the sheen of sweat on Izzy's skin. He rolled his head forward and hoped Holden's attention would relax him. Instead, it reminded him of the second reason he was up here, working out until his arms felt like rubber and his brain no longer functioned.

"It's taking me too long to get back to where I used to be." Izzy pulled away and stood. He was trying to ignore the feeling that Holden was hiding something.

Izzy had tried asking him about it. Told him if they were serious about moving in together, they needed to trust each other. Pointed out six months together was too long to be playing these *I'm fine, you're imagining things* games. And Holden insisted every time that it was nothing for Izzy to worry about.

Then again, he wasn't the only one keeping secrets. Izzy still hadn't figured out how to tell Holden about his angelic past. Was it really a fair comparison? Hard to know without having an idea of what Holden's secret was.

"What happened to your deadline?" Izzy tried to push a lighthearted tone into his voice.

Holden was a journalist and had expected to be locked away for the next couple of days. His love of research was one of the reasons they clicked so well. Doubts aside, Izzy looked forward to this being be his home; so even if he was sequestered and writing, they'd still see each other.

The first few times he visited Izzy in the hospital, he'd been this kind of reserved. Wouldn't meet Izzy's gaze. Couldn't stand still. Except, then it was because he'd been trying to figure out how to ask Izzy out. Now, something darker lined Holden's hesitation.

Or maybe Izzy was scared of commitment.

"I wrapped up my work and sent it to my editor this morning." Holden closed the distance between them again. "I missed you too much to procrastinate." He drew a thumb across Izzy's cheek. "I'm glad I caught you this morning before you shaved."

The hidden compliment made Izzy smile. Holden said scruff of his beard made him rugged.

Something crawled over Izzy's skin, leaving him feeling like he'd stuck a fork in a light socket. Was that really lingering mistrust? "Now that you mention it, I was about to jump in the shower. I might shave if someone isn't there to stop me."

"Tempting offer." Holden kissed him

This time the tingles racing through Izzy were vibrant and delicious, bringing his senses to life.

Through the pleasure, the heavy air sank into his skin, running over his nerves like he was a live wire. What the hell was—

He shoved Holden away as hard as he could and fell back before his brain caught up with instinct. Lightning flashed between them. The crackle filled the air, temporarily blinding Izzy and leaving the heavy scent of ozone in its wake.

His heart hammered in his chest. Doubt. Exhaustion. Every other feeling became background noise. That wasn't a freak electrical storm. Such a precise, targeted strike could only come from a host of heaven or hell.

"Who the hell is that?" Holden's question jerked him out of his rambling thoughts and creeping fear.

Izzy followed his gaze. Anyone who could summon such intense energy from nothing was powerful, so there was no reason they'd stick around instead of vanishing into thin air. Then again, it also didn't make sense they'd only struck once, despite missing.

Abaddon. Izzy's insides turned in on themselves when he saw her. No wonder it was a precision strike. *Powerful* was an understatement. She stood just a few rooftops away, several stories up. Her platinum hair was tied back from her face, and she dressed in a denim jacket and crinoline skirt. Only Abaddon, heaven's top assassin, could simultaneously manifest instant lightning and rock a thrift-shop-chic look.

Izzy swore her eyes met his, even across the hundreds of feet between them. She dipped her head in a short bow, and then vanished.

Anxious dread clawed under his skin. He thought Ronnie was exaggerating about him being in danger. Speaking of, Ronnie needed to know about this. Abaddon only answered to Gabriel, and that meant the original angel was back in action.

Izzy turned back to Holden. "Are you all right?"

"No, really." Holden brushed invisible dirt off his jeans. "Who the hell was that? What kind of electrical storm only hits one house? And how did she vanish into thin air?"

"Magic?" Izzy hid his wince. How did he know she'd been there, and that she'd disappeared just as quickly?

Why didn't Holden assume it was a freak lightning storm, or a power surge? The trick of fogging the mind only worked on people who didn't want to believe what they saw. Anyone who had accepted there was more to the world than what they understood couldn't be so easily swayed. What did that say about Holden?

Izzy extended his hand and pulled Holden to his feet. His hot palm against Izzy's sent racing tingles through him.

He wanted to go after Abaddon. Start making calls. Find out what the hell was going on. But he didn't have the power to chase her down himself, and Holden was his priority. "Do you want a drink? I can make it strong."

"At ten am? If you have iced tea, that'd be great."

Izzy always had a fresh pitcher. The normalcy of the conversation helped soothe him, but not enough. Every inch of him twitched with excess electricity—both from the attack and the questions he suspected Holden was gathering.

They made their way down to Izzy's apartment. He excused himself long enough to call Ronnie, pacing the entire time when she didn't answer. Neither did Irdu, Lucifer, or anyone else he knew in hell or outside Gabe's circle in heaven. Who the fuck knew where Michael was. Izzy left her an insistent message and returned to Holden.

Izzy grabbed glasses, ice, and the pitcher from the fridge. He tried to focus on the conversation. On distracting Holden. Too many concerns hummed through him, carried on waves of stress.

Ronnie had warned Izzy that Gabe would recover quickly from her stripping him of his powers, and that he'd be pissed—go figure—but Izzy had no idea what that had to do with him. Then again, maybe it was Abaddon who had a grudge against him. Just because she was one of those who never acted on her own didn't mean she couldn't start now…

Or maybe this wasn't about Izzy at all. A strange hum vibrated in his ears. Silence. He looked up to find Holden watching him expectantly.

Crap. He'd probably asked Izzy something. "I'm sorry, what?"

Holden shoved aside a few stacks of books on the breakfast bar to make an empty space in front of the stool he sat on. He nodded at a book on his right. "What exactly *did* they believe about angels and possession in thirteenth century South America?"

He was referencing the tome with the worn leather cover, cracked spine, and pages so yellowed Izzy had to turn them with latex gloves to keep the oils on his fingers from damaging them further.

Izzy set Holden's drink in front of him, grabbed the book, and returned it to its sleeve, and then its spot on the top shelf. "It's complicated."

"Complicated like magical girls in tutus who vanish into thin air, fire that guts your house and church, but leaves all the surrounding buildings intact, and freak lightning storms that only strike where you're standing?"

Izzy whirled to face him, anxiousness growing at the direct questions.

Holden raised an eyebrow. "Or a different kind of complicated?"

Izzy had about two seconds to come up with an answer and still look like he meant it. Holden obviously wasn't buying the current excuses, but it wasn't as though the truth sounded any better. *Screw it.*

"They all fall into the same category of complicated," Izzy said.

Angels and demons didn't keep their presence secret from humanity because of some overarching command from above. They mostly kept quiet these days, because people as a whole were cynical. Plastic boxes lined with tiny wires and solder transmitted terabytes of data over oceans in the blink of an eye, and it wasn't a miracle. Not a lot of people were going to believe a random priest who spent his weekends swapping theology with his congregation had wielded an ethereal pike and been an actual muse thousands of years ago.

Holden's cheeks puffed out and then deflated as he exhaled. "So, am I seeing things, or not?"

Was he? Izzy couldn't meet his gaze, and his wandering eyes landed instead on another book on the counter. This one about prophets; people who could see auras. Prophets knew—not just believed but knew with all certainty—something besides the standard world around them existed. The blind faith was gone for those people. Could Holden be…?

No. Izzy just needed to talk him out of what he'd seen. Do a verbal version of the thought clouding an agent would do.

A nagging thought nudged the back of his mind, about how he'd wanted transparency. But this wasn't his secret to share. "Maybe. I didn't see it, so I don't know." He didn't like this.

Creases marred Holden's forehead, and he scowled. "Of course. Just like before your accident, you didn't really glow. I imagined that, too." There was no question in his statement.

Could he really...? Izzy didn't know if he was terrified Holden might have the same gifts as a prophet, or relieved. "What kind of glow?"

A low growl rumbled from Holden's chest. The noise he made when he was frustrated with work, or the world around him, and apparently now Izzy. Holden breathed deep. "The glowing kind of glow. Not like your friend, Ronnie. She might as well be a fucking light bulb. At least now she's ditched that whole visage of leaking chaos thing. Not a good look for someone with her skin, by the way. But you still might as well have been your own power source."

Yeah, that was Ronnie. The chaos Holden described had been her aural reflection of having two separate entities living in the same head. Indecision made Izzy's skull feel like it was full of helium. He should be excited about this. He'd never picked a prophet's brain, and this meant no more lying to Holden. So why did the possibility leave him disconcerted instead?

"How long have you..." Izzy wasn't sure how to phrase his question. His brain moved a million miles a minute.

Holden rubbed his face. "You believe me?"

Poor guy. Part of the reason it was so hard to find prophets, especially these days, was because if they told the wrong people what they saw, they were drugged, institutionalized, or worse.

"Yeah," Izzy said. "I believe you."

The corners of Holden's mouth pulled up. "Thank, God."

Maybe. But He was more of a hands-off, learn-for-yourself kind of deity. The odds He'd pulled strings to push Izzy and Holden together were less than non-existent. Was Izzy going to delve into an explanation or try to keep brushing off Holden's questions?

Izzy's brain had been stuffed full of knowledge as an angel, but only what he needed to do his job. It had never been enough. After he fell, he spent his free time digging up as much as he could about what everyone everywhere believed, and searching for the similarities. With Holden he had a choice—rob him of the same opportunity by convincing him he was a little nuts, or tell him the truth.

Izzy dropped onto an empty stool. "Have you seen it since you were a kid?"

"As long as I can remember. I learned pretty young not to talk about it." He drained his tea in a single swallow. "Am I sane after all, or are we both crazy?"

"Either. Both. But what you saw on the roof, the stuff with Ronnie, with me, is all real." Izzy's thoughts tripped over something, and he stopped to examine it. He'd missed something important about this revelation, but it was just out of his reach.

Holden was staring again, but this time Izzy knew he hadn't missed something he'd said. "What?" Izzy asked.

"There's something else."

The gears in his brain ground to a halt at the intensity of his scrutiny. "Oh?"

"You're outright sexy when you're excited about something," Holden said, resting a hand on Izzy's neck.

Heat spread out from his touch, cranking up a notch when he scraped a thumb over Izzy's stubble.

"I mean, that's not what I wanted to say… When I found your church a year ago, I couldn't believe it. The nondenominational sign on the front door was a nice change, especially since you actually are. Nondenominational I mean. But on top of that, I'd never met someone who glowed, who was just down to earth, and wanted to talk to me. And now, with the way I feel about you, and you have answers for me, too?"

He hesitated, eyes searching Izzy's face, then leaned in and kissed him.

Izzy's body pulsed with need. He pushed past the hesitation and deepened the kiss, intensely aware of Holden's every movement.

He stood and pressed closer, sliding between Izzy's legs, and resting his free hand on Izzy's chest. Izzy fisted his fingers in Holden's hair, holding him captive, tongues exploring each other with fervent want.

When they broke apart, Izzy struggled to find his breath.

Holden traced his thumb over Izzy's stubbled chin. "I've been terrified to bring this up with you. I didn't know what I'd do if you told me I was insane."

"Me too." Izzy winced at the less than stellar response, but his relief at having this out in the open made up for it. Was this what Holden had been hiding? The same topic Izzy was worried about?

Logic listed all the reasons spilling heaven's secrets was a bad idea. But it wasn't as if Izzy was going to sell anyone out. He was just going to answer Holden's questions.

Holden stepped back and jammed his hands in his pockets. "So, will you tell me why your cute friend glows? Wait." He studied Izzy for a moment. "Did you and she ever…?"

"Hook up?" A rush of heat sped through Izzy at the reminder. He had once with Ronnie. More often with Irdu. The reminder left a pit in his chest. Izzy tried to be happy for them, but sometimes it was hard to ignore that he wanted to be a part of what they had. He didn't need that, though. He had Holden. "Not any time that mattered."

"Why not?"

"Angels and demons aren't big on commitment or long-term relationships."

Holden's smirk grew, and he dropped onto the couch. "You make it sound like one big orgy."

"More like several small ones." Izzy hadn't meant to dive into the middle of things with his explanation. It might make more sense if he started at the beginning. Or it might just bore the hell out of Holden. People and their perception of angels and demons entertained Izzy.

The air shifted around them, and his next words died in his throat. This was an identical sensation to what he felt on the roof. Heavy, suffocating, and sparking across every nerve.

"Fuck, she's back." Holden pointed at the window. The glass exploded in million shards. A ball of electricity filled the living room. Izzy didn't have time to react before everything slammed into them full force. His vision blurred at the edges, and consciousness slipping away.

His books. Not again. He forced himself toward Holden's prone form. The room spun and his legs refused to hold his weight. Please. Not with him here.

Chapter Three

Irdu started at his screen, and the row after row of random locations around the globe. *What are you doing, Ronnie?*

He knew the answer. She was using Tracker, the Ubiquity event-finder app, to locate her next high. Agents could feel the emotions of humans. Ever since Metatron and Uriel became one in Ronnie's head, her thirst for that vicarious thrill had grown.

She didn't talk about it, which meant she either didn't recognize the problem, or didn't want to admit one existed. The fact that she made most of her trips during business hours, and didn't mention them to anyone, made Irdu think it was the latter.

He was worried about her. This was the kind of behavior that could trigger cherub warnings. He knew from personal experience she was just dealing with having two sets of memories, one of which hadn't lived for thousands of years. But if she didn't get it under control soon…

Irdu didn't know what would happen. For now, he was purging the records from the database, to keep her out of trouble.

One of his favorite things about immortality was he'd had decades to learn everything. He'd watched technology grow and change for almost a century, and he'd adapted as the world did. Which meant he was perfectly suited as a Development Manager at Ubiquity, and he could watch Ronnie's back without anyone being the wiser.

Her behavior hadn't lessened over the past few months, though. If anything, the instances of her hopping around the world, and hiding it, were getting more frequent. He couldn't just tuck the problem away much longer; he needed to talk to her.

It wasn't as though she was spending her life popping from one high to the next. A couple of times a week. And in between, she was doing some incredible things at Ubiquity, and for Irdu, and his sister, Tia.

She'd taken Tia off Reaping, and given her a new job. Reaping was getting dangerous. Cut-throat. Those angels still loyal to Gabe had access to the best jobs, despite the original angel being gone from Ubiquity. They were growing more powerful, and didn't try to hide that they'd stomp on anyone who got in their way.

Right now, Tia was just watching Izzy, to make sure his new boyfriend wasn't an asshole. Kind of a cushy job, really, but Irdu was fine with that as long as she was safe.

He deleted the records of Ronnie's searches.

He wouldn't mind be Izzy's new boyfriend. They'd fucked a few times over the years, and it was always casual. But Irdu spent a lot of time with him while Izzy recovered, and they'd gotten closer.

Ronnie had some influence there, too. The three of them always had a blast together.

"You ready to meet?" Ronnie's voice carried from the doorway.

It might be fun to believe thinking about her had summoned her, but this appointment was on their calendar. Actual work stuff. "Absolutely."

She shut and locked the door behind her. Instead of taking the chair across from, she moved to his side of the desk and sat on the edge.

He rolled away from his computer to position himself in front of her. He rested his hands on her bare knees and searched her face. Dark red irises stared back, and heavy shadows marred her pale, smooth skin. "You look stressed."

"It's this SEC thing. Nothing to do for it besides comply and hope it ends soon." She sighed heavily. "Like so much of the work here."

He knew the feeling. If Lucifer demanded it, they both were compelled to obey for their own reasons. "I'm here to listen, if you need to talk or babble or whatever."

A smile cracked her expression, but didn't reach her eyes. "I wish I could. I don't know anything yet beyond *Ubiquity might be in trouble.* But I'm not the only one under pressure. What's going on with you?"

This was his opening to talk about her event-finder activity. But was it really such a big deal if she was just blowing off steam? "Everyday work stuff."

"What can I do to help?"

This was one of the many things Irdu loved about Ronnie. They should be doing actual work. But despite that and her own tension, she was sincere about listening to him.

He also loved that she wore more skirts to work these days. The studious exec look was sexy, and offered easy accessibility. He loved her cherry red lips. Her appreciation for the world around her… which included what he was doing with the event-finder. "I wouldn't complain about a brief distraction."

"Hmm… you'll have to be more specific." She rested her foot between his legs on his chair. "Anything you need."

He *needed* to be out from under Lucifer's thumb. And for her to have the same. And Tia. He needed to have every morning be a lazy one in bed, rather than a rush to get into the office. To take his time waking up next to Ronnie. To mingle with the world on their terms, not Ubiquity's or Lucifer's.

"Irdu?" Her voice was sweet. "You still here?"

He met her gaze and her concern stared back. He kissed the inside of her knee. "You. Right now I need you."

"You always have me. And you can always have me. Whenever. However."

Not if this behavior keeps up. Irdu silenced the nagging whisper, and let lust rush in instead. He shoved her skirt to her hips as he stood, and pushed between her legs.

Kissing her, tasting her sugar and spice and desperation, fed his own desire. Amplified need filled him. He nipped hungrily at her lips and tongue, devouring every whimper and sigh.

She dug her fingers into his chest and pressed her body to his. The curve and heat and friction made him instantly hard.

Compulsion overwhelmed him, begging to drown in her body and ignore the outside world, even for just a few minutes.

The way she fumbled with his slacks said she was as hungry for this physical connection as he was. This wouldn't be a sweet, passionate, drawn-out lovemaking session. They could do that any time. Right now, he needed to consume and be consumed.

She wrapped her fingers around his shaft and worked him free. Her soft, hot skin against his drew a long groan from his throat. He covered her hand and guided his cock toward her, using the head to shove her panties aside.

Her hand fell away as she fisted his shirt, and she wrapped her heels around his ass.

He didn't slide inside her yet, despite how wet and inviting her pussy was. Despite how intently he wanted to be buried in her. He stroked his dick along her slit, focusing on her clit. Bumping the swollen nub and stroking himself in the process.

Irdu teased her to the edge of climax. Her pleasure rolled over his skin and wrapped around him. He pushed harder, adding a hint of sensation to roll over her body.

She gasped when she came, and dug her nails into his chest. When she was at the height of climax, he plunged into her. She tightened her legs, pulling him in, thrusting her hips to set a frantic pace.

He was fantastic with that. It didn't matter that this wouldn't last long. He needed to get off. Pleasure prickled his nerves and desire built inside. Feeling her tightness wrapped around him, seeing the gorgeous expression on her face, him biting her lips… it was the perfect orchestra.

His balls tightened. His brain sparked. He came hard, thrusting as he spilled inside her. Pounding hard. Faster.

He didn't slow until he was spent.

Irdu used the desk and Ronnie leaning against him to keep him upright.

"Better?" She asked, his chest muffling her question.

"So very much." It was nice to put aside the world for a little while, and remember the things that made life amazing.

A *snick* reached his ears, like the sound of a latch moving, and the office door that had been locked swung open.

Lucifer strolled in. He barely gave them a glance as he lingered by the doorway. "Do you two do anything here?"

Irritation seared through Irdu. So much for forgetting the world. "You have to ask? She does more for you than anyone, and you can fuck off if you think differently."

"He's got a point." Ronnie straightened and met Irdu's gaze.

Lucifer rolled his eyes. "Yeah, yeah. We're all model workers. Some of you just fuck more than horny teenagers. Ronnie was looking for me? It was urgent?"

"I am and it is." Ronnie gave Irdu a quick kiss, and pushed her skirt down to be modest as she hopped from the desk. She spun to face Lucifer, using her body to block Irdu while he zipped up.

"Let's talk, then." Lucifer jerked his thumb toward the hallway.

Irdu squeezed Ronnie's hand before she followed Lucifer from the room, then sank back into his chair.

He hated seeing her act like Lucifer's lapdog. Irdu didn't have a choice. But Ronnie was an original. She shouldn't be jumping based on anyone's whims.

Besides, Lucifer was manipulative. Deceptive. And had something fairly intense with Metatron back at the beginning of time. Before Michael, even. It should have been one of those love of the ages things.

It probably was for Lucifer, considering he'd somehow carried her spark with him for millennia until he could bring her back.

Irdu didn't care if Lucifer and Ronnie reignited that flame, but if Lucifer hurt her, he'd find a way to destroy Lucifer. Devil or not, Irdu would make it happen.

Chapter Four

"Izzy?" The panicked voice dragged Izzy's mind from a black pit.

"Oh, God." Her concern grew a few decibels. "Please wake up? She's going to kill me. Please be okay."

Izzy would recognize the sweet, genuine panic anywhere. The information helped him shed more of the clouds. He forced his eyes open, and every inch of him creaked in protest.

"Thank you, thank you." Relief trickled into Tia's voice.

Izzy wanted to know what she was doing here, but Holden was a higher priority.

"Let him breathe, miss," Holden said.

Relief spilled through Izzy.

Holden sat on the scorched couch. Black smudges scored large portions of his bare skin, including some new holes in his shirt, and the back of the sofa was the only thing keeping him upright.

The wet, soggy sofa… Damn it. Izzy forced himself into a sitting position.

Where Abaddon preferred lightning, Tia's element was water.

Izzy tried to brace himself as he surveyed the apartment. His gut sank at the sight of singed books dripping with water. *Not again.* He turned to Tia, not wanting to look at the destruction. "Why are you here?"

She wove her fingers together, not meeting his gaze. "I can't say. But I have to tell Ronnie you're okay. Fuck, I should have called her first. But I couldn't tell her you were dead. What if—"

"Tia." Izzy rested a hand on her arm, cutting her off. She'd ramble for hours if he let her. "Don't call anyone yet. First, tell me why you're here." More of the morning rushed back to him on a wave of lightning, making his entire body cringe. "And why a giant ball of electricity crashed through my window."

"I can't. I mean, I can call Ronnie. I have to. She'll be furious if I don't. Do I need to call you an ambulance? But I can't tell you about the why, or the what, or the who, or—"

"Stop." Izzy should have only asked her one question. Tia wasn't flighty. She just lost focus and tended to follow every thought at the same time. He held her gaze, keeping his expression steady, despite the throbbing ache growing behind his eyes. He needed to lie down, but first, she was going to confirm his suspicions, and probably deal a massive blow to his ego in the process. "Why?"

She finally turned away. "You're my assignment."

"Sorry to interrupt." Holden's voice was scratchy and strained. "But I have to ask what you are. Otherwise, I might be jealous that Izzy has so many impossibly attractive women at his beck and call."

She glanced back at him, eyes wide. "I'm—Um … a friend. From church."

"Which is why I've never once seen you in the church. Makes perfect sense." Heavy sarcasm lined Holden's response.

Tia's eyes narrowed, and she was on her feet in a flash, stalking toward him. Any hesitation vanished. "Listen, I didn't have to save you. I don't know you from bubblegum on the bottom of my shoe. But since Izzy likes you, you get a pass. Back off, because your curiosity is pretty fucking insignificant in the grand scope of what's going on here."

Where did that come from? The mini-tirade was extremely not like Tia. "She's a demon," Izzy explained. Maybe he should be more delicate with information like that. Save the conversation until they'd discussed more about what Holden could and couldn't see. But the last few minutes had snapped a few of Izzy's filters.

Tia's pout returned in an instant. "Am not."

And bipolar? "Because it just spontaneously rained in my apartment? Why am I your assignment?"

She spun back to face him, lower lip jutted out in a pout. "Don't take it personally." Now that her panic had ebbed—Izzy assumed over how Ronnie would react if she'd let him die—Tia could carry on a conversation. "You're not the only one with a guardian angel or demon. You're just the only one who's local."

"Did you have to destroy my books?"

"Your apartment was on fire. You're welcome." She pulled her phone from the satchel hanging from her wrist and jabbed the screen several times.

"I told you not to call Ronnie." Izzy wanted answers, not more coddling.

"I didn't. I texted her." Her eyes never left the device. "She's in meetings, this is faster." Her phone beeped. "We're moving you."

"Bullshit we are." He forced himself to stand. The room spun at a dizzying speed, and his legs threatened to give out. "That's not your call.

"Nope. It's hers." Tia held up the phone, screen toward him, to show him the message from Ronnie.

Sometimes having friends in high—or low— places sucked. "It's not her call either. Are you going to knock me out and kidnap me?"

She bit her bottom lip, and her brow furrowed. He could almost hear the debate raging in her head over which instructions were more important, getting him out of here, or keeping him from getting hurt. "I'll be back," she said.

Tia stomped out the front door, slamming it behind her.

Izzy picked his way to the couch and collapsed next to Holden. Wet foam squidged around them, but he was beyond caring. Izzy dropped his head against the back of the sofa.

When Holden brushed a damp lock of hair from Izzy's forehead, a pleasant tingle nudged aside some of his irritation. "You know some interesting people," Holden said.

Interesting was one way to put it. Izzy forced a smile. "It's not as swell as it sounds. Are you sure you want to stick around? Apparently it's not safe here."

"What are *you* going to do? If it's not safe for me, the same goes for you."

The concern in his voice warmed Izzy. Every inch of his body begged him to take a nap. He had things to do, though. He'd pop a couple Aspirin. The urge to survey his apartment threatened to rear its head, and he ignored it. He couldn't stand to see so many damaged books again so soon. "I have to pay a friend a visit."

"Someone who blows things up and vanishes, or drenches rooms in water? What kind of friend?" Holden's dry humor made Izzy laugh in spite of the aches.

"The normal, library kind of friend. I need to research some things up, and—" Izzy nodded at the room, "—I can't do it here."

"Do you want company?"

He did. He wasn't in the mood to be hovered over by Tia, or anyone from heaven or hell, but Holden would keep him sane. Besides, the research Izzy wanted to do revolved around prophets. He wanted to could fit the pieces around Holden together better. Taking a living, breathing, sexy source with him would help.

"I'd love the company," Izzy said. "I have to change first, though." It was tempting to ask if Holden was still interested in joining him in the shower. But physically Izzy was going to have a hard time walking without wincing. He definitely wasn't up for more. "Meet me on the street in thirty?"

Holden gestured around the apartment. "What are you going to do about this? Don't you need to call the cops or something?"

Izzy had no idea what to do. What would he tell police? *A vengeful agent of the archangel Gabriel tried to execute me. Please stop her.* "I'll figure it out."

Holden winced as he stood. He flexed, stretched, and then hesitated. He dipped down, hands on either side of my head, and brushed his lips over mine. "Downstairs, thirty minutes. Don't stand me up. And don't shave."

Chapter Five

Ronnie wondered how, in all the years she'd known Lucifer in both her incarnations, she'd never noticed how closely he resembled a brick wall when she was trying to get answers from him. Had he gotten worse over time? Or was this a face he adopted for colleagues?

She should have stayed with Irdu a few minutes longer. More productive all around, and definitely more fun. And she wished like hell that she could ignore the ache inside at Lucifer's lack of response finding the two of them together. She didn't want him to be jealous, but it would be nice if… what?

It would be nice if he looked at her even a little like he used to. Before he fell.

She blew up a puff of air to force a loose strand of hair from her eyes. "Sammy didn't tell me."

"Is that because you refuse to call him Samael?" Lucifer leaned forward at his desk in the Ubiquity offices, his fingers clasped together.

"He's never minded the nickname before." Sammy wasn't one of those agents who got hung on up the sanctity of a name. As long as she approached him with respect, she tended to get along with him great. "He told me there was nothing for the SEC to find."

"Smart man. Listen to him."

Ronnie growled. "Why are we under investigation? We're supposed to be flying under the radar." That wasn't always possible. It went back to the whole concept of being public-facing. But she'd like to believe the SEC wouldn't be knocking on their door without probable cause. Her phone buzzed in her pocket, and she ignored it.

"Do you know what *plausible deniability* means?" Lucifer asked.

And there was the fucking stone wall again. Moments like this made her miss Michael. Not just emotionally, but he was the one original who was always up front with her. "I'm pretty sure it was part of Basic Deception Training, in hell. Do I need to have it in this case?" Her phone nudged her again.

"No." Lucifer's expression never shifted from neutral, despite the edge in his voice. "But Samael does. Stop pushing his buttons and let him do his job."

The only reason Sammy would need that… Ronnie scowled. "So the allegations are true, but he doesn't realize it."

Lucifer shrugged.

"Way to be noncommittal." This was the thing that frustrated Ronnie about her Ubiquity job more than all the rest combined. She signed on because angels and demons were taking advantage of loopholes in the system. Corruption ran rampant. And she swore in half the cases she tried to uncover or fix, Lucifer stood in her way. Her phone buzzed again, and she itched to reach for it.

He always had reasons, and they always made sense. Then again he was gifted at using logic to spin things his way. This was the key reason she hadn't followed him to hell when he fell. She'd gotten tired of the spin.

"Funding for places like this doesn't happen when the company and its founders appear out of thin air," Lucifer said. "It doesn't matter how good we were at investing; this is a multi-billion-dollar corporation. So yes, there may have been a little smoke and a few mirrors employed. You know why we did it. Do you disagree?"

"With the idealism behind Ubiquity? No." Beyond seeking out rogue cherubs, it was a joint initiative between heaven and hell so both sides could better help humanity. After all, what better way to follow what people were up to than tracking their web browsing habits? "With your tactics? Yes."

"You know why it has to be this way."

Yeah, yeah. She was tired of slamming her head into this wall. "I have to get back to work." She strode out of his office, muttering, *greater good bullshit*, as she reached for her phone. Two missed calls from Izzy. She frowned and played his voicemails.

"Someone tried to blow me up. Call me now?" And then, "Hey. Where is everyone? Call me."

The device vibrated in her hand before she could return his messages. A text from Tia. One of the few people Ronnie knew who was genuine. They'd sat next to each other for months and rarely talked, even though Ronnie was sleeping with Irdu. All because it was a secret that Tia and Irdu were related. Ronnie wished she'd gotten to know the other woman sooner, but was glad they were friends now.

Someone lightninged Izzy's place.

Fuck. Fear tightened in Ronnie's gut.

Half of heaven or hell could summon lightning. Electricity and water were easiest to work with. They existed in most things, so angels or demons who were only strong enough to work with a single element gravitated toward one of those two. Knowing the list of possible attackers was broad amped Ronnie's anxiety.

We're moving him someplace safer, she sent Tia a reply, then called Izzy. Best to soften the blow herself if she could.

No answer. Tia was next.

With each ring, Ronnie clenched her free hand tighter. This couldn't be related to their suspicions about Holden, unless humans had figured a hell of a lot more out about angelic power than Lucifer believed. Where did the attack come from?

"Hey." Tia's stress was evident.

"Is everyone all right?"

"Well… Izzy's pissed because I got all his books wet."

He would be. Ronnie hated that ancient tomes might be ruined, but at least he was well enough to get mad about it. "Why are his books wet?"

"His apartment was on fire, and I had to put it out somehow, and he was unconscious, and I thought he was dead, but he's not dead, and have you met that creepy friend of his with the staring—?"

"Tia." Ronnie hated to hear her so stressed. And Irdu would be furious when he found out his sister had been in a battle zone. "You said it was lightning." Ronnie didn't know which would be worse—two agents, one wielding each element, or one with enough strength to control both.

"It was. And there were books. Did I mention the books? They sparked."

"Did you see who it was?" Not that Ronnie would recognize most of the names Tia might give her.

"Abaddon."

Ronnie's blood turned to ice in her veins. Why was one of Gabriel's soldiers after Izzy? Or was Holden the target? "You're sure?"

Tia huffed. "*Everyone* knows who Abaddon is."

Right. This just got a lot more complicated. "Did you tell Izzy we're moving him? And Holden's going with him."

"Did I mention that Holden guy's doing a creepy-starey thing?"

"He does that." Ronnie racked her brain. Where to put them? It wasn't as if Ubiquity had safe houses; they were a technology company. And heaven and hell didn't have a use for such a thing. Her place was no safer than Izzy's. Anyone who was interested in hurting him knew he and Ronnie were friends.

"He—sorry, *they*—can stay with me for a few hours." Tia sounded reluctant.

"I can't ask you to do that." Really, she couldn't. Irdu would never forgive Ronnie if she didn't pull Tia now, and Ronnie would hate herself if something happened to the demon. "I'm going to send someone else in to relieve you."

"No." Tia's voice grew hard. "Why? Because of my… Irdu?"

No one was supposed to know they were related, or that they'd been human once upon a time. If Gabe found out Lucifer had turned mortals into full-fledged demons, angels blowing up buildings would become the least of Ronnie's worries.

"Yes, because of that," Ronnie said. "And because of what you are. And because I'd hate myself if you got hurt."

"So, you can pull me, and send someone you *don't* care about to take my place?"

Ronnie clenched her jaw. She didn't like that phrasing at all. She cared about every agent at Ubiquity, regardless of who they swore loyalty to. But Tia mattered more. "What am I supposed to say to that?"

"Exactly." Tia was smug. "Argument is over. They'll stay with me for now. You'll find them someplace long term and bring us dinner when you come to move them."

Bribe an agent with a good meal, and all was right in their world. Ronnie didn't like that Tia had so deftly won the argument, but she smiled at the request for food. Still, a million thoughts and questions pounding in her skull. "Deal. I'll be at your place as soon as I can. Promise Izzy whatever it takes to get them to go with you. Please?"

* * * *

Michael's surroundings vanished, and a city street replaced them in a blink. He clouded the thoughts of the dozens of people milling on the sidewalk. Most of them wouldn't notice him appear out of nowhere, but the fogging ensured anyone who did would assume Michael had always been there.

He extended his senses, searching for threats. The world seeped back in response—the warm layer of nighttime humidity against his face; the stench of car exhaust, alcohol, and money; patrons chattering as they entered the art gallery. He wasn't looking for the obvious, though. Disruption would most likely be an aura, spiked and frantic.

He wove his way through the throngs, and stopped at the entrance long enough to show the doorman his invitation to the exhibit opening. Inside, bright white lined the walls and floors, pausing only for the paintings and sculptures on display. The artwork was stark, and horrific in contrast. Beautiful and erotic in its terror. Nudes bound with thorns. Chained by thick, woven cable. Locked with shackles of… was that a human heart?

Michael shook his head, to clear the vivid imagery. It was potent work. Almost haunted or inspired. What would Ronnie think about the art? Would she be drawn to the detail and brush strokes, or zero in on the passion and pain?

He resisted the urge to hover his hand millimeters above the canvas, to see if it emitted its own energy. Potent art shone or bled with its creator's intensity. That would probably hold Ronnie's attention the longest—the chance to *feel* something new. Her appreciation for experiencing everything, whether it was beautiful or raw and visceral, was a big reason he was drawn to her. Why he missed her so much, despite his attempts to set her memories aside.

It was also why distance was necessary. When he lost himself in her awe, it was too tempting to stay there rather than do his job. It would be worse now that he was tasked with execution.

An aura rescued him from his thoughts. Clear and sharp, like a sparkling sea. Almost as beautiful as the woman herself. Abaddon. Her narrow waist and seductive hips breathed life into a calf-length denim skirt, and the way she held herself said she owned the room.

She glanced over her shoulder when he approached, then turned back to the painting in front of her.

To an outside observer, Michael was meeting his date. The charade was fine with him. Abaddon was an old friend, and about as complication free as life got. He needed that. Her loyalties may lie with Gabriel, but subterfuge wasn't in her arsenal.

He stepped up beside her and wrapped his arm around her waist. The physical contact without emotional context was pleasant.

She pressed her warm weight against him. "Shaken, not stirred, Mr. Bond?" Her words were almost a purr.

He suspected she was joking about the suit. Abaddon was what Ronnie would call thrift-store chic. Ronnie's name carried a rush of second-guessing and regret, and presented him with a new question—was he wrong to walk away from her, rather than discovering what their future held?

Lucifer told him she chose to go by Ronnie, rather than Uriel or Metatron, because it was the name both had used. It was also the nickname Michael gave her so long ago. After Lucifer fell from Heaven. After Metatron and Michael fell in love.

Michael focused on his companion for the evening, instead of the past. The faint scent of jasmine teased his senses. "Is there any place in this city that's more crowded tonight?" He kept his tone pleasant, despite the weight of everyone's emotions pushing in on him. An exhibit like this, meant to shock and tantalize, would wreak havoc on an angel if they weren't careful.

"Probably a lot of places." Abaddon looped her hand into the crook of his arm and tugged him to the next painting. "You wanted a spot somewhere besides Nashville, and let's say I'm a patron of the artist's."

He wouldn't take his frustration—the stress of the atmosphere—out on her. She risked a lot by continuing to meet him. "You look good," he said. That was polite. Conversational. "Your glow could be healthier." He couldn't help sliding in the reminder he wasn't happy about her current lifestyle choice. She was his only almost-success.

She held a cherub she shouldn't have. According to his rules, he should have stripped it from her and obliterated her into nothing. It wasn't that simple, though. She was an old friend, which made it harder, but she also supplied him with information about where to find others like her. And she hesitated each time he brought it up, so he *knew* she was closer to surrendering the cherub.

"I heard what happened with Azazel." She trailed a finger down Michael's arm.

He wouldn't call her on the change of subject. "Thanks to media coverage, the world heard what happened with Azazel." He hoped the family who witnessed it was doing all right. Whenever he saw them in an interview, he felt bad for not whisking them somewhere else before leaving.

He caught Abaddon's fingers and traced his thumb over her knuckles. He tried to fall into the physical contact. This was nothing more than a business connection, and he needed to re-learn the difference between an emotional attachment and a physical one. Before Ronnie, he didn't have an issue with casual sex. It was one of the few ways to hang onto sanity for someone who had a mortal form for thousands of years.

Since his time with Ronnie, thinking about hooking up with someone else made her memory surge back lucid and potent, sliding under his skin like silk and stealing away again in an instant.

He'd left Ronnie because when he loved Metatron eons ago, he'd been willing to become mortal in order to experience humanity by her side. He was worried if he learned to love someone now, the temptation to fall would return. Heaven and hell were in too much upheaval for him to make that selfish choice.

If he were tempted to go back to Ronnie, if he weren't worried it would distract him from the matters at hand and make him question where his priorities lay, he'd still hesitate. To him, Metatron died three thousand years ago and Uriel was a separate entity. Now, according to all accounts, they were one and the same. Though he knew that was how the process worked when a full merger happened, he struggled to reconcile the angel he loved and the demon he wanted to.

"You could try a different approach with your targets, you know." Abaddon guided him to another painting. It wasn't as stark as some of the others, but the pain in the model's eyes drove into Michael's core.

"I give everyone a chance to surrender what they shouldn't have."

"Not like that." Amusement ran through her words. "And you don't. Not really. It's kind of an in-your-face thing. You demand they give up their strength or die. What kind of a choice is that?"

"The only choice."

"You did more for me."

"And you still have what I want you to give up." He concentrated on keeping his voice low and teasing, despite the words. It made it easier to keep up the happy-couple illusion.

"But I may not always. I'm saying you should consider something more conversational. Speak with them all friendly like. Try to help them understand."

"I'll think about it." He used a kinder tactic when a cherub latched itself onto an unwitting human. A cherub was naïve, but they were still individuals. If one found a human, Michael talked to both to see if their minds were compatible. The human host always took priority. If there was a clash, he'd extract the cherub and send it back to heaven. However, an angel's primary mission was to help people achieve their true potential. If merging a person with a cherub, who stumbled onto them by mistake, helped rather than hindered that goal, he helped the two become one.

This was different. Angels and demons knew they were taking from someone else's existence. They'd been taught the rules.

She nodded at the painting in front of them. "One of my favorite pieces of his. Almost as if he had a muse."

"You?" Michael asked. Abaddon said she was a patron. Though she never had a lot of respect for angels who metaphorically perched on shoulders and whispered inspiration to people.

She laughed and shook her head. "No. That's not my calling." Her purse chirped. "Excuse me." She fished out her phone, and frowned when she read the screen. "I'm sorry to cut this short, handsome, but I've got to run."

"Is everything all right?"

"It's fine." She kissed him on the cheek. "I have a meeting with a muse."

She vanished. Her words, innocent as they sounded, sank heavily into Michael's bones. If she became part of the problem, rather than helping him with a solution, would he be able to destroy her? What if it was another old friend? There was a breaking point somewhere, and he dreaded the day he had to make that choice.

Chapter Six

A safe house. *Great.* Because Izzy needed another unresolved question to haunt him. Why did Ubiquity have a safe house?

Tia gestured at the studio apartment. "Make yourselves comfortable. The books you wanted are on the table. I'm getting the rest." She'd promised that if Izzy and Holden let her move them to a safe location, she'd go to the library and get the books Izzy wanted.

A mattress sat on the floor in one corner, next to a battered easy chair. There was a kitchenette on the other side of the room, and a dining table with two chairs in the middle of it all. Izzy knew the layout. It looked just like Ronnie's old place—or that of most agents who worked for Ubiquity.

The simplistic, cramped living conditions were Gabriel's idea when he and Lucifer started the company. Back when the two were pretending to be civil. The plainness of the apartments was supposed to keep a brand new angel, one who'd just received a physical form and experienced a rush from interacting with pretty much anything, from sensory overload while they adjusted to their new bodies. And then it was supposed to motivate them to achieve more and earn something better based on their own tastes.

At least, that was what Gabe said. Izzy suspected he didn't feel anyone needed something so fancy as a livable apartment to do a job they were made for anyway.

He hovered in the doorway next to Holden, not sure where they were supposed to sit. Tia nudged him forward, and the latch clicked shut behind him.

"I'm sorry it's not more." Her voice was sheepish.

Izzy turned to face her. She studied her shoes as they traced lines in the carpet. Holden nudged him with his elbow and nodded at the walls. It took Izzy a moment to realize what he was pointing at.

The place wasn't as barren and nondescript as it appeared on the surface. Even though there were only a few appliances in the kitchen, they were all vibrant blue, as if someone had melted a crayon to color them. A handful of prints were thumbtacked to the walls, each of them a brightly colored but abstract interpretation of flowers. And the comforter on the bed—as fluffy as Izzy had ever seen a blanket—was covered with tiny bluebells.

Realization sank in, joined by guilt. This wasn't a safe house. It looked like a Ubiquity apartment because it was Tia's. "It's perfect. I have zero complaints."

She shrugged. "We didn't know where else to bring you, and this place has wards, and I'm only here because my last place was blown up by Ari, which you know a bit about, and I'll be moving out soon. I found the perfect place, but it's not like you can time things like this, and—"

"It's fantastic." Izzy rested a hand on her arm. "Thank you for putting us up. What are you supposed to do while we're here, though?"

She shrugged. "I'll make sure you're settled, and then I have to run some errands, so you can make yourselves at home. And I promised to answer your questions." That was the other condition she had to meet for Izzy to agree to this entire thing.

It felt awkward making himself comfortable in someone else's home under these conditions. But he also didn't want her to think he was turning his nose up at her offer. Izzy grabbed a chair at the table, grateful when Holden followed his lead.

"I'm not sure where to start." Izzy should have been better prepared, since it was his request. "Was that really Abaddon this morning?"

"Abbie-what?" Holden asked.

Tia chewed on her bottom lip, glancing between him and Izzy.

"You told me to bring him." Izzy understood her hesitation, though. He was still coping with the fact that Holden had any idea she was different, let alone how to explain it.

She furrowed her brow. "I know, but I'm supposed to give *you* answers."

"Do you want me to plug my ears?" Sarcasm lined Holden's question.

Izzy had no idea why the two of them were clashing. He did know he'd have to answer Holden's questions either way, which could take a long time.

If he even believed Izzy. "Give me the rundown. It's okay. Blame it on me if anyone asks why you let someone else listen in."

She drummed her fingers against her thigh. "Fine. Cliff Notes version. You know how Ariel kind of went nuts and burned down large portions of the city?"

The time where she'd ripped out the remainder of Izzy's immortality first, and made sure his apartment was one of those impacted? "I'm vaguely familiar with it."

She dragged the easy chair across the room and dropped cross-legged into it. "Anyway, people kind of noticed. Like human people."

"You think?" Holden asked.

She turned her narrowed gaze on him, irritation smearing her face.

Izzy reached across the table and covered his hand. "I promise we'll talk. But I have to hear this first."

Holden glanced at Tia one more time before facing Izzy. "Sure. I'm sorry."

"Anyway." She spat the word out with venom. She glared at Holden again, breathed deep, and turned back to Izzy. "Remember, if anyone asks, it was your idea to let him in on company secrets."

Seriously, what made Holden the one person in the world Tia didn't like?

Tia shook her head. "There are people out there, not just angels and demons, but humans, who—and I don't know how they know this, but supposedly they do—want to figure out how to do what you did."

"I didn't do anything. Someone blew up my apartment. No secrets there." And then what she meant hit Izzy, and his gut sank. "That? Really?"

She nodded.

The secret to how he'd kept his immortality. The rule he broke after he fell. Why had Holden just gone still?

Tia paced. "I've heard rumors of angels being used like batteries, of kidnappings, scary stuff. I don't know how much of it's exaggeration." What was she leaving out?

"And…?"

"You're technically human. You know how you did it. You're a loose end he wants cleared up."

The information sucked the air from Izzy's lungs. Did heaven—Gabriel—want him dead? Izzy had never been on the best terms with the original, but this on top of everything else… And people kidnapping angels? Izzy could barely wrap his head around it.

"I have to go," Tia said abruptly. "Stay here, pretty please, and stay safe. You can have anything in the fridge. I'll bring you the rest of the books you asked for."

Izzy wanted to stop her, to drag as many answers out of her as possible. But regardless of reassurances, she wasn't going to open up completely around Holden. Izzy would find out the rest later. Right now he was still processing the fact that he was on someone's hit list.

He looked at Holden, the one bright spot in all of this mess. At least Izzy could clear some things up for him, even if his own life was muddled.

"So, what *did* you do?" Holden interrupted Izzy's attempt to find a starting point for his thoughts. "This big, vague thing the two of you were talking about."

"I merged with a cherub that wasn't mine." He knew the answer wouldn't make any sense, but it was a segue way in to the conversation.

"Great. My entire life is suddenly clear," Holden teased. "You'll give me more information than that, right?"

Izzy sifted through the stack of books Tia brought, until he found the one he was looking for. A reprint of a fifteenth century scroll from Rome about a man who had been stoned as a heretic, because he claimed he could talk to angels. He slid it across the table.

"Am I searching for something specific?" Holden asked.

"Proof you're not alone." Izzy raked his fingers through his hair. As much as he loved his books, he hated this feeling of impotence. Of having to sit around and wait while someone kept an eye on him.

Even though his job back in the day was as a muse, he'd still had power. He could have protected Holden. He could have put up wards. He could have taken Abaddon. There was no question there. He'd done it before.

And now Izzy was reduced to sitting at someone else's dining table, waiting to be hunted or fetched.

He jumped to his feet and paced the length of the room. Nervous energy coursed through him, carried on whispers of the last couple of hours. There was too much to process. Wondering what Holden was keeping from him had suddenly become the least important thing in his universe.

"When I was three, I told my mother the woman at the grocery store was glowing." Holden's quiet voice broke into Izzy's thoughts and dragged his feet to a halt. "By the time I was seven, I had seen at least five different *specialists*, including clergymen from different churches. That was about the time I figured out my life was easier if I kept my observations to myself."

Izzy turned his attention to Holden, and the pain in his gaze stared back. Holden continued. "When I found your church a little over a year ago, I knew—*knew*—the moment I walked in the the that there was something different about it. There's a calm I've never felt anywhere else.

"And then there was you, with one of those gorgeous glows, wrapped around a stunning, confident man, who passed zero judgment on people or their beliefs."

The compliment warmed Izzy.

"So tell me, Father Izzy, what are you? What are these friends of yours? What have I been seeing my entire life, and does it make me crazy?"

Questions Izzy could answer. After the day they'd had, he owed Holden that much.

Izzy explained to him what cherubs were. How falling worked, and that it wasn't always because an angel broke the rules. That in Izzy's case, it had been a choice. And that just a short while ago, Ariel had ripped his immortality from him, before she destroyed parts of the city.

He left out details about who Ubiquity was. No reason to spill it all.

"Wow." Awe lined Holden's voice. "Just. Wow. What kind of an angel were you?"

Such a simple question in the grand scheme of things, it almost made Izzy laugh in relief. "I was a muse; an angel of music."

"Why am I not surprised?" Holden kissed him. His lips lingered on Izzy's, stealing some of the uneasiness and flooding him with heat. Izzy let out a tiny exhale when he pulled away.

His grin reminded Izzy of a hungry wolf. "What's it going to take for you to convince your demon friend to let you stay with me tonight? You can't sleep here," Holden said.

"I hope you gentlemen are decent." Ronnie's familiar voice carried through the door, interrupting the thought.

Chapter Seven

Ronnie drummed her fingers against her leg, willing the guy behind the counter to prep her order faster. Normally, the scents of onions, peppers, and steak were almost an aphrodisiac. Anything yummy was a mild turn-on. Tonight, they made her gut churn. Or that was anxiety over not knowing why Izzy was attacked or if the lightning was aimed at him.

"Order up." The guy in the white apron chimed a bell on the counter.

She snatched the bag from his hand so hard, something tore. A quick glance told her nothing would fall out before she reached her destination. The cook raised his brows. "Sorry," she spit out, before she rushed out the front door and phased back to Tia's apartment.

Why did she let Lucifer talk her into keeping secrets from Izzy? She wanted to save Izzy the heartbreak, and instead she made a stupid call by not telling him about her suspicions. For all she knew, Holden was a normal guy, aside from the most-likely-a-prophet thing.

Tia sat on the landing, knees pulled up to her chest and a stack of books beside her.

Ronnie frowned. "Why are you out here?"

"I went to fetch these," Tia nodded at the books, "and when I got back they were talking, and I didn't want to interrupt, and the staring is really creepy."

Ronnie hated that Tia was going through all of this. "I know. I've got it from here." She handed Tia a convenience-store bag with a pint of ice cream. "I got you a sandwich too. Thank you so much for doing this."

"It wasn't a problem. You're practically family, after all. " Tia stepped out of the way.

Family was kind of a messed-up concept when it came to heaven and hell, but Ronnie appreciated the sentiment coming from someone who'd been human once-upon-a-time. She knocked on the apartment door and called, "I hope you gentlemen are decent," before pushing inside, Tia on her heel.

Relief swept aside a portion of her angst when she saw Izzy, a bruise glaring and purple on his face, but sitting up and looking coherent. She crossed the room, dropped dinner on the table, and hugged him tight. "I'm glad you're all right."

He returned the hug. "*All right* is a relative term, but all things considered, I'm okay."

She stepped back and met Holden's gaze. He leaned against the kitchen counter, mouth drawn in a thin line. Ronnie forced a smile. "Then, considering Holden saw everything, is everyone up to date on what everyone else is?"

Izzy pinched the bride of his nose. "How long have you known about him?"

"I didn't *know*. I had a feeling." This was the worst part about lies. The truth always came out somehow. Why did Ronnie think she could hide this?

"You couldn't clue me in?"

Ronnie wanted to spill everything—hers and Lucifer's suspicions, why she kept quiet. While she felt bad for lying to Izzy, she didn't trust Holden any more than twenty-four hours ago. She had the same gift for feeling emotion as any angel, but the hostility and fear he radiated could simply be because he didn't trust so many people around him glowing. The best she could give Izzy was a grimace. "Can we talk? Alone?"

"No." Holden stepped forward.

Izzy held up a hand. "It's okay. Give me ten minutes?"

Holden clenched his fist. "Fine."

Ronnie waited until he and Tia left the room. She felt bad banishing them to the hallway, especially since it was Tia's apartment, but she didn't know another way to do this. "I'm sorry about your books. Let me fix the damage Tia did?" She'd draw the water from the pages of his tomes instead of from the air around her.

Izzy crossed his arms. "When you told me people might be watching me, you failed to mention it was your people."

"Technically, we're watching Holden." She didn't want to look him in the eye. Her answer was no better than his suspicion. "This is more about him than you."

Izzy sighed. "What's going on? Tell me everything. And I mean all of it."

"I don't know everything. Just what he is, and that…" Lucifer was going to throw a fit, but Lucifer could go fuck himself. "I don't know where to start."

He his jaw. "A year ago, you were lost, confused, and a friendly-as-hell newbie demon. You hated how much Lucifer and Gabriel kept from you. Now that you have the Metatron part of your life back, you're one of them. Playing office politics. Sending people to watch over me. Pulling strings. Doing the same things you resented them for. At least Michael had the sense to walk away before you sucked him back in."

The words hurt worse than a slap. Not only the accusation—Izzy was right about that. But throwing Michael in her face… The Metatron half of her had loved him with such an intense, burning passion, it had turned to hatred when she thought Michael had betrayed her. Uriel had wanted that, and thought they could have had it again.

Michael disagreed. Walked away from that opportunity because he thought falling in love would be distracting. Okay, that wasn't quite what he said, but that's the way she saw it. She shouldn't miss him. Hadn't known him long enough in this incarnation for the longing to make sense. And she had Irdu, whom she adored. That didn't stop her from missing Michael so much it left a persistent, empty pit in her gut..

She couldn't swallow past the lump in her throat. "Fuck you. What am I supposed to do? Ignore what's going on? Sorry we didn't all choose to surrender responsibility for freedom." This wasn't fair of her, but he'd pushed one too many buttons.

"Freedom? Really?" Disbelief hung heavy in his voice. He shook his head. "Forget it. I'm tired. It's been a long day."

"Me too. I didn't want things to unfold this way. I wanted to be wrong about this—which I probably still am—and let you be happy with your new guy." The last bit was harder to force out than Ronnie wanted. She'd rather Izzy was happy with her and Irdu… and Michael. Maybe with a little Lucifer on the side. Since most of that scenario wasn't happening…

"Wanted to be wrong about what?" Izzy asked.

Right. She was explaining as best she could. "Something's happening to us. To demons and angels. We don't know what. Agents are disappearing. Rumor is"—she didn't like to think about the rumors, the implications—"a group of mortals saw the clips of what happened with Ariel. If people are looking for answers, for a way to get to us…"

Izzy's irritation shifted to anger. "And you think Holden might—"

"I don't know. I can't rule out his involvement, but like I said, I want to think he's here for you."

"You want to, but you don't."

She had so hoped to avoid this conversation. "He spilled his heart out to you right after the incident with Ariel, and you know how I feel about coincidences."

"I know *Michael* feels coincidences don't exist."

There was that name again. Why did it dig so deep? She knew him in this incarnation for a month, and hadn't seen him in the several since. She tried to shrug it off. "Anyway. I don't think Holden attacked himself, and if it was Abaddon, it's not like her to hurt other agents. Keeping you and him safe is more important than theories."

"You can't have us stay here."

Ronnie agreed. It was too much of an imposition on Tia. "There's an empty apartment upstairs. It's not much, but I can put wards on it. Stay there for tonight, and we'll get you something longer term in the morning."

"Yeah. Okay." He didn't look happy about it, and she didn't blame him. Until they knew what was going on, there weren't a lot of options. She had all night to make some headway on her research, though. She liked sleep, but if she stayed in her ethereal form rather than her mortal one, she didn't need it.

Ronnie asked Tia to keep an eye on things, then set up wards around the apartments. They were a series of ever-shifting puzzles that had to be solved before they changed, in order to be brought down. Or destroyed—but it took more power than most angels or demons had to make that happen.

When Ronnie was at least a little comfortable with Izzy's safety, she headed home. Fortunately, that was only a few blocks away, and she was in the mood to walk. The humid night air might help clear her thoughts.

She reached the building where Michael's condo was. The place she'd been staying, convincing herself she'd look for a new place tomorrow. She

kept walking. Her mind still whirred too quickly for her to process any single concept.

Two hours later the situation hadn't improved. Her feet were sore, but the pain would go away if she lost her physical form for half a second. Too bad phasing wouldn't give her answers.

She grabbed her phone and dialed.

"Hey, hot stuff." Irdu's greeting made her smile.

"Can I come over?" Visiting him wouldn't give her answers either, but it would be a fun distraction.

****

A low hum dragged Izzy toward consciousness. Correction—it wasn't humming, it was a voice. He forced his eyes open. Every inch of him ached as if he'd been caught in an explosion less than twenty-four hours ago. Why hadn't he gone to the hospital? Oh, right, because he was sick of hospitals, and he'd been certain he could shake it off.

And who was talking? Light from the hallway spilled under the door, and a crack in the curtains let in more from outside. Holden stood near the window, silhouetted, phone to his ear. His voice was low, most of his words vanishing in the whir of the air conditioner. Izzy caught snippets, though.

"It's possible." Holden pressed his palm to his forehead. "He knows how…." He stumbled, and his hand shot to the windowsill, holding him up.

Apparently Izzy wasn't the only one who had faked their way through a series of injuries. But Holden seemed fine earlier. Hadn't even had any scratches from when my living room window exploded.

"Don't know..." More of Holden's words floated to Izzy. "He doesn't, but I think his demon friend does... Mortal, yes... Lucifer."

None of the words made sense. He could be talking to a friend, but with the names he threw around, that was disconcerting. He turned back toward Izzy, who snapped his eyes shut.

Something hard pressed against Izzy's temple, and Holden's voice was close and clear now. "I'm sorry. We have to go."

The genuine regret only set Izzy further on edge. He made a show of forcing his eyes open. "Huh?"

Holden's sigh echoed with the climate control. "I wish it hadn't come to this. I just needed a little more time. But the gun is loaded, and you know as well as I do you can't survive something like a bullet hole to the head these days."

Betrayal, hurt, and fury shoved aside the aches in Izzy's joints. This was bullshit. He'd fought with Ronnie about keeping secrets, when the man he loved was prepared to hold a gun to his head. Izzy didn't know if he wanted to roar in fury, or break things. Maybe both. Anything to not have to acknowledge the hollow pit in his chest.

"Your angel friend was wrong." Holden kept the gun trained on Izzy. A slight tremor ran through him. Or was the dim lighting playing tricks on Izzy's eyes? "This is all about you, not me. And yeah, I heard most of what she said. Do they have any idea how shitty the thin walls in this place are?"

That explained why Holden was talking softly now. Screw this. Instinct, driven by fury and betrayal, coursed through Izzy, and he let it have its way. His hand shot up and grabbed Holden's wrist. He twisted at the same time that he kicked a leg to the side to propel Holden away. The gun clattered loose, struck the nightstand with a horrific clunk, and landed on the ground. Izzy kept his attention on Holden.

The move knocked Holden's support out from underneath him and flattened him. He was on his feet again before Izzy finished rolling to his.

They both lunged for the weapon. Izzy's reactions were sluggish, even given what had happened earlier. He couldn't shake off the haze around his thoughts. This wasn't how things were supposed to go.

Holden's fingers closed around the pistol grip, but Izzy kicked it aside. Holden elbowed him in the gut. Izzy stumbled into the small space between the window and bed, ducking when a fist flew at his head. He drove a shoulder into Holden's gut, and used momentum to flip the other man.

This was hard work as a mortal. Izzy fought to catch his breath as he grabbed for the weapon, rolled onto his back, and leveled the barrel at Holden. Speaking of paper-thin walls, where was everyone? If he and Holden were here to be watched, shouldn't they at least be drenched by Tia *saving* them right about now?

Damn it, why hadn't Izzy seen this coming? Why didn't Ronnie say something sooner? Why couldn't Holden just be the wonderfully perfect boyfriend he'd pretended to be?

Holden struggled to stand, then sank back to the floor again. His chest heaved with each breath. At least Izzy wasn't the only one struggling.

He wasn't as assured by the thought as he wanted to be. There was still the huge looming question of *why did Holden turn on me*?

Izzy leaned against the bed for support, keeping the gun trained on Holden.

"The wards your angel put in place are gone," Holden said. "Replaced with something different. In case you're wondering why no one has come running."

Well, fuck. Izzy licked his lips. He needed something to drink, and was desperate for a different something to take away the pounding in his head and body. He also wouldn't complain about anything going the way he expected. "You could have just asked me to leave with you. Until you pulled a gun on me, I probably would have agreed without a second thought."

Holden shrugged. "You might have been compliant, until we crossed into another state. Then you would have started asking questions, and gotten suspicious… I wish you'd finished your drink. It would have knocked you out all night, and we'd be gone by now. But you had to let your irritation with Ronnie distract you."

Realization spread through Izzy, amplifying the hammering in his skull. "You… slipped me a roofie?" Bad news under the best of circumstances.

Now, the information pushed out a bitter laugh of rage. "Are you serious?"

"I didn't want to hurt you." Holden scrubbed his face. The regret in his voice had to be fake. "Read what you want into the sentiment, but I don't have a choice. We're out of time."

Izzy let the gun droop. Killing of any kind was high on his list of *Things to Avoid*. Could he make an exception if he had to? "You're not leaving me with many choices either."

"Call one of your angel friends. For backup." Holden's suggestion came too quickly, setting Izzy further on edge.

"I think I'll hold on off on that." As much as Izzy wanted to, he wouldn't draw anyone else into this… whatever it was.

A sharp *crack* split the calm air in the room, rocketing in his skull. The door slammed open, connecting with the wall at high speed. Someone grabbed Izzy from behind, hooking their arms under his and resting their hands at the base of his skull. Electricity crackled over his skin.

"Izrafel. Oh how far the mighty have fallen." The familiar voice brushed his ear, summoning centuries of regret, and a healthy dose of fear.

Abaddon. Shit. Apparently things could get worse. And the only reason for her to blast the door open was to make an entrance. She was powerful enough to phase into the room without a second thought.

The assassination attempts earlier were for show as well… The fact that only Izzy was surprised by her presence here implied Holden was working with Abaddon. Which also meant Gabe knew about it. But Ronnie said they were kidnapping angels. Even though Izzy could see so many pieces, none of them made sense when he tried to snap them together. What the fuck was going on?

He needed to get out of here, find answers, and reconcile this abrupt desire to make Holden suffer. He resumed his struggling—twisting, testing for a weak spot. He jerked his head, and his gaze landed on her left wrist. If he hadn't been certain before, he knew for sure now.

Most angels and demons wore their names on their backs in stark, tattoo-like marks. Abaddon kept hers on her wrist, which currently peeked out between her sleeve and glove. She wanted people to see who destroyed them without having to expose herself.

He brought his heel down on her toe. And not any further. Of course, she was wearing Docs. This wasn't a sparring workout with Ronnie. Abaddon wouldn't hold back. He ignored the reminder, especially the part asking why she hadn't snapped his neck yet.

"What are you waiting for?" Her bark tattered his eardrums.

Holden stared at them, jaw set. "You told me you weren't working for Gabriel anymore."

Abaddon's sigh echoed in Izzy's skull. "And who told you otherwise? A flakey little demon with poor intel? Besides, *you* told *me* you could bring this one in without having to blow anyone's cover."

Why the hell did she want Izzy? Wait, so Ronnie really had lied, and this was about him after all? He should feel grateful he wasn't dead yet, but he didn't find as much comfort in it as he wanted. Holden climbed to his feet and vanished behind them. Panic surged inside Izzy when Abaddon tightened her grip.

"You don't get to do this one unconscious." Was that regret in her voice?

"I'm sorry." That was Holden. Hands that didn't yield pulled Izzy's arms back, and rough plastic bit into his wrists and bound them. Zip tie? Maybe. The sharp edges cut his skin with even the slightest movement.

"No car ride." Ice lined Abaddon's words. "You took too long."

Seconds later, Izzy's entire world shifted, and the dimly lit apartment faded from view. He closed his eyes before it vanished completely, already knowing what was going on and not wanting to watch the nothingness. It was the same sensation as falling in a dream, a spiraling free fall where his brain didn't have a spot to land. Except he wasn't falling, he'd just temporarily ceased to be physical. His feet hit solid ground again. The overwhelming stench of ocean during a storm, mixed with stale grease made his stomach churn.

She'd moved Izzy with her. Not a lot of angels could phase a mortal. It required too much energy.

"God, I love that feeling." The exhaustion was gone from Holden's voice.

And apparently, Abaddon was strong enough to phase herself plus two mortals at the same time. Fuck.

Chapter Eight

When Lucifer found Irdu, years ago, with a hitchhiking cherub, he gave Irdu a choice. Asked him if he could be any kind of demon or angel, what would he be?

Irdu was twenty-five, horny constantly, and an awkward nerd who was convinced he'd never get laid. His answer seemed easy and straightforward at the time. He wanted to be an incubus.

He'd never complained about the choice. There were a lot of things he didn't like about being beholden to Lucifer, but the ability to seduce anyone who was interested, and the confidence he needed to go along with it? He'd never wasted that gift.

But having Ronnie in his life was comforting. Knowing when she knocked on his apartment door and he let her in, there was a good chance sex was on the table, but cuddling was nice too.

Neither of those was happening right now, since she was pacing his living room and raking her fingers through her hair.

"Talk to me," he said. When she'd called, he meant to make tonight when he talked to her about her event-finder activity.

That would wait until she was a little calmer.

"I don't know where to start. This shit with Izzy and his boyfriend… Have you met him? Creepy, creepy fucker. He just stares."

Irdu stepped up behind Ronnie and settled his hands on her shoulders. She paused. When he kneaded into the muscle, she groaned. Technically she shouldn't have any aches from stress, but the gesture would feel good regardless. "Most people stare when it comes to me. Gay guys too. So… can't say I noticed."

She leaned her weight back into him, and pulled his arms to drape over her shoulders. The contact was pleasant, as was the trust it implied. He was glad she'd come here and not invited him to her place.

Correction—Michael's place. Irdu didn't blame her for staying there. It was huge. Free rent. The keys were literally just handed to her. He was a little jealous that she still missed Michael. She didn't talk about it much, but the sentiment was there. Michael hadn't earned her adoration. His missing presence didn't deserve to be mourned.

But that wasn't why Irdu stayed away. The place reeked of heaven and it made his skin crawl.

"It's just…" she sighed. "As if this whole *agents are going missing* thing wasn't stressful enough, today it's all falling apart."

Between Tia and Ronnie, Irdu knew most of the story, and why Ronnie had suspicions about Holden.

He understood exactly why it added to her tension, so he squeezed her tight instead of interrupting.

"And then today, out of the blue, Abaddon showed up and—"

"Wait." Irdu's entire body went rigid. "Abaddon? *The* assassin of heaven?"

Ronnie pulled away and turned to face him. "Yes…"

"And you left Tia there? Alone? Watching someone being hunted by a vengeful angel? One of Gabriel's most loyal?"

Ronnie winced. "She's capable. I trust her. And she's got strict instructions to observe only. Not to engage. They're in a separate apartment that's warded, and so is her place."

Irdu wasn't reassured. He clenched and unclenched his fists as he stepped back. Flashes from that night, so many months ago, filled his memories. "Ariel took out an entire Ubiquity apartment block. If Tia is in the same city, I'm worried. You left her a few feet away."

"We're all in the same city. And she's creeping up on a century old. You have to let her grow up sometime."

He didn't appreciate the scolding. "I'd be just as worried about you being in that situation if you didn't have the power of an original at your fingertips. You'd worry about the same for me. Why. Is she, Still there?"

"I tried to pull her." Defensiveness slid into Ronnie's voice. She insisted I leave her in place, and refused to let me put someone else in that situation just because I know her personally. As soon as I found out Abaddon was involved, I told her I was taking her off the assignment. She told me *no*."

"You could have pulled rank. Done it anyway." Why were they still talking? Someone needed to take action.

"Really?" Ronnie crossed her arms. "I should have forced her? She made a compelling point. This was her decision. We don't take away free will."

"No. We just twist the truth to get people to make the decisions we want them to. She's my sister. It doesn't matter that she's an adult and immortal. She's the only person in the world I can trust."

Hurt splashed across Ronnie's face, and he realized how cruel he sounded. He hadn't meant it that way. So why couldn't he take the words back?

"Tia will be fine." Ronnie clipped off her reply. She frowned then wobbled. Her hand flew to her forehead.

"Ronnie?" Concern flared through Irdu.

"My wards around the apartment just shattered."

He was gone before she finished the thought, phasing to the landing in front of Tia's. Ronnie appeared next to him a blink later.

Tia's apartment door hung open, hinges and frame broken. Lingering traces of broken magic littered the air. The distinct scent of ozone singed his sinuses like a dry storm on a summer's night. Lightning. *Abaddon.*

He ran into the room, heart racing. "Where is she?"

"I don't know." Ronnie searched the other half of the apartment. The entire process only took a few seconds, and then she blinked out of sight. She returned a heartbeat later, face drawn and pale. "Izzy and Holden are gone too."

"*Fuck.*" Irdu didn't care that he was shouting. Didn't give a damn if the entire block heard him. Whoever—whatever—had been here was powerful. Strong enough to blow through Ronnie's wards. Fear and the unknown clenched in his chest. Threatening to choke off his breath. "If anything happens to Tia, there's going to be a serious lack of forgiveness going around."

"I'm calling Lucifer." Ronnie had her phone out, and was pressing it to her ear. "We have a problem," she said into the receiver.

Damn right they did.

* * * *

Izzy forced his eyes open, despite the clawing desire to curl up and sleep away this bad dream. The room was pitch black. Someone shoved him and he stumbled, but complied with the insistence he move forward. The restraints on his wrists were cut. He rubbed the slices in his skin while he searched the darkness for a hint of light.

"Izzy." Tia. She couldn't be in on this.

Though, why was he surprised at this point? The door latched shut behind him, and the bare bulb in the center of the room assaulted his vision. He cringed and blinked at the sudden brightness, trying to bring things back into focus. He almost lost his balance when Tia tossed her arms around his neck and hugged him tight.

80

"I'm so sorry. I'm glad to see you, but I'm sorry I didn't protect you," she said.

Apparently everyone was sorry today. Yet shitty things kept happening. Izzy's world solidified into more than blurry shapes. The only furniture was a handful of folding chairs. The room was even smaller than the Ubiquity studio apartments.

Something cool and damp rested against his cheek. "You look like shit," Tia said.

Izzy might have been offended by the comment if its direct nature wasn't a relief. His tongue didn't work. Whatever Holden drugged him with had sunk into his mouth, leaving everything feeling like cotton. Izzy focused on Tia. The cheer was gone from her eyes, and smudges of grease marred normally porcelain skin. She wasn't in here of her own free will any more than he was.

"Your wrists." She traced along his wounds. More of the strange damp feeling rolled over his arms, and a faint spark seeped into his skin. He knew the sensation. It was angelic power—or demonic in this case. Something Ronnie had given him so he could heal himself in the hospital. But this was weaker than he expected, even from Tia. Like melted ice cubes with traces of soda mixed in.

He fought to tug all the pieces of their situation together. None of what he'd seen and heard in the last twenty-four hours made sense on a larger scale. Why were he and Tia locked in a room? And why were her palms wet?

Izzy grabbed her hands, studying them. A thin metal band—nothing more than a bangle, but cutting into her skin—circled each wrist. "What are these?" he asked.

She tugged him toward a chair at the far end of the room. A whole two or three feet away. "Sit down before you pass out."

He didn't argue, but it was more to keep her happy. The tiny lick of power she'd fed him—he didn't know if she'd done it on purpose—had refreshed him. He felt better than he had in weeks. He tucked the reaction away until he could get a better grip on the current situation. "What's on your wrists?" he asked again.

She sank into a second chair, a soft growl escaping her throat. "I don't know. It's making me weak, and my wrists hurt. I can't believe they caught me. There's more of us in here, you know, and I'm going to kill those fucking assholes when I figure out what they did to me. Does anyone know where you are? This sucks, by the way. Do you feel like this all the time? All weak and helpless and stuff? I mean, sorry, but you know what I mean, and—"

"She's a battery." Holden's voice came from nowhere and everywhere all at the same time.

Battery. Ronnie used the same word earlier. Rage roared inside Izzy.

Apparently the chairs weren't the only things in the room. It was wired with a speaker, and Izzy assumed mics. "Cameras too?" He asked the empty air.

"In every cell." Holden's reply echoed off the exposed ceiling and concrete floor. "We have to keep an eye on our power sources and make sure they're balanced. Too much drain kills them before we can find replacements. Too much slack and they break free. So the cameras let us personalize and adjust the restraints as needed."

They were draining Tia of her energy—and she wasn't the only one. Izzy wrapped his hands around hers, which didn't seem to be drying. Whatever Holden and his buddies were doing focused all her energy in her hands. But there were no wires. Nothing binding her to an external source.

The heat of anger raced over his skin. There was also the question of why he was here, but Tia and any other agents were a bigger concern. *Kill them before we can find replacements*. Holden's words echoed in Izzy's head and clenched his chest until it ached. These people—his boyfriend among them—were destroying agents to assume their power.

"How many?" Izzy demanded.

"No." Holden's disembodied voice was sharp. "Once Abaddon is sure you're not a threat, we'll talk. Until then, sit tight."

Izzy wasn't sitting on his ass and hoping things just magically turned out all right. He surveyed the room again while his brain ticked off the possibilities. His fury made it difficult to sit still. So did the tiny amount of Tia's power coursing through him. It set his fingers and toes on edge. He had to concentrate to keep his knee from bouncing.

"I tried the door." Despair lined Tia's voice. She held up her hands. "Whatever this is, it's turned on just high enough I can't do anything."

They'd drain her eventually. Like any circuit, she wasn't meant to be on non-stop. How long had Holden been at this? How many others had they done it to? And what were they doing with the results? More anxiety joined Izzy's anger.

"Izzy?" Tia's soft tone barely reached his ears.

Izzy glanced at her. Was this making her so weak she couldn't talk?

She reached out a hand, palm up, gaze holding his.

She wanted to feed him more power. So she did know what she'd done. He couldn't, though. She needed to hold onto her strength as long as possible. He gave her what he hoped was an imperceptible shake of his head.

"It's okay," she whispered.

Hesitation warred with his desire to do something, *anything,* besides just sit there. He lifted his hand to meet hers.

"Don't touch her." Holden shouted.

Tia screamed and crumpled, wrapping her arms around her knees and sliding to the floor. At the same time, the door slammed open, hitting the wall with enough force to match her torment.

An ear-splitting bang filled the room, and Tia's yell spiked. A gunshot. They'd shot her. She grabbed her arm around the wound, but it wasn't enough to stop the blood from spreading across her skin and oozing between her fingers. The bullet should have torn through her arm without leaving a mark.

Rage licked the edges of Izzy's vision and he lunged toward her. He slammed into an invisible wall.

"Hands off." Abaddon stood in the door next to the gunman. Izzy struggled, but whatever she was doing held him captive.

Holden stepped into the room next to her.

"You told me he wouldn't be a problem," she growled.

"You told me when to bring him in was my choice."

"Do something for her."Izzy roared and lunged again, not making it any farther before. His invisible prison appeared to be four sided and barely bigger than him.

Abaddon locked her gaze on Izzy. "We need him here now, not when you'd sweet talked him into a Sunday drive."

Tia's cries faded to soft whimpers. She knelt, one palm on the ground, the other clutching her arm, and her hair draped around her face.

Abaddon stepped closer, finally turning toward Holden. "And I told you not to put him with her."

"Sorry, *Abbie*. I'll remember that next time." Holden's upper lip pulled into a sneer.

Even if Izzy hadn't seen her jaw tighten he knew the nickname would infuriate her. Some angels regarded their names with the highest reverence. A name was a gift, a purpose. And those few never shortened them. Abaddon was one of those. Why the hell was she deferring to Holden? What had happened to Gabriel wanting Izzy dead for his knowledge?

Who was pulling the strings here—angels or humans?

Holden nodded at the gunman, who holstered the gun. The shooter crossed the room and twisted Izzy's hands behind his back, yanking a new set of plastic bindings tighter than the last one. He jerked

Izzy toward the door, and Abaddon's invisible wall fell away. Options raced through Izzy's head. A kick to his captor's shin, and the right twist of their legs, and the shooter's head would meet the concrete.

Beyond being satisfying, the move wouldn't get Izzy any thing else. Holden had a pistol trained on him, too, and Abaddon was an unknown. She brushed past, heading for Tia, and a new kind of fear raged inside.

"Don't touch her," Izzy shouted over his shoulder as they dragged him from the room.

Before the door closed, he swore he heard Abaddon mutter, "Shh, I've got you."

He glanced at his captors, but if they'd heard what Abaddon said to Tia, it didn't faze them. Izzy continued to assess his situation as they made their way down a short hall. He tested his bindings. The pain was gone. If he tugged a little harder, the ties would snap, thanks to Tia. If she'd saved him at the cost of her own life, he'd never forgive himself.

They were in a warehouse. A wide open room in the middle housed several machines that looked like giant tubs or cylinders—all chrome and reaching up three stories. They resembled unmarked batteries. He shook the disconcerting thought aside. Doors lined the hallway. Which were offices and which had more angels and demons?

Holden held one of the side doors open and gestured. Unlike the barren cell Izzy'd shared with Tia, a couch sat against one wall and a foosball table in the middle. There was even a small fridge at the opposite end of the room. How cozy.

Holden shut himself and Izzy off from the rest of the building, and nodded to the couch. "Have a seat."

This was so much bullshit. If Izzy eliminated Holden here, could he get to the gunman and move through the facility before they retaliated and hurt their captives? Unlikely. Besides, he couldn't fathom having to shoot anyone. Rage was one thing, but death… Being responsible for someone else's demise? Even before he fell, he struggled with the idea of ending lives. Orders from Michael himself made Izzy queasy back then. Now that he understood firsthand how fragile mortal lives were, the decision was impossible.

"I'll stand, thanks," Izzy said flatly.

Holden dropped onto the sofa. "This is the one room not wired with cameras. We need a place where we can be us."

Be us? The idea chilled Izzy. What did kidnappers and angel killers do to unwind? He didn't want to know.

"Why are you still wearing those?" Holden asked.

He knew Izzy could snap his bonds. No reason to let on he was right. Let Holden be the one with unanswered suspicions for once. "What am I doing here? What are *you* doing here?"

The way Holden studied him, with compassion and sadness, dragged back memories of what they'd shared; the intensity, the promises, and apparently— lies. It pissed Izzy off even more. He couldn't believe he'd be so completely taken in.

Holden shook his head, as if clearing away an errant thought. "I see it. The moment she touched you I saw it. The faint traces of her aura flickered off your skin. I know with what you have flowing through you right now, and it's enough strength to do more than snap a plastic restraint. Why haven't you broken free? Why haven't you run?"

"How do you know that's what you're seeing?" Izzy wouldn't give him the satisfaction of an explanation. He was furious at Holden for fooling him, and at himself for falling into it. Nausea rolled inside at the thought of what was happening to the angels and demons here.

Holden's laugh sounded tired. "Everything I told you earlier is true. I see what's happening to you right now, and I know it because I've watched it happen to everyone here."

Izzy didn't know what kind of technology allowed them to snap a couple bracelets on someone's wrist and drain them of their power, but that was what was happening. The large devices on the main floor of the warehouse must be storing power from the agents held captive, and feeding it into mortal forms.

Except Izzy knew from experience that without a cherub, without a direct link back to the power source, a temporary charge wore off quickly. Holden's behavior, the way he'd appeared miraculously better after the explosion, how drained he'd been in the apartment… It was all a result of him using agents as quick pick-me-ups, and then crashing after.

It also meant their entire conversation about why Tia glowed, his fear about Abaddon vanishing into thin air, was all an act. He already knew this shit. *Lying asshole.* Raging at Holden was easier than admitting how much his deception tore at Izzy.

"So, you've figured out the temporary juice doesn't last. And you feel just as crappy once it's gone as you did before you imbibed." Izzy couldn't keep the fury and disdain from his voice.

Holden glowered. "I'll tell you why you didn't run. You're concerned about those *things* in the other rooms." He said *things* with so much disdain and disgust, the word gnawed at Izzy's soul.

"Of course I am."

"You shouldn't be." The words were hard and edged, slicing through the air. "They have this gift, this power, and they hold it over us. They never even help us."

"They help people every day. You remember the demon who broke into my house this morning and put out a fire? The one you have locked in a room back there? The one you had shot?" Izzy's voice rose with each question.

"Who also destroyed your most prized possessions? Who was only at your apartment because your friends in high places have an idea what we're up to?"

"I—" Izzy stalled as Ronnie's words rushed back to him. *This isn't just about you. It's about him.* They had been watching Holden. She'd had a feeling he was involved and hadn't told Izzy. Would he have listened even if she had? More frustration flowed through him, and the plastic restraints snapped without him intending to break them. His hands dropped by his sides, fists clenched.

"They don't deserve your help, because they aren't helping you." Holden's words were full of conviction.

He was wrong. Ubiquity hadn't done anything, because they weren't certain of their suspicions. Ronnie wasn't letting this happen just to see the results. She couldn't be. Could she?

Holden crossed the distance between them, stopping less than a foot away, his gaze boring into Izzy's. "I've never lied about my feelings for you. I love you deeply, and I wanted to tell you all this without force. But things fell apart. You have information that will let us fight them off, instead of letting them destroy our cities. I want you by my side through this."

A selfish part of Izzy wanted to wrap himself in the assurance. But he didn't slip into it. "You lied about everything else. Why should your words mean anything? How long have you known who I was?"

"Since before I walked into your chapel for the first time. But my attraction to you, my feelings for you, are all real." He raised a hand toward Izzy's face.

"Don't." Izzy grabbed his wrist and pushed him back.

Holden jerked away. "You're going to have to choose, and soon. If you do it today, it's going to hurt a lot less."

"Choose?"

"Whether you embrace that you're human now, or continue to serve those who look down on you."

Izzy couldn't hold back his disbelief. "You're going to declare war on heaven and hell? *You*?"

"Yes." Holden's smirk grew. "And you can fight by our side. Abbie? She has a cherub. You could take it. You could teach me how to take it. We could do so much more with their gift than they do. She was already given immortality. She needs more?"

Great. Now Holden had gone all movie super villain. Izzy could almost taste his disdain every time he mentioned Abaddon. Did she have any idea Holden had used her as much as he had Izzy? And why was she working for him? She was a powerful assassin; there was no way she'd been reduced to *Mortal's Errand Girl*.

"You know this is bordering on sounding insane," Izzy said.

Holden raised his brows. "Really? Why did you want all the books about prophets, then? What was your ultimate purpose? You wouldn't have used me to find yourself a new link to immortality?"

The idea of using him for such a thing made Izzy furious. "I never—"

"Or, if you're going to parry my question again, tell me this instead. Who was there for you when you were in the hospital? Even though some psychotic little immortal put you there—someone like Abaddon—*I* was the one who came to visit."

Ronnie and Irdu were there whenever they could find time. "I'm not interested in extending my life at the cost of someone else's existence or sanity."

"Are you sure? You hate what you've become. Weak. Capable of feeling pain. Taking forever to heal." His voice was passion mixed with madness. "You felt the rush when Tiamet touched you. You dove into the energy headfirst. You'd really surrender immortality because someone else, who wouldn't think twice about destroying you, might be unhappy afterward?"

Izzy wouldn't—couldn't—betray those who had been by his side for eons. Holden was asking him to pick between immortality and loyalty. It was an easy decision. The answer should have flown from Izzy's throat before Holden finished. He had one thing right though.

Izzy hated himself for thinking it. He was far more tempted by the possibilities than he should be. He liked the rush of Tia's touch. The energy she'd shared. And he missed having that feeling full time.

That didn't mean Izzy could fathom torturing and possibly killing anyone for power. Angel, demon, human—none of them deserved to suffer because he wanted the best of both worlds.

Before he could process an answer, a series of explosions tore through the air. Four concussions shook the ground. His eardrums rang in response, and he struggled to keep his balance as the floor rolled under him.

Chapter Nine

Ronnie leaned back in her chair. Ubiquity was the last place she wanted to be in the middle of the night. First choice would be in Tia and Izzy's place, with them safe at home and her kicking the ass of whoever took them.

Her second pick was going door-to-door, to every single door in the world, until she found their auras or something that could block her from seeing such a thing.

They were here because Irdu pointed out Ubiquity had the resources and connections to search the world from a single spot instead. That was about the only thing he'd said to her, beyond grunts and monosyllabic instructions, since they left the apartments where Tia was staying.

He'd adjusted the cherub algorithms and tightened them to look for specific indicators. Mostly, large electrical storms that could indicate Abaddon was in an area.

Lucifer had been no help. His response was to blame Gabriel. *Maybe he's trying to plug holes,*

Lucifer said. *Izzy's a loose end. A mortal who knows how to achieve immortality.*

Ronnie was fighting off flashbacks of the night Ari ripped Izzy's cherub from him, and almost killed him in the process. The memory of Ariel's betrayal notched Ronnie's anxiety higher. A friend who lied to get what she needed. Who tried to kill Ronnie in the process. Had she just done the same to Izzy to further Lucifer's plans?

If so, Irdu was right to be furious with her. But she hadn't done any of that consciously. And Tia was there of her own free will.

"*Damn it,*" she screamed into the empty air.

Irdu glared at her, then turned back to his laptop. He was sitting at the small conference table in her office, as far away from her as possible. They'd done a lot of things on that table. She didn't know how she'd cope if *breaking up* was added to the list.

Things were supposed to be better now that she'd assumed her place as an original. She was one of the four most powerful angels in existence. Created before all others. Top tier. And through it all, she felt more powerless than ever. She couldn't even build a ward that could keep another angel from crashing through it.

She could save the tumble into self-pity until after she knew Izzy and Tia were all right. Sick dread slid under her skin at the thought of something bad happening to them.

Being in charge wasn't this stressful three-thousand years ago.

The minutes bled into hours, and she was no closer to answers. The clack of Irdu's fingers on the keyboard drilled into her thoughts. A constant reminder of the lack of communication.

She could go after Gabriel if she knew where he was. That didn't guarantee he had or would give her any information. And it wasn't as though agents come with a built-in homing device.

Freak lightning storms as a search term would have to do. In a different program, she had the system scanning for isolated floods. As in, a city block or two, when there was no rain. Maybe if Tia had tried to help again…

Her computer chimed. Another hit on the flood query. She tried to grasp at hope, but a night of disappointment and dead ends made it difficult.

****

A series of gunshots punctuated with screams rattled Izzy's nerves.

"What the hell?" Holden was on his feet in an instant and running toward the door.

It all stopped before Holden reached the exit, and an eerie silence settled.

Izzy's heart hammered in his chest, his pulse racing with unanswered questions. Who was hurt? What did he need to do to get as many people and angels out as quickly as possible—

The door slammed open, hitting the wall behind it. Abaddon really seemed to like that as an entrance. She stood there with Tia.

Abaddon growled. "Let's see how you like it."

Holden's feet lifted off the air as an unseen force threw him back. He slammed into the far wall with a grunt and slid to the floor.

Izzy didn't know which way to run. Toward Abaddon to stop her—not that he could—or toward Holden to see if he was all right. Part of Izzy wanted him to suffer endlessly for his betrayal. If Izzy let violence justify more of the same, he wouldn't be able to live with himself. There were other punishments for Holden, and losing access to immortality would be one of the worst for him.

Something flashed past Izzy, bright and white like a miniature bolt of lightning. Holden's scream seemed to shake every inch of the building, a sound more horrific than the entirety of the last few seconds combined. His right arm fell limply to his side, and dark red blood seeped through his shirt near his shoulder.

Izzy rushed Abaddon. She held a hand up, and he slammed into an invisible wall. Electricity crackled over every inch of his skin.

"Izrafel." Her voice was hard, but something wavered in her eyes. "Please don't do this."

He pushed against the barrier she'd created, probing for a weakness. She couldn't maintain the wall for long. "What did you do?" he asked more to distract her than because he thought she'd answer.

"Weren't you paying attention? I gave him a taste of his own medicine. Turns out he gives better than he receives." She stepped aside so Izzy could see Tia. The demon's arm was healed, and the color had returned to her face.

"Fucking bitch, I'll kill you." Holden's words were strained. Izzy turned long enough to see him struggle to stand, but his right arm was still useless, and the blood flowed freely now.

"You're welcome to try." Abaddon snapped her fingers and the bracelets on Tia's wrists fell away. "Not that it's necessary at this point." Abaddon's gaze never left Izzy's. A slight smile played on her face, making ice join the heat of rage in his veins. "The explosions just now? The generators are gone. What I'm doing with you is a show." She stepped closer. "A show for you, Izrafel."

Izzy's gut twisted in on itself. The screams and the fact they'd stopped so quickly probably meant anyone human was dead. So much death. For what? "Why?"

"Do you know why I have a problem with what Ariel did?" Abaddon might as well have been discussing bad weather.

Holden needed medical attention. Even if he was borderline psychotic, he didn't deserve to be tortured. Izzy wasn't surprised, but was grateful, Abaddon had rescued Tia and whoever else was here. He understood her reasons for killing their captors. He didn't fault her for the rapid executions, though lingering on the details would make him ill.

However, it devoured him to know *what* the humans surrendered their lives for. It was their choice to make, but he didn't understand how stealing someone else's existence to further their own made sense. Then again, fanaticism had always baffled Izzy.

"You mean besides the fact she blew up half the city?" Izzy asked.

Abaddon's eyes narrowed. "I'm not insane like she was, if that's what you're implying. Her biggest problem is she grew an ego. She thought she knew better than Gabriel. That she deserved more than she was given. She was too young to think big and spilled our secrets to every camera, phone, and computer within the city limits."

Abaddon gestured around her, not pointing to anything specific. "This is what happens when you let humanity think for themselves. This is the chaos it brings, and this is only the tip of the iceberg. You were stupid to become one of them, but because you were created as one of us, because you and I have a history, I'm giving you one chance.

"You're only here to see what they've done. Because you're one of the few who can help them, and this is your one warning to stay out of things. They'll destroy every agent of heaven and hell if they can. And we're your true brothers and sisters, regardless of where we came from. Lucifer doesn't understand this is what anarchy truly is."

Abaddon's voice was cold. "Yes, I still answer to Gabriel. He has plans, and the world will burn if it doesn't submit. I will track down any mortal who thinks they deserve to stand as our equal and show them their place."

The air around Izzy weakened, and he stumbled forward. The invisible wall was gone. He rushed forward. He didn't know what he was going to do, but tackling Abaddon was a good starting place.

Her eyes grew wide, and time seemed to slow.

"She's got one." Holden's rough reminder became part of Izzy's plan before he could process what Holden meant.

Instead of tackling Abaddon, Izzy lunged for her bare wrists, the hint of flesh exposed between sleeve and glove, and grabbed tight.

Skin met skin, and eons of training rushed back. What angels and demons did with cherubs—taking them in, and then exorcising them and sending them back home—didn't require power. If it had, none of the fallen would be able to do it. It was just knowledge, and Izzy had that. He let instinct drive and visualized in his mind the cherub she had wrapped around her. He mentally yanked for all he was worth.

If Izzy thought Holden's scream was painful, Abaddon's sounded like it might peel the soul from the core of the earth. He grabbed harder, despite her attempts to shake him off. The foreign power flowed into him, filling every inch of his thoughts and being. He stumbled back as a flood of emotion that wasn't his rocketed through his skull.

He expected a separate voice in his head, similar to what Ronnie described when Uriel and Metatron had shared a body. Instead he felt all of Abaddon's hatred and jealousy. He stumbled and sank to his knees at the wash of unfamiliar venom.

All of her emotion was there though, not just the negative. Her passion for her job. Her knowledge that what she was doing was right. It filled him, whispering to his thoughts. And it was incredible. Power he hadn't touched in ages—so much stronger than the cherub he had after he fell—sealed the cracks of his doubt. This was what he'd been missing. Abaddon was right. Humanity didn't deserve this gift.

No. That thought wasn't Izzy's.

But it had a point. The whisper of emotion spoke to every doubt he'd suppressed over the past day. Had it really only been a day? It didn't matter. Linear time was a stupid, primitive way to measure reality.

It wouldn't take much to make this feeling his forever. He knew how to integrate. He could be whole again. Immortal. Powerful. He could have everything He wanted with just a few focused thoughts. Gabriel would take him in. Izzy would apologize for the folly of wanting mortality. Tell Gabriel how much of a mistake it was to fall. Then serve, as he was meant to do.

Out of the corner of his eye, Izzy saw Abaddon struggling too. She'd collapsed, her breathing heavy. He needed to help her. She was his sister. Why did he hurt her?

No.

The single syllable echoed in his skull, in his own voice.

Those thoughts aren't yours.

These compulsions were Abaddon—her influence and emotions. Izzy shoved the drive for destruction and control aside.

Tia rushed past him, in Holden's direction. Izzy grabbed every ounce of strength to push to his feet. Concern for the safety of everyone else in the building helped him ground himself. He didn't know if Tia was going to hurt or help Holden, but he couldn't take that chance.

Izzy's thoughts echoed that Holden didn't matter. Izzy stumbled, and panic filled him as Tia reached Holden's side.

Tia rested a palm on the side of Holden's face. Izzy saw the fractured flow of blue between them. The energy she trickled into Holden. She was helping. It was as if Izzy had been blind for the last several months.

Holden had kidnapped her, bound her, and drained her of her energy, and she was trying to ease his pain. It made Izzy smile with sadness to see her blind compassion.

Abaddon's roar dragged his attention back to the immediate threat. The power flowing through him was incredible. He needed to keep it. To integrate it. Which meant keeping Abaddon's hands off him.

Don't.

The tiny whisper was Izzy. But it was wrong. He wasn't going to go back to Gabriel, but he needed to keep this power. Didn't he? Confusion rocked in his skull. He didn't know which thoughts were his, and which belonged to the cherub.

Abaddon lunged, and Izzy hopped aside. Yellow flowed and raced around her, a vibrant aura. She was so powerful, even without the extra help. He needed to figure out a way to get out of here without her touching him. Without her following.

Considering his T-shirt left his arms bare, preventing her from making skin on skin contact seemed as impossible as hoping she'd give up. She tightened her stance and kicked at his legs. He rolled, came up behind her, and swung at her head. She had already moved and spun to face him.

Each time she jabbed, he parried, ducked, or dodged. She matched him strike for strike. It was more intense than anything he'd done in centuries. Abaddon was at least Ronnie's equal, and since she'd been around non-stop for the last several thousand years, far more practiced. But at the same time, Izzy had her cherub, a part of her. If he let his instinct drive his limbs, his muscle memory knew what came next. He just had to not think about it too much.

The rush was incredible. He wanted this. Needed it.

I need my humanity.

No. This was what he was made for, this kind of power.

"Izzy." Tia's panic cut into his enjoyment of the fight. "I can't make this better. I can only slow it down. He needs a hospital."

Holden.

No. Holden betrayed Izzy. Lied to him. Used him.

Adored me. Showed me affection. Loved me for who I am.

The words, Izzy's thoughts, hit him hard, and he stumbled. The emotion dragged back his memories of all the moments he and Holden shared. Of everything he enjoyed about humanity. He slid around a feint and blocked Abaddon's strike to his gut.

If Izzy kept this cherub, if he yielded to this power, he'd surrender everything he worked for in the year since he lost his last link to immortality. But it felt so good.

Not as good as what I had after I fell.

It was true. Izzy made this decision a century ago. Mortality, humanity, that was what he wanted. He ducked a flying kick, closed his eyes, and muttered the brief words needed to exorcise the cherub.

"Fucking bastard." Abaddon's yell shook the walls. "How dare you?"

She'd seen the light leave him. Maybe he should have resolved this situation before he exorcised the cherub. He dropped to his knees, no strength left. She was going to kill him and most likely Holden and Tia. Sending the cherub back was the right decision, but doing it so quickly was stupid in retrospect.

Except he could think now, which meant the extra voice was gone. And that Abaddon hadn't severed his head from his shoulders.

He looked up to find her watching him, eyes narrowed, jaw clenched.

The corner of her mouth pulled up, and his blood froze in his veins. Her voice was low and cool. "I can do the same to you."

Take his cherub? The threat almost made Izzy laugh. "Ariel already did."

Her chilling smirk grew, and she raised her hand in Holden's direction. Izzy didn't have time to move before Holden slumped forward with a soft, "Oof."

"He's not breathing." Panic filled Tia's voice. "He's not … What do I do?"

Shit, no. Izzy's clenched his fists and jumped to his feet.

"Goodbye, Izrafel." Abaddon vanished from the room.

A giant lump grew in his throat, spreading to his chest. He was by Holden's side in an instant, laying him down. Izzy pumped his chest, trying to ignore the mounting panic. Izzy hated Holden for his part in all of this. But part of Izzy still loved the Holden in his memories and loathed any senseless death, even if Holden brought it on himself.

Izzy performed the motions of CPR over and over. He wouldn't give into despair. Holden would come back.

"Izzy." Tia wrapped a hand around his arm. Izzy tried to shake her off, but her grip was tight. "We need to leave."

"We need to help him." Speaking gave the hopelessness something to cling to. It pounded in his joints, and he sank back on my haunches.

She tugged Izzy to his feet, gently but leaving no room for argument. "We can't. We need to do something else, instead."

He wanted to resist as she half-dragged him from the building, but too much of him knew it didn't matter. They cleared the building and paused. She turned back to face the warehouse. From the outside it was like all the others—worn, boxy, and sitting along the edge of the water.

"I'm sorry," she said. She raised a hand, and a giant wave climbed from the ocean. It was focused, as if it had been sliced from the water. It crashed down over the building, and then receded, taking remnants of aluminum, steel, wood, and broken generators.

Izzy couldn't think about what else was in there. He'd rather focus on the fact Tia shouldn't have been powerful enough or skilled enough to wipe out a single building without touching any of those around it.

They sank onto a nearby curb. Why did making the right decisions have to hurt so much?

Tia leaned her head on his shoulder, voice soft. "I'm calling Ronnie. Do you have any complaints this time?"

Izzy fished his phone out of his pocket, careful not to jostle her. At least it was still intact. He had no idea how, but there it was. He handed it over without another word.

Chapter Ten

The atmosphere in Ronnie's office shifted, and she jerked her head up. Jasmine and ozone filled her nostrils, and a tall, blonde angel appeared in the middle of the room, wearing a tutu, leggings, and denim jacket.

"I thought you'd be taller. This is a good look for you." Abaddon's voice wavered, and she swayed on her feet before righting herself.

Ronnie would be envious of the clothes, if she weren't furious at Abaddon—who glowed a lot more faintly than Ronnie expected for someone who had pulled the stunts she did last night. It didn't matter. Swords materializing with the slightest thought, Ronnie was on her feet in an instant and pressing the tip of the shorter blade to Abaddon's throat.

She couldn't hide her surprise when Irdu charged Abaddon from behind, a dagger of his own pressed to her back. No one but originals could summon weapons. It took immense power. She'd worry later about how he'd done it.

Abaddon held her hands up, palms out. "I surrender, and your people are safe."

Ronnie didn't know if the appearance of weakness was the truth or a feint, but she wasn't taking any chances. She finally had control of something. *Safe*. Was that both Tia and Izzy?

"What did you do?" Irdu growled.

"Your demon friend will tell you. Tiamet, right? Keep an eye on her and tell her again, I'm sorry. Izrafel is fine, too. They're in Boston." Abaddon fished a piece of paper from the breast pocket of her jacket, and held it up between two fingers.

Relief flooded Ronnie. Her cellphone rang, jarring her, and Abaddon faded from sight. It took her several seconds longer than it should have to vanish completely

Irdu snatched the card from the air before it could hit the ground, and disappeared. *Fuck*.

Ronnie extended her senses through the building. Both auras were gone. Her weapons dissolved into piles of glitter at her feet, and then disappeared as she dove for her phone. "Hello?"

"It's me." Tia sounded exhausted. "Can you come… Never mind. Irdu is here. How did you find us?" her question was muffled, as if she'd covered the receiver.

"Tia." Ronnie shouted, panic leaking into her voice. "Give me an address?"

"What? Oh yeah." Tia rattled off the information. "See you soon."

The line went dead. Ronnie let relief trickle in, and tried to ignore the hurt from Irdu leaving without her. If this was the extent of the request and there was no babbling, Tia and Izzy were probably okay, and

Holden should be with them. Though, if he was behind this, he'd suffer.

Moments later, Ronnie sat with Tia and Izzy at a coffee shop by the harbor. Irdu stood behind Tia, arms crossed and scowl etched onto his face.

Tia kept rubbing her wrists, though she didn't sport any injuries, and Izzy wouldn't look at Ronnie. He hadn't spoken since she found them here, wearing torn clothing torn and matching looks of exhaustion.

Ronnie had ordered them coffee and snacks. It was the only thing she could think of to do, given her lack of information. Guilt and frustration warred inside. She was trying hard not to push for answers, allowing them time to think. At the same time, her emotion clogged her senses. Where was Holden. What happened? Why was Abaddon involved?

Once again, she hadn't been able to help. The feeling of powerlessness was the same as it had been with Ariel, when Michael had to step in and save her. Ronnie wasn't able to stop the angel as Ari destroyed the city.

The reminder of both added to the void growing inside. Missing Michael. Hating the conflicting memories of Ari's friendship and betrayal. Two of the only people she'd trusted, both turned against her in their own way.

That wasn't a great place to linger, but trying to shift her thoughts led her to Gabe. She still had no idea how she survived the fight with him. And now she'd sat in her office, looking at a fucking computer screen, while Tia and Izzy went through what her imagination told her was an Inferno-like ordeal.

"So, I…" Tia traced the scratches on the plastic table. Unlike Abaddon, who looked about to burn out in Ronnie's office, she glowed violent and blue against the sunrise. "I destroyed the place. Water. A big wave of it. I don't think anyone saw, but I wasn't paying attention."

Ronnie wanted to grab the information and dig out everything else she could. That kind of power… With what Irdu did to Abaddon, she had a whole new set of questions on top of everything else. Those would wait, though.

She didn't want to stop the conversation as it started, and settled for, "What place?"

Izzy shook his head, and then buried his face in his arms.

"It was a warehouse." Tia squeezed his arm. "Run by agents. They… um… They had these bracelets." She massaged her wrists again. "I wasn't the only demon there. They bound us from using our power. Like out of a freaking science fiction movie. They wanted Izzy's friend because he could see things, I guess? It didn't make any sense. The humans wanted to figure out how to be more powerful. Like, we were their lab rats. And Abbie was there. She was furious they had other angels and demons. She killed every human there, except Izzy."

Holy shit. Ronnie's gut churned at the idea of so much death. "But the agents lived?"

Tia shrugged. "Those who were still alive when Abbie went full-blown Terminator.

The table vibrated, and Ronnie realized Izzy was shaking. This didn't have anything to do with humans, the way Lucifer thought, and that was impressive considering his ability to see conspiracies in everything. She didn't want to ask her next question. She had an idea, but it needed to be spelled out. "Holden?"

Izzy made a sound like a bark, jerked back from his seat, and paced several feet away.

Ambivalence filled Ronnie. She hated to see Izzy in pain, but if Holden was in on this entire thing…

Tia swallowed. "Someone shot me, to see how much the bracelets were restricting me. Have you ever been shot? It fucking hurts. Holden tackled them. Someone fried him. There was so much chaos, I don't know who. I just…" She sobbed.

Fuck. Nausea rolled through Ronnie. Angels and demons attacking each other, and prophets. Why?

Irdu crouched next to Tia and she fell into his embrace. The daggers he glared at Ronnie cut through her as much as Tia and Izzy's distress.

"This is what happens when you keep secrets," he growled.

That wasn't fair. Ronnie wanted to argue this was what happened when humans were assholes. Something told her that wouldn't go over well.

She kept her mouth shut, jaw clenched tight, until Tia's crying became small hiccups for air.

"Are you all right now?" Ronnie asked softly.

"Abbie helped me."

Any other day, Ronnie would correct her and point out Abaddon hated that name. "But what about you?"

"I'm alive." Tia shrugged.

That was something Ronnie couldn't be grateful enough for. Even without Irdu, she wouldn't have forgiven herself if something happened to Tia.

Ronnie pushed back from the table and approached Izzy. He stepped out of reach as she drew closer. "Don't." A sharp warning ran through his words.

"I'm—"

"I said, *don't.*" He spoke through clenched teeth, his gaze frozen on the ocean. "Give me time and space. I don't want to say anything I'll regret, and trust me, you don't want to hear it. Leave us here. Go back to work."

"How are you going to get home?"

"*Home* was torched and then flooded. The man I love was killed by a psychotic fucking agent of heaven. This is the second time my apartment's been blown up since I met you. I know you're not to blame, but you're always here, and no one else is around for me to yell at. So leave me here. I'll find my own way home. Give. Me. Space."

"I've got them." Irdu's cold words hit her back. "Go back to the office. We're fine without you here."

"Yeah." Ronnie couldn't make this better. She couldn't take it back. She didn't even know where to start with an apology. She blinked away from the group, impotence, and grief on their behalf clouding her thoughts.

Chapter Eleven

Michael rolled from under the Datsun station wagon, and dragged the back of his arm across his forehead. He felt the smear of grease take the place of sweat.

When he did restorations in bigger towns, he rented garage space with a pit, hydraulic lifts—the works. This was a remote location in northern California, with a population of a couple thousand at the most. He didn't mind driving the beater up onto ramps and using a creeper to get underneath, if it meant having his latest project towed to a local shop and lease one of their bays.

He'd restored cars off and on for a couple of decades, but dove into it full-force after his time with Ronnie. There was that name again, clenching in his chest. The memories that flooded him overlapped his surroundings, the scent of flowers mingling with motor oil, and the taste of strawberry waffles teasing his tongue and dancing with grime.

He shuffled to a nearby sink, to wash away the dirt. Phasing would get rid of it all, but this was about the tactile experience. Every step of the way, from finding an old car for under five thousand dollars, to breathing new life into it to make it good as new, and then giving it to a deserving person.

Surrounding himself with so many sensations made it easier to block out memories of her.

The water grew warmer as it spilled from the faucet, over his hands, and into the basin below. Usually this helped him achieve an almost meditative state, but today his mind still wandered. If he pushed it beyond Ronnie, it drifted to Azazel. He had no leads on where the demon was nor any idea where to look next. His resources for new leads were tapped. Not even Abaddon had anything for him.

"*Damn it.*" He jerked his hands out from under the water when it scalded him. *I need to pay attention.*

He forced himself to be back in the now, and slid behind the wheel of the car. He smiled when the engine rolled over and kicked to life, purring like large cat. The mechanical work was done. Next up— installing replacement seats, which he custom ordered, fixing the side panels, and then painting it. For now, he backed it off the stands. It would sit in the lot out back until he was ready for it again. He cleaned up his rented space and stripped off his coveralls before wandering into the front office, to tell the guys he was done.

Voices, almost shouting, floated out to meet him.

"No, dude. Play it again."

"I'm working on it. It's dog-ass slow."

Michael frowned.

"I'm telling you. Act of God, man."

"No. Way. Something like that? Fucking wizard."

"That's stupid. Wizards don't exist."

"Giant wave of water—"

Meant an agent. And if it made news, one who was doing something they shouldn't' be. Michael's threatening tension snapped and cranked several notches, and he increased his pace. He found Rob and Carl, the brothers who owned the place, hunched over a laptop.

"Anything interesting?" Michael wasn't sure he wanted to know, but he needed to.

"*Dude.* You gotta see this." Rob stepped back and gestured to the screen.

Michael watched the shaky U-View video. Camera phone? Voices in the background directed the action, and the shot swung toward a warehouse. Unlike most of the other buildings in the clip, its windows were intact. The bricks clean. As if it were the only inhabited spot on the block. Smoke spilled from upstairs, and a rush of flames exploded from the top story.

Too many voices overlapped in the video, to tell how many people were watching.

"The fuck?"

"Check it out."

"Why is the ground shaking?"

Then he saw what the fuss was about. A huge wave rose from the water and crashed over the single building. Splashes hit the neighbors, a few drops landed on the lens filming, but it was controlled and precise otherwise.

Every foul word, in every language he'd ever spoken, spilled through Michael's head. If there were another Ariel out there, destroying and paying no mind to public scrutiny, there was a good chance they didn't care about human casualty, either. Michael needed to put a stop to that.

"What do you think it was?" Carl asked. "Act of God, right?"

"Definitely not. I need to make a call."

"Whatever." Rob stepped back into his spot and slapped Carl on the back. "Play it again."

Michael's neck was tight as he strode from the building. His next cherub-laden agent was leaving a trail. Something to be grateful for, right? Why hadn't Ubiquity pulled that video? U-View was their subsidiary.

His fingers itched at his side, as he debated calling the corporate office to find out what was going on over there. No. He didn't agree with Ubiquity when it was created, and the brief time he'd worked there, he saw Gabriel and Lucifer used it more as a red-tape machine than to help humanity. Their mess, their solutions. His decision had nothing to do with needing to resist the temptation to talk Ronnie. She was the only person there who might take his call.

Instead, he pulled up Abaddon's number. She must know something. If the video went viral, everyone had heard about it by now.

"Hey." Her exhaustion bled over the line.

He frowned. "Are you all right?"

"Really tired. I'll be good with some rest. What's up?"

"What do you know about Boston?"

"It's a big-ass city on the harbor." An irritated edge lined her question. Or that was defensiveness?

Michael was never great at telling the difference. "There's a video circulating, and I was hoping you had the inside scoop on who was there."

"It's not the kind of thing that will help your cause." Definitely defensiveness.

"So you do know."

"I can't…" She sighed. "If I give you a different name, will you drop it?"

His tension grew. "It doesn't work that way. *I* don't work that way."

"There's a café in Moscow. East of Red Square, gorgeous view of the Kremlin. Be there at six in the evening local time, two days from now. And try and keep in mind what I said about the pleasant approach."

"Abaddon—"

"I'm not your personal Rolodex. This is what you get." With that, the line went dead.

Michael snarled at his phone, pocketed it, and then rolled his neck.

"Hey. Wait up." Rob's voice and the slap of sneakers on pavement drew Michael's attention. He turned as the man came to a stop, and held up a piece of paper. "A guy was looking for you while you were under. Asked me to give you this."

"Are you sure it's for me?" No one knew Michael was in Springfield except the local people he'd met, and they didn't know specifically when he was in town. He tended to blink in and out as his schedule allowed.

Rob extended the note closer. "It's got your name on it."

So it did. "Thank you." Michael furrowed his brow as he unfolded the lined paper. Handwritten in block letters across the middle of the sheet, it read, *Surprise.* He looked back at Rob. "What did he look like?"

"Wasn't paying attention. See you around, man."

Michael felt the change in the air, as if all the heat fled toward the building and a chill rushed in to replace it. His instincts kicked in and he shifted to an ethereal form before he registered what the disruption meant. Flame erupted from the garage and roared onto the street. In this state, Michael couldn't feel, hear, or see any of it. His ethereal form removed all physical senses, and left him with a grayscale interpretation of the world around him. His brain told him it was an inferno, and for one of the few times in his existence, he was grateful for the loss of his senses.

Fire swept in and incinerated everything in its focused path—another alarm to the jangling mess in his head. The explosion was concentrated on the building. Horror sank in, clenching his mind and stalling his thoughts, as Rob vanished in the heat so quickly, he didn't have time to scream.

In the seconds it took for Michael to process everything and focus enough to draw the heat from the air and dissipate the fire, everything was consumed—the garage, the brothers—leaving shadows of ash and melted, twisted piles of steel in their place.

Grief choked him worse than the lingering smoke. Agony for the lives lost. It surged inside, hotter than the fire, and stole his reason, until all he could think about was the loss of life. The tragedy smoldering in front of him.

He grasped for a sense of calm, clawing through disbelief and sorrow. Alarms blared, jarring him back to the now.

He didn't know any agent with this kind of control over flame, outside of an original. And he knew nobody with such a desire for baseless destruction.

"Pretty." Azazel's voice drew Michael's attention. The demon appeared in front of him. "That worked better than I thought."

Rage filled Michael. He was done asking for surrender. No angel or demon had the right to destroy life without an order from Him. Senseless execution was unforgiveable. Fury destroyed the mental center he'd found. He extended his energy, binding Azazel to the earthly plane, and grabbed his wrist. Michael reached inside the demon and yanked out two… correction, three—that explained the blast—distinct entities. It only took a flick of his mind to send two back to heaven and twist Azazel out of existence. With the demon gone, his body ceased to be as well.

Rob and Carl were merely acquaintances, but the loss of human life, especially as a result of his actions, even if indirect, ached through every inch of him—physical and ethereal. Michael dropped to one knee, exhaustion and grief roaring inside.

* * * *

A lot of people—agents and humans—would kill for a job like Ronnie's. Most of them not literally, though Gabe probably had in order to keep it. She should be grateful. Act professional. Feel fortunate to be in such a position.

She adjusted her weight in her seat, trying not to let it look like fidgeting, and kept her smile pasted in place. This was high on her list of things she never wanted to do, even on the best of days. Today, she wanted to be groveling for Irdu's forgiveness. Comforting Izzy and making sure he was all right.

Putting her own life back on track.

Instead, she was kissing SEC ass.

Mr. Gimbel—he refused to give a first name— sat across from her, firing off questions about her recent rise to the position of Chief Operations Officer. When he trailed his gaze over her for the bazillionth time, the lust he radiated felt like slime over her breasts. "We don't usually see people of your… With your… Who have such limited business experiences slide into a position like this."

She was grateful she wore the suit coat and slacks, and left the camisole and skirt she would have preferred in the closet. This guy made a cherub hopped up on sensory addiction seem tame. At least with a cherub, she wouldn't have felt the associated emotion.

"Ubiquity has a unique policy when it comes to advancement," she said. "As long as someone demonstrates they can do the job, through actions and knowledge, they shouldn't be passed over because of seniority or lack thereof."

"I see." He made a note on his tablet. "And what kind of experience and actions have you demonstrated?"

Could she deck him and claim it was an accident? When Lucifer told her the company wouldn't hold up to close scrutiny, he'd understated things. No one here had any history. They all had paperwork and legal documentation, which made tax time easier, but when it came to investigating their past, there were no previous jobs or places of residence. She couldn't fathom how someone had overlooked that, but apparently either Lucifer or Gabe—whoever was in charge of that detail—did.

It wouldn't matter on a normal day. It was an issue when the SEC wanted to know why she'd only been with the company for six months as a Data Analyst—what Reapers were called on paper—and nowhere before this, and then achieved a top-ranking position.

She fought the urge to tell Mr. Gimbel she was older than the continental divide, rather than the twenty-three years her birth certificate claimed. He'd laugh at her, but that didn't matter. If he believed her, it'd lead to an entirely new set of problems, like having to explain why the angels and demons here had falsified documents. All of them.

Someone knocked, and she swallowed her sigh of relief. "Yes?" She used her sweetest voice.

Tia stuck her head into the room. "We have an emergency."

"Can someone else handle it?" Ronnie hoped not. This was better than an excuse to leave. It was a chance to talk to Tia and at least get one person to hear her out. "Mr. Gimbel and I are in the middle of an important conversation."

"I'm afraid not. This is something only you have the knowledge to address."

Ronnie wanted to kiss Tia for the phrasing. She turned to her guest. "I apologize. We'll have to pick this up later."

"Of course." Mr. Gimbel's tone implied this was anything but acceptable. "Perhaps this afternoon. You understand my questions are critical as well."

She never let her smile waver. "I do. It's been a pleasure. I assume you can find your way to your next meeting?" She stood, and he followed suit and shook her hand when offered.

"I can."

Ronnie almost let the door hit him in the ass when she locked it behind him. She nodded Tia toward the now empty chair across from her desk. "I owe you lunch. Your choice."

Tia's worried expression eased a little. "I'll hold you to it. This really is critical, though."

"That's fine. Anything's better than him."

Tia cringed. "You say that…" Instead of taking a seat, she hovered at Ronnie's computer. "May I?"

Ronnie nodded.

Tia typed a phrase into the browser, and then clicked *Play* on a U-View video. Despite there being no sound, Ronnie swore she could hear the rush of water crashing over the single warehouse, in what she knew from yesterday's experience was Boston.

"Holy shit." Ronnie dropped her voice. "Did *you* do that?"

Pink dotted Tia's cheeks, and she ducked her head. "Yes."

"Double shit." Ronnie's gut clenched and churned, as the implications sank in. First Irdu with the weapons, and now Tia with this kind of immense power and control over water… They were stronger than almost any natural-born agent. And the world could see the proof in Tia's case. "This is on a public-facing… Why hasn't this been taken down yet? We can't have this kind of stuff out there."

"I didn't know who to talk to, so I came to you as soon as I found it. You know what happened, and I could have pulled it myself—" Tia snapped her jaw shut.

Ronnie was stunned to hear Tia had access to do that. U-View might be a child company, but it operated under independent management. Or as independent as was possible in a structure like this. Tia shouldn't have access to yank videos. "We'll talk about that in a minute." Ronnie was already dialing a familiar extension.

"Not a good time." Raphael's irritation echoed over the speakerphone.

Ronnie rolled her eyes. He had been her boss before, and they'd never gotten along. They reached a tentative understanding when she promoted him to manage development and information technology at U-View, in that she understood he didn't like her, and he understood she'd been promoted ahead of everyone else. Again. He didn't seem to care much that she was an incarnation of an original angel.

She wasn't in the mood for niceties. "You'll make time for this. You've got a video on your site."

She rattled off the number in her address bar. "You'll know what it is when you see it. It comes down now."

"I don't have—"

"*Now.*" Ronnie disconnected. She turned back to Tia. "What do you mean, you could have pulled it yourself?"

Tia moved to the other side of the desk, fiddling with her fingers. She didn't sit. "I've been learning on my own, and…"

"And what?"

"There are a few security holes, so I gave myself access to the databases."

Ronnie shouldn't entertain the teensy hint of pride amid her concern. This was bad news. If Tia found the hole, someone else could. "You have to let us know about these things, so we can patch them."

"I was going to. But I was having fun."

"I won't write you up this time." Largely because Ronnie had so much guilt about what led up to the incident in the video. "But we also have to fix it." She was already calling Raph back.

"It's pulled." Raphael's irritation was almost tangible.

"This is about a different problem. I need you to assign me a developer to work directly with Tiamet."

"That goofy little imp who used to sit next to you? I liked her. She never made waves."

Ronnie didn't know which part of his comment bothered her the most. If she thought Raphael had a sense of humor, she'd wonder if he was trying to make a joke. "She's in the room with me."

Tia didn't look fazed. "Hello."

"You can't have someone if you don't tell me what it's for," Raph said.

Ronnie learned long ago that getting the job done drove him, but there were heavy doses of ego mixed in. It was a delicate line to walk. "Tia's my best; you can spare someone who can keep up with her. Besides, wouldn't you rather be the guy who plugged the security hole she found, than the person she had to step around to get it done?"

"We don't have a security hole."

"It's a big one." Tia sounded pleased.

"How do you know? You're not development."

Ronnie didn't have time for this. It was like talking to Mr. Gimbel, minus the visual undressing. "We don't do things that way anymore."

"Right. Everyone there rises to their own level of incompetence instead."

"Give me a developer, or I'll pull rank." Ronnie hated to play that card.

"Like that would be new."

God. She wanted to reach through the phone and throttle him. "Yes or no?"

"Fine. I'll send Tiamet a name and copy you. We'll schedule something, but my person determines how much time this deserves, not yours."

"Thank you." Tia sounded more chipper than she should. Her grin implied she was looking forward to this and not terribly bothered by the tense conversation.

Ronnie disconnected again. "You're too nice."

"You used to be too." Tia winced, and looked away.

Ronnie sank back in her chair. "About what happened in Boston. Not the video; I mean to you. I'm sorry. I—"

"Don't," Tia said kindly. "You did what you thought was best, and I was the one who insisted on staying. Izzy though…"

Yeah. Everything with him was wrong. Ronnie had no idea where to start in making it right, especially since he wouldn't talk to her. "I don't know what to do. And Irdu is so angry too."

Tia patted Ronnie's hand. "You'll make things right. I know you will. What I meant came out wrong. You're still good and kind."

"I know what you meant." And that was the issue. Ronnie understood all too well this job was sucking from her the person she wanted to be. She was at Ubiquity to make a difference, but hadn't expected to surrender her soul in the process.

Chapter Twelve

Michael phased in several blocks from Red Square but didn't assume a physical form. The incident from two days ago haunted him. The fire. Lives lost with no motive he could see. Two sparks ended before they could become more.

Dwelling on that wouldn't help him here, but he needed to keep it in mind. Abaddon's request danced with the impression of an ashen shadow on the sidewalk, telling Michael to try this politely. Reminding him he lost control with Azazel, not only by letting him get away the first time, but also with Michael's response to seeing him again. The execution was appropriate. His rage while delivering it wasn't.

He scanned the rows of shops and people. Staying ethereal wouldn't hide him from other agents. If he could see them, they could see him. But it removed the distractions of his senses and made it easier to spot an aura in the midst of the crowds. He didn't know how Abaddon expected him to find someone with so few details. Or perhaps she didn't.

His gaze landed on a rainbow of colors, bright and vivid compared to the surroundings his mind interpreted as visual. A ripple, like water over stained glass. He knew the demon. Vine was Abaddon's equivalent in Hell. An assassin. A soldier. And old enough he'd been in heaven when Lucifer left and took a third of the agents with him. Vine was a force to be reckoned with, even without the cherub he held.

Michael solidified, and the rest of the world bled in around him. The chill combined with sunshine on his face. Blooming flowers, fragrant and blanketing their beds. The chatter of hundreds of voices vying to be heard.

Ronnie would love it here.

The abrupt thought, combined with the shock to his senses, jarred his thoughts. How long would it take before her memory was just another in the sea of billions? Until her name didn't squeeze his lungs, and beautiful places didn't summon thoughts of her laughing face?

He stashed the surge of longing, and headed for the table where Vine sat. Michael wouldn't lose control here. Not again, and not in a public place. Was that why Abaddon suggested the location? To reinforce her idea of *talking it out*? Michael would have stuck to his word anyway. This was a negotiation. A conversation with an old acquaintance. No reason to risk lives.

Except for his aura, no one looking at Vine would think *demon*, going by cultural definitions. His hair was cropped short, and he stood about five foot five inches. The logo on his University sweatshirt was faded, obscuring the school name, and it hung off his thin, spindly frame. "I wondered if you'd show." Vine stood and extended a handshake and smile.

Michael returned both, and they took their seats. The cold of the wrought iron bit through Michael's clothes. He must be spending more time than usual in his ethereal form to notice so much about how his environment felt. "I am on a mission."

"So I've heard." Vine waved over the waiter. "Same thing for my friend." His Russian was flawless. At least to Michael's unpracticed ears. He hadn't been there in several centuries.

They made small talk until the waiter returned and set a *pirozhky* drizzled with honey in front of Michael. Of course it would be sweets. It almost always was. Not that he was complaining.

"How's life? Up to anything interesting, besides your *mission*?" Vine asked. He partially reclined in his seat, one ankle over the other knee, occasionally sipping his coffee or taking a bite of pastry.

Michael wasn't in the mood to blather, but that was mostly the anxiety of the last few days crawling through him. "I do a bit of this and that." Not so much of the *that*, with the garage and his latest restoration project gone. It would be a while before he was comfortable picking up a car project again. "How about you?"

"Life keeps me busy. I spend a lot of time inspiring people to follow their dreams."

It sounded noble. All angels and demons were tasked with helping humanity grow and evolve as individuals. Hell's definition of what that required was looser. "In other words, promoting rebellion?"

"Only when there's no other option. To each their own, you know?"

Michael did know. "No matter who gets hurt?"

"People get hurt, regardless." The shift in Vine's posture was subtle. The way his spine straightened wasn't as obvious as his aura growing brighter, indicating he drew on power from within. "They hurt each other. They get offended by anything that doesn't agree with them. I'm not doing anything but helping people shed their inhibitions and realize those around them choose to be hurt. An individual can't hold themselves responsible for how others react. They'd never improve if they did that."

"Unless there's physical pain involved." Michael knew the argument. What sounded logical quickly fell apart in the hands of someone selfish or sadistic.

Vine shrugged. "Some people get off on that. But I know what you mean. It's not as if I motivate people to go on killing sprees. There's no personal growth in wholesale slaughter." He focused on Michael, eyes narrowing, and icy blue streaking the light around him. Vine shifted his gaze to something behind Michael. "So glad you could join us, love."

Michael felt the angel before he saw her. Her aura was jagged and fractured, pushing at the edges of his power, as if probing him for weakness. She wore chaos better than Azazel had. She took the seat next to Vine, and Michael's tension skyrocketed. He didn't know her, which wasn't as odd as it should be.

It meant Gabriel had trained and named her. Gabriel had done a lot of that over the past century.

Her appearance was a sharp contrast to Vine's. Her curves were apparent in her black and violet corset and leggings, and she had her wings out. Another reason for Michael to be on edge. She wore them like a costume, but the flickers of purple racing over them said they were anything but an accessory.

"Cassiel, this is Michael."

Her eyes grew wide, and she rested manicured nails in front of her lips. "Not *the* Michael."

Michael tried to be subtle about reaching deep into the ether and calling his power. "The one and only."

"He's here to convince us to change our wicked ways and go back to serving." Taunting seeped into Vine's tone.

"We already serve," Michael corrected him. "That's what we were made for, and regardless of your methods, that's what you do."

"No." Cassiel shook her head and laughed. "*We* don't. It's time humanity took on that role and paid homage to their creator."

Michael extended his shields. As the force moved out, people stood to leave. Nothing like a mass exodus. One by one, diners agreed it was time to go. None of them was sure why, except it felt like the smart thing to do. "It doesn't work that way," Michael said.

Vine's smile morphed into a sneer. "It will."

This time, Michael was prepared when the energy around him shifted. He'd learned his lesson with Azazel. He cast out a second bubble of a shield, inside the previous one. Vine's explosion collided with the invisible wall, which wrapped it up and snuffed it before it connected with the surrounding buildings. Before the blast of flame dissipated, Michael projected a third wave to keep Vine and Cassiel from drawing power from the air around them.

"Stalemate." Vine chuckled.

He was right, but Michael wasn't going to admit it out loud. This kind of display—redirecting people, stopping damage, and preventing his counterparts from accessing energy—took a force of will. Even an original had limits, and he was nearing his. Which led to his next problem. In order to strip Vine or Cassiel of their cherubs, he had to refocus and touch one of them long enough to perform the exorcism. Those precious seconds would be all it took for the other to attack Michael, or worse, the surrounding city.

In short, he was in trouble. Did Abaddon set him up? He didn't like thinking that. She was one of the few angels or demons he felt he could trust.

His shields flexed, and then the one surrounding Vine shattered, snapping through Michael with a jolt of pain that reached from his head to his toes, as if his insides split into a million tiny pebbles.

Vine's smirk grew.

As Ronnie would say, Michael was double fucked.

* * * *

Ronnie couldn't stop thinking about what Izzy said. It had only been three days since he told her off, and it wasn't as though they had the kind of friendship where they spoke daily, but she missed him. And Irdu. She saw him daily. Passed him in the halls. Sat in meetings with him.

He gave her brief nods. He was polite. When she asked him to pull her a list of victims from the warehouse explosion, he didn't question her. *It'll take some time.*

She didn't have time, but she also didn't have a choice.

They were both busy at work, and he'd been *busy* outside of office hours. There was no sex. Barely any talking. It was the friendship that she missed most of all. Irdu understood her. And it ached to the core of her soul that there was a rupture in their relationship.

If Michael were here. He'd what? Brush her aside again? She had that already. And why was she even thinking about him?

Because his name popped into her head more frequently, not less, as time passed. Memories of his voice, deep and reassuring, sang in her mind. They mingled with ghosts of his fingers dancing across his skin, his breath caressing, and that he seemed to know the right things to say to make her smile and think.

"You're not listening, are you?" Samael's question cut into her mental rambling.

They sat in her office, talking about his latest gripes. "The SEC wants a whole bunch of paperwork and you want to know why you can't give it to them."

He raised his brows. "Exactly."

Because when Lucifer and Gabe created Ubiquity, they didn't cover their tracks as well as they should've. Not the answer Sammy needed to hear. "You give them what they ask for. No more, no less. And you run it all by me first," she said.

"Since when do you have a say in financial matters?"

"Since now." She hated the answer but didn't have a better one. Everything in her experience— recently and in the past—told her giving him all the information was the right way to go, but then Lucifer's voice echoed in her head. *Plausible deniability.* If she withheld the details, Samael wouldn't have to lie to the auditors.

"How's that working out for you?" he asked.

"What's that?"

"Throwing your weight around and pretending you believe what you're telling us. You're not Gabriel; everyone knows it. You'll get a lot further if you stop trying to be." The harsh words caught her off-guard. "I'm sorry. That was out of line."

Everyone knew what had happened with Gabe. It was hard to hide the truth about something like a rampaging angel, or the return of Metatron. What she didn't understand was why people were still loyal to Gabe. Regardless of their reasons, the last thing she tried—or wanted to be—was him. "Thanks for the advice." She let the sarcasm leak into her words. "Nothing goes to the SEC without my approval, and you don't offer anything they don't ask for."

"Yes, ma'am."

She kept her posture straight and her gaze directed forward as she strode out of his office. There was no reason to let the words get to her, but they burrowed deep inside and gnawed at her gut. Gabe tried to kill her. Twice. He spent his time subverting the structure. Lying for his own gain. Manipulating the system to get what *he* wanted. She had no desire to imitate him. She just wanted to be respected in her new position, and recognized for the memories she held. She *was* Metatron, damn it.

"Do you have a minute?" Tia called from her cubicle.

That was another thing Ronnie liked about Tia. It didn't matter they both started at the same place—demons working the cherub queue. Tia never questioned Ronnie's promotion or responsibility. "Sure." She strode to Tia's desk.

Tia gave her a sympathetic glance. "He misses you," she said softly.

A lump rose in Ronnie's throat at the words. "Thanks. I wish he'd tell me himself."

"Give him a little more time." Tia turned back to her computer. "I'm getting hits you're going to want to see," she said at normal volume.

She'd come up with a series of automated searches and algorithms that looked in videos for keywords and image patterns similar to those of her handiwork in Boston. Ronnie had no idea how she programmed it so quickly. It was both a relief and disconcerting that, in the last two days, Tia's code had captured a tornado touching down in a city where it shouldn't be possible, and a firestorm wiping out a single auto shop in the middle of nowhere.

Two wasn't a lot, except combined with the video of Tia's wave, it was three more than in the previous decades of U-View. Sure, there was always something out there, but these were big. Unnatural. Damning.

And Tia had another one on her screen now. Ronnie's rattled thoughts crashed in on each other. This one was different. The destruction hadn't started yet. Three individuals stared each other down.

"Why did your filters pull this?" Ronnie asked.

"It has the right keywords."

Someone wanted this discovered quickly. Ronnie recognized the angel with the wings. Cassiel was one of the retrieval analysts who topped the capture lists early on and had been gone before Ronnie's first month at Ubiquity was up. Lightning sparked over her skin, which meant it was visible to the naked eye. A camera wouldn't pick up any auras. Ronnie wasn't sure she was grateful for that.

She knew Vine, too, from her time as Metatron. A close friend back in the day, thousands of years ago.

It was the third person who screwed with her head the most. *Michael.* Her stomach dropped into her shoes, not only at seeing him again, but that he appeared to be the odd man out. None of the three moved, beyond slight twitches. The most active thing onscreen was the power dancing around Cassiel.

Ronnie forced her voice to work. "How long ago was this was taken?"

"This is streaming live. And it's everywhere."

A chill swept over Ronnie when the camera panned out and the Kremlin swam into focus.

Michael, Vine, and Cassiel were in the middle of what should be a crowded city. No one else was on screen. That meant whoever was holding the camera was inside the force keeping the people out. Michael shouldn't be in any danger. He had more power than Vine and Cassiel. Why wasn't he doing something? An irrational fear crept over her. He couldn't be destroyed or anything like that, so where did this concern come from? "Can you shut the feed down?"

"Working on it. It's hitting new sites faster than I can block it, but I'm tracing and canceling as quickly as I can."

That was something. And if Ronnie found the source, she could stop it from spreading. "Keep on it. Here. From your desk. Don't go anywhere."

Less than a second later, she was across the globe. She stood alongside her colleagues, on a length of sidewalk that should have been cluttered with people, but only held four others. She didn't recognize the person with the camera. She flicked her fingers in his direction, and the device exploded in his hand, shards of plastic and glass clattering everywhere. He jerked back in surprise, and the movement gave her enough time to grab his wrist, and banish him to hell.

The other agents didn't give her more than a glance. She was surprised they could see anything, with the bright glows all of them radiated and the heavy tension weighing down the air.

Michael's sigh bothered her more than any of it. "I've got this," he said.

He'd cut ties with her for months—going so far as to ensure she didn't know where he was or what he was up to—under the premise he *didn't want to fall in love.* And *that* was the first thing out of his mouth? Bitterness and hurt tinged the joy of seeing him again.

They'd talk later about gratitude. Or not. If he was so under-joyed to see her, she'd put a stop to this and let him go back to whatever the fuck it was he did. "Obviously." Convincing herself his greeting didn't sting would take more time.

Cassiel laughed—a sharp, piercing sound that reminded Ronnie too much of Ariel, and sank into her veins like concrete. "Oh look. The impostor." Taunting filled Cassiel's words.

Irritation, spurred by days of being unable to act, spilled through Ronnie and materialized as twin blades in her hands—one long and curved, and the other a dagger. Her wings spread from her back, and without looking she knew they were glorious and black, devouring the light that touched them. The ground rumbled under her feet.

"I am *not* an impostor."

Chapter Thirteen

Michael knew Ronnie was a blend of two beings. The original angel, Metatron—whom he loved completely, millennia ago—and a demon who served Lucifer for centuries before ever acquiring a physical form. Last time he saw her, she was struggling to come to terms with being both.

Now, she looked comfortable with it. Red and gold flowed around her like liquid, and her presence singed the air with the scent of burnt sugar and champagne. She was stunning. A Valkyrie wrapped in glory and grace. He wanted to embrace her, fight by her side, and whisk them both away to someplace they could spend decades getting reacquainted.

And she was about to bring this event crumbling down in a disaster of epic damage. If she distracted him and he dropped his shields, Vine or Cassiel would retaliate. If she took one of them on without full understanding of the situation, odds were someone would destroy the landscape.

"Stand down." He spoke through clenched teeth, his resources pushed past their limits even before she arrived. "I have this under control."

"Oh yeah. I see that." She ducked under a fist-sized fireball thrown by Vine. It hit the side of a building and sent chunks of rock and mortar spraying everywhere. "No, wait. I don't buy it for a second."

Michael couldn't spare more energy to stop Vine. Fragments of brick clattered to the ground around them. At least it was physical, so it didn't hurt. Ronnie's words, her posture, the way she ducked and dove and exchanged swipes with Vine—this wasn't the same agent he remembered from either time in his life. She was far more confident. And that didn't stop the surge inside of wanting to protect her. Putting time and distance between them hadn't done anything to diminish his desire for her. "How did you know we were here?"

"You're trending." She twisted and spun, catching most of Vine's projectiles with her blades. A swipe with her right arm, and she destroyed another ball of flame with the longer sword. A block with her dagger hand, and the lightning he summoned faded to nothing. Her moves were complicated. Too showy. And outside the realm of Metatron's knowledge. She'd been taking lessons. "Duck, by the way."

He was already twisting aside, away from Cassiel. He pulled back the restraints that held her, to grab her arm. This would be a risk, but with Ronnie here, he could take it. He paused. Ronnie was making him hesitate to fulfill his objective. What would she say if she knew he was executing their people, regardless of his reasons?

Cassiel's power surged through Michael, and she broke his grip before he could act. "I was starting to think you wouldn't let me play," she said.

"I won't." He bound her again. He had more energy to devote to her with Ronnie distracting Vine, and even with a cherub, she wasn't as powerful as he was. Her aura flickered and danced in protest. "What do you mean, trending?" he asked Ronnie.

Vine rolled when Ronnie dove at him with her sword extended. As if expecting the dodge, she whirled and brought her secondary weapon up for the follow-through. He didn't spin back to face her. Instead, he planted a palm on the ground. Electricity—both physical and ethereal—crackled over his skin and along concrete, rumbling through the sidewalk and making the other three stumble.

Fear for Ronnie's safety and instinct clenched in Michael's chest, and he nudged out enough air to keep her from falling before he realized he was doing it. It meant letting Cassiel go again.

A wash of lightning mixed with ether slammed into his back.

He snarled at himself when he realized his *help* threw Ronnie off balance.

"Old man doesn't have any concept of how this world works," Cassiel taunted.

"Have some respect for your superiors, you stupid twat." Vine glared at Cassiel, then lunged at an off-kilter Ronnie, who twisted and rolled at the last minute. She landed on her back, blocking him with her right arm and aiming the left at his gut. He blinked out of sight before she could connect, and reappeared several feet back.

"A little help here?" Irritation underlined Ronnie's words. "Or are you a spectator today?"

She was right; the fight was taking too long. With each new blast, more of the cityscape was destroyed, leaving gaping wounds in the street and sidewalk, and rending the buildings within his shields near collapse. This was what Michael wanted to avoid, but he wouldn't lose his temper. He'd made a miscalculation, trying to hold the other agents' forces, rather than eliminating the threats quickly. He pulled all his power back to him and forced it through his limbs and body.

"I don't think she's an impostor. The Great and Mighty Michael doesn't let just anyone throw him off his game." Vine lobbed another fireball at Ronnie. Except it flew wide and took out half a shack a block away. He'd missed on purpose.

Michael reached for Cassiel, but she cast out an invisible wave that sent him stumbling back. "I'm not convinced either of them is that great." Cassiel sounded bored. "We're both still here." She fired at Michael again, this time a vibrant stream of electric blue that singed the air and left the scent of ozone in its wake.

Michael copied the tactic he'd witnessed, blinking out of sight, and reappearing next to her.

"Holy *fuck*. Do you ever stop talking?" Vine shouted. He vanished and reappeared at the same time, beating Michael to the target. Vine grasped Cassiel by the throat, and an array of lights passed between them. Her screams lasted less than a second as he absorbed her cherub, and she was gone. He turned to Michael. "I really hoped you'd kill her sooner. She never fucking shut up."

Michael stepped back, his concern multiplying threefold. Why had Vine done that? Taken out an ally without a second thought?

Vine flickered from view, and then reappeared a few feet away. The non-pattern continued, with Vine vanishing and reappearing in a new spot with every blink, making him impossible to track. Each time he phased into sight, the glow around him was brighter. He was building up a reserve of strength for something. He'd taken Cassiel's cherub and drawn it into himself.

"We have to stop him," Michael said.

Ronnie growled. "No shit, Sherlock." Her scowl melted to a wicked smile that sent ice running through him. "Gotcha."

No she didn't. Vine blinked into sight and back out. Whatever he was summoning would take everything down. Michael could throw up another shield to minimize damage—and risk drawing this out longer—or gather enough power to exorcise the ancient demon, but not both.

Vine reappeared, a scream tearing from him that threatened Michael's eardrums even in a quasi-mortal form. Vine stayed tangible for more than a heartbeat, and Ronnie phased in front of him.

She rested a hand on his cheek. "And now she's talking in your head, isn't she?" An odd combination of taunting and sympathy filled her words. "Your last steal didn't have much of a personality, did it? God. This must suck for you."

Whatever he pulled from Cassiel would think and sound like her, if she'd shared a head with it for any amount of time. If he thought she talked too much face to face, having her voice in his head must be wreaking havoc on his sanity.

Similar to Vine touching Cassiel, power flowed between him and Ronnie, but it left her again in a blink. Despite it only lasting a second, Michael saw she didn't take all of Vine. Only what didn't belong to him. And then Vine was gone. Vanished into thin air.

The lightshow blinked away from Ronnie, and she shook her head with a shudder. "And I thought one voice was bad." When she looked up again, her eyes were clear and narrowed, her gaze focused on Michael. "Was that so hard? Maybe Cassiel had a point. You *are* slipping."

"What did you do?" he asked. With the immediate threat gone, he was free to focus on her. How fierce she looked with her hair windblown. How tempting and delicious the anger was that flashed in her eyes.

She rolled her neck, and her body solidified, becoming mortal again. "I sent him home. What was I supposed to do? Buy him coffee?"

Definitely not the same demon he left all those months ago. The adrenaline racing through him didn't ebb. It focused into a narrow point of desire, and he struggled to quench it. "As in, to his apartment?"

Now he had more time to observe and process, he realized she wore a pinstriped jacket and matching slacks. She shed the coat, which left her in a shimmery camisole, and flexed her shoulder blades. Didn't matter which incarnation she was, she hated having her back covered. An agent's wings were ethereal, but she swore she could feel them suffocating. The familiarity, combined with these new aspects of her, amplified his want. Did she taste like the burnt sugar of her aura? Would the ferocity follow her into the bedroom?

"As in, to hell." She brushed the dust from her pants.

"You can do that?" he asked.

"Can't you?" She uprighted a chair and dropped into it. Around them, people milled back in. The screaming started and the phones came out when they realized how much had been damaged.

"Not to hell. Only to heaven." It was the way the power flowed. He was an angel. He could take himself to hell, but not send others there. "We need to have this conversation somewhere else." He'd also like the chance to talk about other things. Despite his resolve to keep his distance, having her here made it difficult to watch her leave.

"Lucky me, I have one foot in either place. Special little snowflake and all that. What makes you think we have more to discuss?"

*

"Because you haven't left yet." Michael extended his hand.

Presumptuous ass. He had a point, though. Chaos was exploding here, and the damage was

144

already done. Seeing the destruction made Ronnie's heart hurt. She settled her palm against Michael's.

She was supposed to push him away—tell him *have a nice immortality* and leave. When she took his hand so he could phase them, images skated through her mind. Meeting him in a temple in Israel, millennia ago. Sparring with him in heaven just a few months back, as he tried to coax her memories to the surface. Talking until the early hours of the morning.

She swallowed the longing that came with memories from two lives. "Fine. Let's talk."

In a blink, sand and sun replaced their surroundings. The crash of waves carried the scent of the sea and calmed her. *Did he bring me here on purpose? No.* He shouldn't remember a random comment she made at a random point about loving the beach. It had to be a coincidence, and wasn't at all because he was considerate, or that he was failing as hard at forgetting her as she was him. He looked incredible, and the strength in his grip. It wasn't fair that seeing him made her miss their past even more.

He got them here quickly, which meant he was more powerful than she remembered. Then again, these days everyone was. They'd have to start measuring ability on a scale of how many buildings an agent could destroy with a wave of their hand, rather than whether or not they could make a spark of lightning flow over their skin without breaking a sweat.

She spared him an appraising glance. Almost a head taller than her five-foot five-inches. Dark hair, pale eyes, and fashion sense three decades old. It didn't matter that his clothing was out of date. Seeing him in the faded jeans and grungy plaid shirt did dangerously tantalizing things to her.

He let go of her and disappointment rushed in. This was ridiculous. He was sexy, but so were lots of beings. Like the two currently pissed off at her for being inconsiderate—

"Ever heard of collateral damage?" The irritation in his question made it easier for her to cut off her gawking.

"Funny you should mention that. I found you on U-View, and that's some fairly serious damage. Do you know what kind of PR nightmare this is?"

"What?" He stared at her, eyes wide for a second, before giving a disgusted snort. "I mean the people. You know—*human beings*, not a company image? Buildings were destroyed. Lives put at risk."

If she wanted this kind of shit, she'd have stayed at the office. He was supposed to be relieved to see her. Be more than irritated with her. "It would have been worse if you'd continued to stand there hiding behind your invisible bubbles of nothingness."

"Things didn't start exploding until you arrived."

There was no way he was turning this on her. "Including your opponents. And yeah, things blew up, but no one died. Were you going to stand there forever, hoping neither of them got the drop on you? Vine was free when I showed up."

"They'd get tired before me."

"You were expending more energy than they were. None of us are limitless." She clenched her hands until her nails dug into her palms. When he was being a self-righteous prick, it was simpler remembering how *just another guy* he was.

"You'd know."

He meant what she did to Gabe, draining of him of his power reserves to the point it took him months to recover. "He literally stabbed me in the back. I did what I had to do." Her own words echoed in her head. She was saying that too often, and the sentiment tasted sour.

"So did I." He turned away. "Thank you for your help. Am I keep you from PR damage control, or do you have time to have an actual conversation?"

She didn't want this. It was good to see him, despite the argument. She missed him enough it clawed at her throat. More than was reasonable. Putting a name to the pit behind her ribs made the desire to spend time with him stronger. "I'd like to talk. Please?"

He looked at her, brows raised in expectation.

"I'm sorry there was so much destruction." Not that she saw a way to avoid it, but it hurt to see things wrecked. "I wish there was another way."

"What do you know about what's going on?"

"Nothing." She hated admitting that, more because it meant she didn't have next steps than because she was worried Michael would judge her. He didn't work that way. "Or close enough. Humans are kidnapping agents. Gabe might be involved. Agents are hunting people. There are explosions that could only be ours. More than one, as if Ariel wasn't enough. My best guess is this is going to get worse before it gets better."

"It will, unless I can keep it from happening."

"Alone?" That wasn't what she meant to say. Not that she had any sort of plan, but she was pretty sure somewhere in her head that letting him walk away should be the end result.

"Less red tape this way. Fewer"—he dragged his gaze over her—"distractions."

So she wasn't the only one this meeting was impacting. Heat flooded her under his gaze. She didn't know if that made her feel smug or not. She never meant to be a distraction—not before, and not now. Memories teased her—his hands roaming her body in the shower, the way she molded against him when he held her. On second thought, *that* kind of distraction sounded nice. "We can help each other." Was she offering to keep him around, or to get more information from him? She didn't know.

"You're part of the machine." His disdain squashed her pleasant fantasies.

"I have to do something." The argument felt weaker aloud than when she used it to convince herself. This was why Irdu and Izzy were mad at her too. How much denial was she in about what she was doing? No. She made the decisions she needed to with the information she had. "Ubiquity has resources, information—"

"Corruption. Bureaucracy." He might as well have plucked the words from the top of her thoughts.

An ache spread in her chest. Familiarity mixed with frustration and longing. It was a bitter cocktail. "*God.* You're infuriating. How did I forget that? I missed you."

"I—" He scrubbed his face with his hand. "I miss you too. I struggle to keep my distance, even though it was my idea."

"Come back and work with us?" This wasn't fair of her. If she was miserable dealing with all the second-guessing and corporate politics, he'd hate it more. Michael preferred straight-forward. At least part of her more or less grew up in the system.

"Why don't you quit? Do this on your own."

That wasn't an option. "There are thousands of agents of heaven and hell, because there need to be that many. There are also four originals for a reason. We're not made to be independent entities."

"And Gabriel shot that notion to pieces. The rules have changed over the millennia."

"The rules have changed over the last six months." She couldn't keep the frustration and pleading from her voice. "And you put up a good front, but you're not following any rules."

"Personal growth, for ourselves and humanity?" He made it sound so straightforward. "I'm certain I've got that covered."

Had he always been so stubborn? She didn't know. The realization hit her hard. As Metatron, she was head-over-heels for Michael. Together, the two of them could do no wrong. As Uriel, Metatron flooded her with emotions from the past. Uriel spent so much time questioning who felt what, that Michael left before they had a chance to rediscover each other. "It's not that simple."

"It never is. If I go back to Ubiquity—which I tried once if you remember—I won't have the freedom to pursue what really needs to be done."

"So you're going to keep doing this acting on your own thing, even though it's too much for even you to handle solo, and not share whatever it is you know?" Something nudged the back of her mind. A thought from earlier that flitted away before she could grasp it. It solidified and dropped in a heavy pit in her gut. *No.* "What did you think I was going to do with Vine? You were surprised I sent him to hell. You couldn't have done that, so what was your plan?" It wasn't true. He wouldn't have. He wasn't… "I might have a gap a few thousand years gap in my knowledge, but we don't kill our own."

He clenched his jaw. "Times have changed."

"Not like that. We don't kill our own." She was repeating herself, but it was better than giving into the urge to sink into the sand. There were too many implications when it came to killing angels and demons. A sharp stab, invisible but vivid, spread through her gut as if she'd been run through. An old wound from when Gabriel stabbed her three-thousand years ago, intent on destroying her.

She stepped back. "Are you really taking agent lives? Izzy said that wasn't possible." Dread pooled around an ancient wound that wasn't there. "You've figured out how."

"You said it yourself—I can't send demons back to hell. If they've taken a cherub for the purpose of gaining power and skirting the system, they've lost their chance at reform." His face was an impassive mask, and his voice never wavered.

Up until now, she assumed Ariel had been stripped of her rank and name but existed in some form in heaven. Metatron survived an attempt on her life; Ronnie thought it worked that way for everyone. "You don't know they can't change. Did you figure out how to do it before or after Ariel?" If Gabe knew how to kill, Ronnie wouldn't be here.

Michael dropped his gaze.

"Oh God. You… She's…" It hit her harder than she expected. True, Ariel tried to take a part of Ronnie, but they were friends before that. Ronnie remembered that bond. Missed that connection. Dreaded trusting anyone else enough to try again.

Michael was killing immortal beings, and thought it was all right. Banishing them to non-existence. Bile and tears rose in her throat. She needed to process, but not in front of him. She blinked from his sight without another word.

Chapter Fourteen

Ronnie's thoughts were a muddled mess. *Are you free?* As she clicked *Send* on the text to Irdu, she remembered they weren't quite on speaking terms.

This was a good time to fix that. She needed to stop burning bridges and start rebuilding foundations.

Working.

His single word reply wasn't surprising, but it still hurt. She was about to pocket her phone when it buzzed in her hand again. He'd sent a follow up.

Maybe after work. I saw the video. I'm glad you're safe.

A sad smile slipped out without her permission. What was she supposed to say to that? *Thanks.*

In that case, Ronnie wasn't going back to the office. She should—it was her job, and she tried to be responsible—but the revelations of the day spilled inside. She thought she'd put most of this behind her, but apparently she'd tucked it away instead of coping.

She took herself to the middle of a crowded casino in Las Vegas. The highs and lows, good and

bad, and all the lights and noise flowed over and through her—an external source of chaos to lose herself in.

Michael had always been a pillar of everything good. It was one of the things that drew her to him. He had empathy, and understanding, and he *cared*. When he was with Metatron, he listened. When he met Uriel, even before he knew who she was, he went out of his way to make sure she was all right.

Now he was snuffing out something that was meant to be eternal. Like someone had tried to do to her. Was she supposed to be okay with that? In a single revelation, he'd fallen from his pedestal, and summoned her most painful memories.

This sucked. Once upon a time, a bad day would mean sneaking away for some alone time with Irdu at work, and then going dancing with Ariel. The names ached in every inch of her.

She needed to be somewhere like the clubs she and Ari used to frequent, surrounding herself in the emotions of the people. Someplace she could be herself but vanish in the crowds. And not home, since she'd come up with a string of excuses about why she never moved out of Michael's vacated condo—the place she was only supposed to be until she got back on her feet.

When she was exhausted and it felt like no one believed she deserved her position, she liked to curl up in the master bed, and lose herself in the traces of his presence. Wow, she was a child. Tomorrow seemed like a good time to get her shit together and move out. Today, she was clearing her head.

It was barely nine a.m. in Nevada. The casino shops weren't open, but the floors were packed. This was a temporary place to collect her thoughts, but Ronnie didn't want to stay. She pulled up a Ubiquity app on her phone. It was one of their most popular. It had global lists of events. For instance, if someone wanted to know where all the soccer games, gun shows, or flea markets currently took place, they could find them here. The app missed smaller venues, but like everything about Ubiquity, the standard user's needs came second. The purpose of this was to help track cherubs, sensory addicts, and these days, rogue agents who felt they were above the rules.

Ronnie might worry they had a several-gig file on her, if she didn't trust Irdu to have her back. He was so good to her.

And if she couldn't see him, she wanted a fantasy convention. A big one. Where she could dress as an impish demon and keep her wings out, and no one would think for a moment they were real. *Bingo*. There was one going on in the UK right now. She wasn't going looking like this, though.

The shops wouldn't open until ten, but she was enjoying the rush. The not being in her own head. She meandered through the rows of machines, lingering on the clatter of digital noises and the sparkle of lights. It was better than watching dimming and spiking auras. Non-threatening. No expectations.

Waves of joy swept past her, tasting like fruit, and mingled with the bitter of disappointment and gloom. She tried to shrug off the negative. To rid her mouth of the flavor. She quickened her pace and moved toward the pit and the small group of people watching a roulette wheel.

"Hey, angel." One of the guys gestured to her. He had no idea how appropriate the nickname was. "Come be my good luck charm."

She supposed she could tweak the air currents, make sure he won, but she wasn't interested in fixing the odds. The way he raked his gaze over her though, lingering on her hips and chest… She liked some emotions more than others. Grief, ambivalence… they weighed her down. Lust was one of her favorites, and it spilled from him like decadence in sweet cream.

"I'd love to." She stepped up next to him at the table and let his desire wash over her, rich, dense, and flowing across her skin with seductive grace.

"Red or black?"

She furrowed her brow. "I'm fond of both. Evens?"

"Playing it safe. We can start there." He placed his bet, and the dealer spun the wheel. He won. Only his money back, but it was enough of a confidence boost to raise his mood. He wrapped an arm around Ronnie's hips and tugged her closer. "Nice suit. You been up all night or skipping work?"

"Either. Both. Place a bet on the middle dozen." She didn't want to talk about what brought her here, even in the vaguest terms.

He won again, doubling his money, and continued to take her advice, shifting his chips with each spin of the wheel. Each time his stack grew, so did the desire he radiated. She liked that feeling. The way it caressed her cheeks. Danced along her spine. Flowed along her fingertips and every inch of her body. The minutes crept up on ten. She'd tell him *farewell* soon, and they'd both be happier with their mornings.

"I'm on a hot streak." He traced a thumb over the back of her hand. "I can't fucking lose." Because she did a decent job of calculating the odds. It wouldn't hold up, but she wasn't going to tell him and spoil the mood. "What's your favorite number, angel?"

"Four." The answer slipped out before she could consider why he asked.

He gave the dealer his bet and thanked him.

"Don't..." She let pleading leak into her voice.

"No more bets," the dealer called.

"Don't look so stressed." The player squeezed her hand. "You're my good luck charm."

Because she was pushing someone's limits for a contact high. She hadn't done anything special, but he was about to lose everything on the table. The wheel seemed to turn in slow motion. She watched the ball bounce and clatter and click over four. Before the spinning stopped, her companion's mood plummeted toward depression. The fresh cloud settled around Ronnie, bringing back a reminder of what she wanted to escape.

She vanished before he could turn to her, and reappeared in her office at Ubiquity. Her mood plummeted too low to have an interest in the convention. Might as well work after all. Here the gnawing of pending disaster always sat in her gut.

She expected it. Maybe that was fatalistic, but she struggled to shake it off.

She sank into her chair. Everything she tried to push aside rushed back. Michael was destroying angels and demons. Erasing them from existence. And Ariel had been one of them. She knew Ari had been too far gone to save. Cassiel was the same; Ronnie didn't question that. Even for the flash of a second Cassiel's already crumbling essence remained in Ronnie's head, she'd felt the instability.

If she used logic to process the situation, she knew where Michael was coming from. He represented His Will and wouldn't act outside of that. But her past—both that she'd been on Gabe's hit list twice, and the loss of Ariel, made the revelation ache.

She logged into her computer and scanned her email. A message from Irdu caught her attention.

The list you asked for.

That was vague. There was a document attached, with a list of addresses across the country and corresponding times. After he'd found the victims she asked for, she'd asked him to get funeral locations for all the people impacted by the different disasters of the last few days. There wasn't a good record of who died in Boston, but the explosion and then the tornado... Ronnie didn't know why, but she needed to see those people were laid to rest. Whatever awaited them in the next life, she needed to know they had closure in this one.

She sent him back a sincere *Thank you. We on for tonight? I'd like to talk.*

Don't know. His reply came through seconds later.

The ache in her chest grew.

* * * *

Michael didn't know how it was possible for one little encounter to wreak so much havoc on his thoughts. One nice thing about being an angel was that when he got an order from above—and it didn't happen often—he didn't need to draw on faith; he *knew* it was real. That didn't stop him from feeling guilty when Ronnie turned that wounded look on him. He didn't question his orders, just her reaction to them.

Which he shouldn't do. This was the reason he put distance between them in the first place. He never wanted to have to choose between her and duty. He could have done a better job explaining to her why he had to kill their own kind, though.

And speaking of playing the executioner—the word rang in his head with bitterness—he wanted to talk to the person who sent him to Russia, and he wouldn't settle for a phone call. He didn't want to believe Abaddon set him up, but from the moment she stepped back into his life, he knew there was a chance of that. A breath later, he stood in front of a tiny beach cottage in Ostia, Italy. It was early evening, just past five. He had no idea if she'd be there, but he'd call if he had to. He hoped for the element of surprise.

When she answered the door, he couldn't hide his shock. Her glow was barely visible in the evening light, and dark circles lived under her eyes.

"Abaddon?"

"At least that answers the *how bad do I look* question." She gave him a flat smile. "Do you want to come in?"

The cherub she carried for so long, the additional source of power she insisted she'd think about giving up *when this was all over*, was gone. He stepped inside but hovered in the doorway. "Did you...?"

"Give up my cherub? Technically. I told you when I gave you the Red Square information it was a bad time. I'm still recovering. Do you want something to drink?"

"No. Thank you." Curiosity nagged him. He wanted to find out what happened, but he wasn't sure he could cope with more stories.

"I suppose not." She leaned against the wall, arms crossed. "How's Vine?"

"Banished." He studied her in the dimly lit room. Why did she have the curtains drawn? She didn't radiate enough of a glow to see her face clearly.

Her eyes grew wide, and she shook her head. "He... What...? You don't— What happened?"

"I was hoping you'd tell me." He expected a more guarded reaction from her. Less stunned.

She raked her fingers through her hair. "He told me he wanted to talk to you. And I knew he was probably lying, but when you called, I was having an off day, and it was easier to pretend he was being sincere. I'm guessing he wasn't? I figured you'd handle him either way. But banished? What happened?"

She looked shocked, but he wasn't ready to give her the whole story. He didn't know if it was because he didn't trust her, or because the details of what happened in Moscow bothered him. "He brought a friend, and Ubiquity got to him before I did."

"Ubiquity sounds less than ideal. I promise I thought his intentions were good, but I'm sorry I sent you there without warning you."

It would be easy to let her take the blame. He'd known from her vague description something was up, and he went in anyway. Maybe he was looking for the excuse to destroy another agent, despite his promise to try and talk things out. He wasn't sure anymore. "What made you give up the cherub?"

"An old friend inspired me." Her aura flickered, and she wobbled.

Her comment tugged at their conversation from the art gallery, but he couldn't place why.

"I need to lie down. You're welcome to stick around and grill me after. I won't have any more answers for you, but if it convinces you I'm sorry about Moscow, make yourself at home."

He didn't question her sincerity. He wanted more, but she didn't have it for him. "Get some rest."

He wasn't sure what his next step was, but it nagged at him that the encounter with Ronnie had him second-guessing himself. Or perhaps he was already doing that. The incident at the garage, letting Azazel escape the first time… A subtle prompting from above to remove those who violated life this way was a different matter entirely from a detailed chart of how to accomplish it. He didn't have the latter, and he didn't like this feeling of floundering.

Chapter Fifteen

Someone knocked on Ronnie's office door.

"Yeah?" She didn't turn her attention from her screen. It turned out throwing herself back into work was a fabulous way to block out the rest of the world, and with the clock rolling past five, soon she'd have the building to herself to catch up on a backlog of messages and requests. And at the same time, she could ignore that Irdu had decided he wasn't free after work after all.

"So you *are* here." Samael stepped into the room. "Are you ignoring everyone, or am I a special case?"

"You're next on my list." It sounded like a weak excuse, but it was true. She was staring at his latest note, detailing what information he needed to hand over to auditors and reinforcing how critical it was.

"Great. Then I'll have that before tomorrow morning? Or will you cut the tape, so I can do this without having to wait on your schedule?" Irritation and disdain ran through his every word.

The way his words echoed Michael's stuck in her head and made her falter. No, she wasn't thinking about that. "I'm getting to it. This is for your—" *own good.* The words died on her lips and looped in her thoughts, in Lucifer's voice. The number of times he told her that… The information he kept from her that could have helped her or destroyed her, because he had to have his secrets.

And now he had her doing the same on his behalf. It pushed away Irdu and Izzy, and it was preventing Samael from keeping Ubiquity out of hotter water. Lucifer had his reasons, right?

"For my what?" Samael asked. He tapped his foot hard enough his entire leg bounced.

Fuck this. Even if she couldn't get a handle on work, on her personal life, on what was up with this onslaught of very public, very destructive agent displays of power, she could take control somewhere. She shut down her computer and grabbed her purse from her desk drawer. "You know what? Let's go get dinner."

He crossed his arms and leaned back, blocking the door. "I think you missed the bit of my email where I said how critical this is. All I need is your signature. You can eat when you've signed off."

"This is a business meeting." She didn't want to have the conversation here. Not because she was worried about someone eavesdropping—though maybe she should be, she hated the thought—but because she was tired of being on the outs with everyone. It would be nice to make things right with Samael.

He liked good food. He was an aficionado. And she wanted him in a better mood when she gave him the choice about whether or not to hear what she knew about why the SEC was investigating them. She definitely wasn't looking forward to telling him why she kept it to herself.

"Which is a shitty way of saying you'd rather expense your meal than pay for it."

Fucking accountants. The thought almost made her smile. "The meal's on me. No expense reports. No company card. You can pick anywhere you'd like."

"Anywhere?"

Was she mumbling? "Yes."

"Breakfast in Japan?"

"Do you speak Japanese?" Unless they learned on their own time, agents only knew the languages relevant to their jobs.

He smirked and uncrossed his arms. Of course he did.

"I assume you have a place in mind," she said.

He closed the distance between them and held out his hand, palm up. "Of course I do. We're not wandering Tokyo aimlessly at seven in the morning."

She and Irdu would. They had. She needed to make things right with him.

The seconds dragged on as Ronnie's office faded and became a crowded street, as if they were stuck in a slow-wipe animation on a poorly edited film. Sammy wasn't as powerful as the angels and demons she'd run into lately. It was a nice reminder the entire world wasn't off kilter and looking to rule something.

As she surveyed their destination, her grumbles evaporated. Awnings stretched in both directions, lining the walkway and covering an assortment of shops with fruit, books, sunglasses, and everything she would have scrimped and saved for, in order to splurge when she was in retrieval. People chattered and shouted. Cool morning air found its way between the buildings, but the sun couldn't. The smell was the best though. She caught ginger in the air, half a dozen types of meat, and so many spices it almost made her drool.

"Over here." Samael led her toward one of the stands with curtain draped from the top and a series of stools next to a bar. There was no one there this time of morning, except the man and woman cooking.

"I told you anywhere, and you picked this?"

"You're complaining? Trust me. Best miso soup you'll ever have."

She she settled on the stool next to his. He chatted with the woman, Japanese rolling off his tongue like a first language. He wasn't kidding. The guy was full of surprises. Then again, she'd made it a point to keep her distance from almost everyone since she was promoted. Not because she thought she was above them, but everything that happened with Ari and Gabe and Michael made her edgy about trusting again. For all she knew, Raph was interesting outside the office.

"Your Japanese is really good," she said when Sammy turned back to her.

"You speak it?"

"No. I understand it. Apparently, there are a lot of languages like that. I know what I'm hearing, but I can't make my tongue and lips form the words. I think it's a side-effect of the whole having-two-sets-of-memories thing."

He furrowed his brow and studied her. "So it's true."

"Of course it is." She couldn't keep the defensiveness from her voice. She was so sick of defending herself from everyone who said she was nothing more than a little demon intern.

"Whoa." He held up his hands in a surrender posture. "I'm not trying to be mean. See it from my perspective. I've never seen this happen before, and I've been around a long time."

The woman set two bowls down and poured them each tea. Ronnie inhaled the vivid scent from the pale-green soup and sipped the hot tea. She'd have to get more dining recommendations from Sammy… if they made it through this conversation and managed to be on vague speaking terms after. Ronnie let the heat sear down her throat and forced herself to back away from the ledge of defensiveness. "It's true. I was a demon, housing Metatron"—she didn't want to go into the details—"and we became one."

"Fascinating." Samael sounded like he meant it. He sipped his soup and studied her for a moment. "So you have all her memories?"

"Technically, they're mine."

"Okay, but… that means you remember all those sensual nights we spent together."

Whispers of memories spilled through her. Both of them with Lucifer. The nights that faded into days and back into night again. The intensity in it all… "I remember it was never just you and me."

Sadness flashed across his face and vanished again. "No. But I always liked having you there." He trailed a light touch up her arm.

She shook her head. "So you haven't become a total dick over the years. I was starting to wonder if you left your personality in heaven when you followed Lucifer to hell."

"You do remember."

"Of course. You would have followed…" She trailed off, leaving the *Lucifer anywhere* unspoken. It was her day for unfinished sentences.

His grief lingered longer this time. "Things change. Look at you." The teasing in his voice sounded forced. He cleared his throat. "Anyway. This is a business dinner."

Right. Now that the impulse to spill her guts had settled, she wondered if this was a good idea. She couldn't think like that. This was Samael's decision. That didn't make it any easier for her to summon the words.

She took a few more sips of her food, savoring the flavor and building her confidence. "I'm willing to tell you everything I know about the mess at work. The investigation. What we're not saying. But you have to understand it's one of those things you won't be able to unknow."

"That's most things." His usual disdain was gone. "Why now and not before?"

She didn't want to second-guess her delivery but couldn't help trying to make it sound as bland and nonthreatening as possible. Apparently this management thing was sinking in. "We felt it was best to not put you in that position. That way, if someone asked you something, you could honestly tell them you didn't have the answer."

"*We* felt?" He scoffed. "You're good."

She pursed her lips. "I know what it's like to be stonewalled, and it sucks. So it's your choice if you want the truth or if you'd rather your denial continues to be honest."

He slurped his meal. Drained his tea cup. Had more soup. Then he looked at her. "This information—does Ubiquity crumble if the SEC finds out?"

"Unless you convince them we're beings placed here by a higher power, to keep humanity safe so they evolve as individuals." She tried to force out a laugh, but it ended in a sigh. "And even then, this information isn't legal."

He wiped his palms on the legs of his jeans, rubbing to the point of obsession. "I wondered. I hoped this wasn't the case, but I was afraid it would be. Yes. Tell me everything you know. I'll use my super-accountant sleuthing powers to uncover more if I need."

She spent the rest of the meal telling him about questionable sources they got investment capital from, that no single employee's ID held up to deeper scrutiny, and everything else she'd gleaned over the past few months in her position. He sighed a lot, shook his head almost as much, and pinched the bridge of his nose every couple of seconds.

"So who talked?" he asked when she finished.

"Talked about what? To whom?"

"Think about it. I work with our books and records every day. I had no idea this was going on.

Lucifer buried this in a way only he could. So who told the SEC?"

Ronnie hadn't considered the possibility of an inside informant. "I don't know if anyone did. Ubiquity is growing. There are always anti-trust rumors. We've got corporate competition, like any business. The dart hit our name when they spun their random-audit wheel?"

"Remind me never to play darts with you, if you think that's how the game works." Samael hopped from his seat. "Walk with me?"

"Yeah." She fell into step beside him as they strolled the shops. So much beauty and fun. She and Irdu needed to come back here. Maybe resetting their environment would help them talk things out.

"Their charges are specific." He paused to sift through a stack of T-shirts before moving on again. "When they came knocking on our door, it wasn't a you-might-need-a-slap-on-the-wrist kind of thing. They asked up front about diverted funds, and falsified employee records."

She hadn't considered someone would sell them out. Ronnie didn't know what this was, but the way Samael phrased it sounded a lot more malicious than she thought her colleagues capable of. Then again, a couple of them were destroying city blocks for fun lately. This was tame in comparison.

"What now?" she asked.

"Now that I know—thank you, by the way—I can minimize damage. But you have to stop babysitting, and let me take care of this."

"Minimize damage how?"

He shrugged. "I'll figure it out as we go. You, Ms. Public Face, need to worry about your own damage control. Like those explosions you've been tracking, and making sure they don't get linked back to us."

She didn't know how they would, but it was a good point. "I'm going to catch up on work. Do you want a lift?"

"Nah. I'm going to wander here for a while. I'll see you in the office."

That went better than Ronnie expected. Could she make a similar apology to Izzy, but with a lot more begging and groveling on her part? She'd make another face-to-face plea with Irdu.

She watched Sammy walk away as she dialed Izzy's number. Two rings, and then to voicemail. She frowned.

"It's Ronnie. I miss you, and I'm more sorry than I can say. Call me, please?"

Chapter Sixteen

The way Michael's mind raced thousands of miles a minute over every random thought, he'd rather spend a few hours meditating in the chapel downstairs. Except the First Angelic Non-Denominational Church of Faith didn't hold the same presence it had for the last century. It was as if the place was in mourning. Then again, it underwent serious reconstruction a few months back, after Ariel tore portions of it to the ground in her maddened rampage.

He knocked on Izrafel's apartment door, on the second floor, and adjusted the laptop bag on his shoulder while he waited.

The man who answered barely resembled the Izrafel Michael remembered. With dark shadows under his eyes and gaze downcast, Izrafel looked a lot like Abaddon had, but without the telltale glow of a celestial being.

"Are you certain this is a good time?" Michael asked.

Izrafel managed a weak smile and opened the door wider. "Now is fine. I'm sorry about the mess."

That didn't sound right. Michael stepped inside and stalled. He was used to seeing books lining the walls, piled in stacks on the floor, and filling all available table space. Now it seemed as though more than half of them were gone, and the remainder lay open, pages rippled and warped. "What happened?"

"Long story. You needed help with something?"

"Yes." Michael took the hint to stay away from the mess topic. "Is there somewhere we can set up?"

Izrafel gestured to an empty spot on the bar dividing the kitchen from the living room. "Power's in the wall."

After Ronnie's comment about *trending*, it occurred to Michael it might be to his advantage to plug into the digital world more often. That was the only decision he'd been able to make after days of poring over the conversation with her. He wished the non-stop pondering yielded more, but it was something.

He was here to get Izrafel's help implementing a U-Lert, to warn him each time events like those of the past week popped up. Michael set up his laptop and stepped aside. He didn't have a problem with technology, but Izrafel had a knack for searching, and this was going to require some magic research intuition.

"Tell me what you're looking for. Specifically." Izrafel pulled up a stool and poised his fingers over the keyboard. "We'll build your search from there, based on keywords. It may take some fine-tuning, but we'll figure it out."

"Anything that's destructive, but not a natural disaster. Isolated. The kind of thing only one of us could do."

Izrafel's laugh was flat and lacked humor. "I'm not sure I can make a search term from that, but I'll try."

"Thank you." This wouldn't lead him directly to others like Azazel and Vine, but it would give him a heads-up they were out there. He didn't want to wait for something fatal to give him a direction, but he needed to jump on it immediately if it did happen.

As he watched Izrafel work, Ronnie's words bled back to taunt him again. Before Michael set out on this seek and destroy mission, he'd spent his time finding humans and fallen angels with cherubs, and determining whether to send the cherub home, or help it integrate with the host. The decision to integrate was based on if it would drive the host insane or not. Izrafel was one of those he helped.

Michael took out Ariel and Azazel, and had tried to take out Vine. So why did he help Izrafel all those years ago and let Abaddon carry on the way she had?

On the surface, the answer seemed obvious. Izrafel never would have destroyed an entire city block, or hurt anyone. Except, as much as Michael hated to admit it, Abaddon might. She didn't have the extra source of power now, but she took it once. There was nothing to stop her from doing it again.

Still, each of the others cost the world so much. He was right to act as he did. But would that always be the case? He realized Izrafel was watching him with expectation. "I apologize. What?" Michael asked.

"I asked if you're looking for things like the showdown in Moscow. The garage explosion…"

"The freak tornado. The flood in Boston. Exactly."

Izrafel's back went stiff. "Boston was Ubiquity."

"As in, they sanctioned it?" That made no sense.

"As in—" Izrafel's voice rose in volume before he snapped his jaw shut. He inhaled a few times through his nose. "That one's a bit hard for me to talk about."

"You were there." This got more interesting every minute.

"Yeah. I can give you an overview but I'm not ready to discuss details yet."

As much as Michael wanted to know it all, he wouldn't push unless he deemed it necessary in order to continue his mission. "Whatever you're comfortable with."

"There are agents who know what Ronnie did to Gabe. The way she drained him of his power. Supposedly Abaddon got the information directly from Gabriel. But her fury at seeing any agent hurt— whether they stood with her or not—I have a hard time believing she'd share …" He trailed off with a shudder.

Shock raced through Michael. "She was there too?"

Izrafel nodded. "Gabe's people know how to capture demons and angels. Bind them, so they can't access their power. But the restraints are physical." He furrowed his brow and clenched his fist. "They wanted to see if they could do something similar to Holden. To other prophets. Abaddon was furious when she found out they were hurting agents. She decided killing the prophets was better than the alternative. She said something about not making them suffer, and death being more surefire than cutting them off from their gift. I couldn't watch her do that. So I took something from her. Something she shouldn't have had to begin with. It didn't stop her."

That explained why Abaddon looked so pale when Michael visited. The entire story chilled him to the core, and he didn't know which part bothered him the most. "But Abaddon doesn't work with water. Or with Ubiquity."

"No. Her death and destruction was hands on. Tia brought the place down when it was all over. The agents fled, and the humans were already dead"—Izrafel's voice cracked—"by the time the wave hit."

Michael wouldn't push for more details if it caused Izrafel this much grief. He was curious about one thing, though. "Tiamet? Petite demon, pale skin, likes to gossip, does retrieval?"

"*Did* retrieval. Does Ronnie's dirty work now. Sorry—that's not fair. But Tia does have an in with the boss lady."

Michael had enough information to move forward without dragging out details that were torturing Izzy to recall. He could investigate the flood further, but if Abaddon and Ronnie knew about it, he'd be blocked from two sides unless one of them gave him answers. It was a chance to see Ronnie again. Taste the burnt sugar of her aura. The temptation was strong enough, it drown out any reasons it was bad idea.

Silence fell between them as Izrafel worked, weighing down the air and pressing in on Michael. Minutes ticked away. He should have scheduled this for another time, but he didn't expect it to take so long or carry such heavy information.

"That's odd." Izrafel's voice in the midst of the stillness startled Michael.

"What is?"

"There were more videos out there this morning that matched your criteria. They're gone. No cached copies, either. They say everything is permanent on the internet. This wasn't."

If Michael were capable of getting headaches, one would be forming at the base of his skull. "Which means…" Someone at Ubiquity got to the videos first and wiped all traces of their existence. Would he need to go back, or re-establish connections there, in order to find what he needed? He couldn't imagine things were better on the inside. One hand never knew what the other was doing at Ubiquity, and the odds that had changed in the last few months were low.

"Yeah. It does."

"Am I set otherwise?" Michael asked.

Izrafel snapped the laptop shut. "I can't test it without content, and it'll probably return a lot more than you need, but you've got a starting point."

It would do for now. It had to.

* * * *

Irdu didn't blame Ronnie for what happened at the warehouse. Not anymore. But he was still upset about the secrets she'd kept. That she'd played a part in the grieving Izzy was going through.

That each time he turned down her request to talk, she used that fucking app to vanish to some high-energy spot on the other side of the planet.

He wanted to talk to her, but hadn't figured out what to say. So when Izzy asked if Irdu wanted to join him for dinner tonight, it was easy for Irdu to tell himself this was important. Turned out Karma didn't appreciate his logic, because Izzy cancelled a short while later.

Now Irdu was working late, because it kept him from thinking about anything else. That was the theory, anyway. His mind was wandering so much, he'd been staring at the same documentation for half an hour.

He looked up at a knock, to find Tia standing in his office doorway. "Go home," she said.

"You're one to talk." He couldn't help but laugh at the teasing command. "Why are you still here?"

"It's the best time to practice what I'm learning about coding. Against a real system instead of some made up thing at home. You?"

He pushed back from his desk and stood. "I honestly don't know. Wanna get out of here?"

"Yes. Definitely yes. Pizza. Movies. Your place, your treat?"

He shook his head, but was still smiling. "All right. Chicago or New York?"

She twisted her face in exaggerated thought. "Chicago."

"Deal." Less than half an hour later, after a quick phase to their favorite pizza place in downtown Chicago, they were back in his apartment. Tia loaded up *Psycho*, while Irdu fetched plates and soda.

They settled on the couch, but she didn't hit *Play*. "Wouldn't you rather have someone else here?" Tia asked.

"I love your company." Irdu glanced at her sideways. Where did the question come from… Oh. She meant Ronnie.

"She's done a lot of good things for me, so I'm biased." Tia fiddled with the remote, staring at her fingers as they traced over the buttons. "Getting me out of Reaping. Helping me move into development. But I think you should forgive her."

Irdu didn't know if he appreciated her echoing his earlier thoughts. "It's not as easy as that. She lied. She put you in danger."

"She did keep secrets. So have we. There's a reason she and Lucifer are the only people who know we're related. It was my decision to stay on the job, despite her wanting to pull me. I'm as adult as adult gets. You can't shelter me forever."

"You're my sister. I'm allowed to be upset that it was you in that situation. We only have each other." He winced as the words passed his lips. It wasn't true now anymore than when he said something similar to Ronnie. He knew she was there for him.

"You have Ronnie too."

He raised an eyebrow, and resisted the urge to demand she stay out of his head.

"Besides, I handled myself. I survived," Tia said. "Would you rather it was another demon in there?"

"Yes." Without question. "*Besides*, Abaddon let everyone go, not just you. It's not like sending another demon would have had a different result."

"Exactly."

"She almost got Izzy killed, lying to him." Irdu switched tactics. Why was he still arguing? He still had issues with the whole thing. Logic aside, Ronnie's attitude about it bothered him.

"I won't argue that. Do you want to stay mad at her forever?"

He didn't. But things needed to change.

"Call her. Talk this through with her, not me." Tia stood and grabbed the pizza box.

Irdu reached for it and she jerked away. "You can't take the food," he argued.

"You bought it for me." Her grin was impish. "Call Ronnie."

"Fine. Go." He shooed her out the door.

My night cleared up. Are you free? He texted Ronnie.

Her answer came through seconds later, in a series of short replies. *Yes.*

Definitely yes.

When and where?

He typed, *My place.*

The message didn't even show *Delivered* yet when there was a knock.

Irdu let Ronnie in, and familiarity surged through him. Any other day, he'd pin her to the wall and kiss long and hard. The impulse was still there, but he shoved it back down.

The frown that lingered on her face, and the twitch of her fingers toward him, before she dropped her arm, said he wasn't the only one conflicted.

She settled into one of the chairs in his living room, and he made himself comfortable on the couch. This felt so wrong.

"The funerals start tomorrow." He should have put some more thought into how he wanted this conversation to go.

She nodded.

"Do you want me to go with you?"

Ronnie looked up, eyes wide, and studied him. "No. I need to go alone."

"You don't have to do anything alone. I'm here to support you. I need you here for the same."

"I know." Her reply came out on a puff of breath. "And I want to be. I have to do this bit by myself, though."

"Okay." This wasn't going anywhere. He could ask her to apologize again, but he believed she was sincere the first several times. He needed to bring up her event-finder indulgences. This was as good a time for that as any. "How's Michael?" Not what he meant to ask.

Ronnie's expression almost looked pained. "Aloof."

"And…?" Irdu wasn't looking for any sort of confession of attraction. He knew how much Ronnie missed Michael. But the face she'd made.

She wrung her hands together. "He's killing us."

Irdu had to be misunderstanding. "As in, his actions are harmful in some way?"

"As in, he knows how to kill angels and demons, and he's doing it."

Shock raced through Irdu. That explained her look. "I didn't think that was possible. Why? How?"

"I don't know the how. I don't want to. He's trying to prevent situations like Ariel from happening again."

"He's not doing a great job."

Ronnie shrugged. "Unless it would be worse if he wasn't doing anything. Think about it—what are we accomplishing at Ubiquity?"

Irdu stared at her, stunned. "Are you saying you agree with it?"

"No. *God* no. I hate the idea of him killing us. I want to talk him out of it. But I like the idea of stopping the chaos. What if I could help him, and change his mind about punishment at the same time? After what he did for Izzy… What he's done for humans…"

Irdu did approve of that. Given he'd become a demon under similar circumstances. "What if Michael had found me first instead of Lucifer?"

"You wouldn't be beholden to a contract with an unspecified term," Ronnie said. "But I probably wouldn't have met you, so… tough call. He wouldn't have destroyed you."

"Do you know that?"

Ronnie frowned. "I have to believe it."

He walked up to her, tugged her to her feet, and brushed his lips over her forehead. "If you trust him, I trust him." Though, the clawing dread inside disagreed. He'd never been impressed with any original.

Did that include Ronnie?

Of course not. She was different. Except when she sided with them, despite evidence she shouldn't.

* * * *

Ronnie phased into view of the next cemetery on her list. This would be her third funeral today, but fortunately her last until tomorrow. It didn't matter that she didn't know these people; watching their families mourn was taking its toll.

This one was no different. Grief radiated from those huddled around the open grave. She kept her distance, not wanting to raise questions or cause problems, but for selfish reasons as well. Getting too close would suffocate her in mourning.

Something else stood out from this group, though. She didn't recognize it at first, because the scent of pine and fresh air should be coming from her surroundings, but the underlying current of something stronger, like sunshine in the middle of the drizzle, was a feeling she wished she didn't know this well. From her spot several yards back, she scanned the crowd, until her gaze met Michael's. What was he doing here, with them, no less?

She should leave. He bowed his head and said something to the woman next to him, then peeled away and walked toward Ronnie. She should definitely go. The desire clawing inside wouldn't let her. She wanted to talk to him. To dive into his arms and seek comfort. To pretend they could block out the world together. It wouldn't happen, but knowing that didn't stop her from needing it.

He stopped next to her, his attention fixed on the funeral.

"I'm not here to cause problems." She kept her voice low out of respect. "These people don't deserve that."

"I'd never assume that, but why *are* you here? A sense of obligation?"

The words cut deep, adding to layers of sadness building inside from her day's activities. "Why does anyone attend a funeral?" She didn't want to let the edge slide into her voice, but she couldn't help it.

"I'm sorry. I shouldn't have said that." He sounded sincere.

"I'm paying my respects, and then I'll be gone. You?" Not that it was any of her business, but curiosity was a bitch.

"I knew them."

The simple statement clenched like a fist around her gut. These men died in an explosion that turned their bodies to ash in an instant; it burned so hot and fast. "I'm sorry. Regardless of how I came across the other day, I feel for these people. For anyone involved." She shouldn't be explaining herself. Didn't owe him anything. As much as she didn't want his opinion to matter, it did. "I had Irdu pull the list of those impacted before you and I spoke. I'm not heartless."

"I don't think that. Give me a chance to explain what I'm doing?"

She shook her head, not sure if it was at him or herself. She wasn't in the mood to hear whatever weak justification he had for killing. "I won't argue with you at a funeral."

"I'll buy you—"

"And you can't bribe me with lunch." She should get back to the office. Too much work waited for her. She risked a glance sideways at his silence. She wanted to say yes. To spend time with him and get to know him. Any other old acquaintance, she'd join them in a heartbeat. But she already hurt too much to be pushed away again because he didn't want to get close.

He wore a dry smile, and when he spoke his tone was flat. "There's a diner down the street with amazing strawberry waffles. You don't have to join me."

Despite her resolve to leave, she fell into step beside him as he strolled down the street. Neither spoke. It felt like the past —breakfast before work and sharing stories of being angels before humanity was created—but drawn wrong. As if whoever witnessed it painted it in grays and browns instead of vibrant clarity.

He chatted with the hostess, their moods somber and voices low, and then pointed Ronnie toward a booth in back. The place was mostly empty. Ronnie suspected most of the town was working or at the funeral.

"Do you need a menu?" Michael asked.

"Not if they have strawberry waffles." The scene mingled with her past. Her demon half, exhausted and frustrated thanks to the voice in her head, wandering into Izzy's chapel. Finding Michael, the first person who had answers for her, who wanted to help. The way their relationship grew after that, and the stolen moments they managed before he left.

"Fresh strawberries, and whipped cream they make when you order."

God. He knew her too well. It wasn't fair. Their waitress took their orders almost right away, then left them in silence.

Michael finally spoke. "I'm not acting out of some misplaced notion of vengeance. My orders came from above."

Orders. She smirked but felt no amusement. "We both know it doesn't work that way. You were given a vague directive and left to your own devices, to figure out how to accomplish it."

"During the battle with Ariel, He gave me the knowledge I needed to destroy her. It wasn't something I figured out on my own."

For the most part, how agents chose to do their jobs was open to interpretation—*He* was more of a hands-off kind of manager, as long as the job got done. There wasn't a lot of guesswork involved in something like showing an angel how to kill in the middle of a fight with one of their own. It didn't make Ronnie like it any more, though. Had they all fallen so far, sunk so low, that destroying angels and demons was the only answer?

"Regardless, that's your goal, not mine. I'd rather do this without any loss of life if at all possible," she said.

"I would, too. And when I think I can get away with it, I do." He worked his jaw up and down, then gritted his teeth. "Why are you here?"

"I told you. To pay my respects."

"That's not what I'm asking."

He wanted to know why she didn't leave. Why she joined him for lunch. Was it that she missed him? That was a strong part of it, but not everything. "When I asked you the other day to come back to Ubiquity? I was wrong." She hadn't realized she felt that way until the words spilled out. "The last thing Ubiquity needs is for you to step in like last time, long enough to make a mess and dump it on someone else."

He raised his brows. "I didn't make a mess last time. I happened to be there as everything was falling apart."

This wasn't going right. Her thoughts were fragmented. Part of her wanted to scream and yell and blame him. The rest knew he was the least of her concerns, and unlike some of the other agents, he was reasonable and honest. "You're right. I'm sorry. To tell the truth, I think you're smart to keep your distance."

"But you're staying there."

She shrugged. "They have the information I need. They have what you need, too. And you know it."

"It's true."

"I'll share what I find with you, if you can stand to see me on a regular basis." Was that what she was doing? Finding a way to worm herself back into his life? Yes. Maybe he'd see her anyway, but too many old friends had turned away from her. She wasn't too proud to admit she'd use excuses to see him until she could figure out where they stood. Besides, her hands were tied at Ubiquity, and while she didn't like his methods, Michael had enough freedom to get things done.

"You know that's not why I left—my not being able to stand you."

The confession kneaded away invisible knots in her neck and shoulders. "I still like to hear it."

She didn't agree with his actual reason for going, even after all this time. She loved her immortality. Couldn't see surrendering this life for anything. Sure, the work got tedious and the bullshit flowed thick on occasion, but overall she wanted to be here. Her memories from Metatron's life, combined with her experiences as Uriel and what Michael told her, filled in his reasons. He walked too close to the edge of humanity, only resisting the urge to fall, because the infrastructure needed him. Given the right reason—which supposedly included loving her—he'd surrender it all for a chance to experience a short, mortal life, burn hot and fast, and flash out of existence in a century or so.

"Why would you share company information with me?" he asked.

"I think you're right to do this on your own. I can't leave Ubiquity, for the same reasons you can't let yourself fall. The structure will crumble."

He gave a sad laugh. "I'm sorry you have to make that choice."

"I'm not sorry. I mean, I don't like that there aren't a lot of options, but I'm the one making the decision, instead of having someone else make it for me."

"There is that."

Their lunch arrived, and her mouth watered at the sight. It looked as good as he'd promised. A bite proved it tasted even better. They ate in silence for a few minutes, and she glanced at her phone out of habit.

"Do they expect you back at the office soon?" He sounded disappointed.

She nodded. "But I'm free tonight." That probably wasn't why he asked. What was she doing?

"Then it's a date." For the first time this afternoon, his smile looked genuine.

She didn't know if she was thrilled or terrified. A little of both. Last time they went down this road, they got close enough she felt something for him, but didn't know what. That was before she merged with Metatron. Before her memories of shopping in foreign markets eons before the Middle East knew its current incarnation. He never forgot fresh fruit was her favorite, even though it was difficult to get in that part of the world. She didn't know if she could walk away if she started spending time with him.

Oh, hell, who am I kidding? She already couldn't walk away.

Chapter Seventeen

Irdu watched the expressions flash across Ronnie's face. A flicker of a smile. A ghost of a frown. The twist of her lips. None of her reactions corresponded to what he was saying.

They were having an *actual* meeting that probably wouldn't end with sex on the desk. Not that he didn't want it to. But he was working with her to figure out why rouge angels and demons were slipping through their searches, and it was a priority. Then he had plans tonight, and so did she, but not in the same place.

There was a splash of jealousy when she'd told him she was seeing Michael. Irdu was reconciling it, though. He'd known for months it was going to happen. He was more okay with it than he expected to me.

She smiled then frowned again, just as he was explaining the intricacies of the cherub algorithm and why it was failing to find Gabe's people.

"You're completely not here, are you?" Irdu teased. "Fantasizing about your hot date, perhaps?"

She met his gaze, looking sheepish. "I'm sorry. What?"

"They're old agents." He'd try to stay away from the technical details. "Some of them have been around almost as long as humanity. They know how to hide."

"Everyone has tells. They must, as well."

"Like your crowd fetish?" He mentally winced. That wasn't how he wanted to broach this subject.

Pink dotted her cheeks. "It's not a fetish."

He'd brought it up. Time to get this out of the way. He didn't want it to feel like an attack, though. He could tie it back to the conversation, and make two points at once. "Do you remember working the queue? How many false positives we got? Leads who had done shit-tons of something? Bought hundreds of pounds of candy? Porn DVDs. Stuff like that?"

They used search engine data to track cherubs by finding people who looked for a lot of anything. A cherub had an intense lust to experience everything physical, and that meant they tended to form addictions to everything from sweets to sex to jewelry. It also meant false positives came from people just price shopping, looking for gifts, or bored at work.

She nodded. "Of course." Some of the tension faded from her posture. "But we also have the tech that returns more specific results. Pegged those targets who weren't as obvious. Why doesn't it pick these up?"

"It does, but this requires the computer to tell the difference between a cherub-laden agent, and someone who drinks coffee for each meal because they enjoy it. Or if you prefer, an angel who gets off on rubbing wings with geeks, and a geek who gets off on it." He hoped she'd get it.

"Right. I'm the example. Fair enough." She let out a long breath. "Except unlike your standard mortal user, my pings come from all over the world."

"And if you were in the system, you'd trigger our flags on a regular basis. Your activity is exactly the kind of thing the algorithms look for."

"Oh. I'm not that bad. Am I?"

Irdu didn't want to make accusations. This was to help her, not push her away. "I'm not exaggerating. And I worry about you. You know how to deal with the impulses, and it's like some days you stop trying. I don't know what you're looking for."

"I don't either. It's like… I don't know what it's like."

"You spend a lot of time in Las Vegas." He kept his voice kind. "Why there?"

"Everyone feels everything there. So much of it." She stared at her hands. "And none of it is mine. I don't have to try to sort through it. I don't have to pretend that feelings from two separate sources both belong to me, and at the same time, that between the two of them, I don't feel whole."

And it clicked. She was still fighting having both Metatron and Uriel in her head. He knew a lot about that, since the cherub that found him so long ago already had its own personality. Unlike so many out there.

His integration hadn't been as rough as Ronnie's, but it wasn't easy. He moved to her side of the desk, and took her hands. "You don't have to do this alone."

"Don't I? Do you want me to call you because I'm missing Michael? Because I'm sulking about whether or not people respect me at work? And what if you don't answer?"

He crouched, putting himself at eye-level, and kissed her knuckles. "Then tell me where you're going, and I'll meet you there. Or send me a text that says *SOS* and I'll find you."

She hesitated. "I'll try."

"That's fair." He leaned in and brushed his lips over hers.

She pressed in, deepening the kiss. When they broke apart, he nipped at her bottom lip. Most of the lines had faded from her forehead.

"So, why aren't these agents hitting your algorithms the way I do?" Her voice was clear and all-business again, but the edge was gone.

He rocked back onto his heels, not letting go of her hand. "Most of them call someplace *home* and stay there. We don't see movement until it's too late, and there hasn't been enough big stuff for us to base algorithms on. The new disasters in Fiji and Perth will help."

"Except we can't keep waiting for things to blow up in order to gather information. There has to be a pattern. Something we can track before the mass destruction happens."

"There is. We simply have to find it. We've got the code from Gabriel's outsource group—the stuff we had access to before he… left." It seemed like a bad time to say *before he tried to kill you again, and you made him temporarily impotent.* "But they never gave us everything."

"I know. I just want…"

To stop celestial agents from destroying the world which they existed to nurture. It sounded simple and impossible at the same time. "I do, too."

Someone knocked, and Irdu's office door swung open. Tia poked her head in. "Are you ready to go, Irdu?" She trailed off when her gaze landed on Ronnie. "I thought you were done. Sorry."

"Is it that late?" Ronnie glanced at her phone. "I didn't mean to keep you. We'll pick back up on Monday."

"Come with us," Irdu said.

She wasn't meeting Michael for a couple of hours, and Irdu wanted to spend some more time with her.

"Oh, do. It's so much fun." Tia pushed the door open wider and looked at Ronnie. "I know you elite-types don't associate with us plebes, but you used to be one of us." Her tone was playful.

Ronnie shook her head, but she didn't look certain. "I can't intrude. And I have plans."

"Later, but not now. We're going to PigSkins," Irdu said. He and Tia used to do this all the time. It had been a while, and Ronnie hadn't been introduced to the experience yet.

"We order bottomless chips and salsa, and make our way down the menu of froofy drinks." Tia crossed the room and grabbed Ronnie's other hand. "You have to come with."

"You do remember we're incapable of getting drunk." Ronnie looked between them.

"It's like caffeine or sugar," Irdu said. "The effects are in your head. It's about the experience. Besides, the drinks taste good."

"So go with us." Tia tugged Ronnie her to her feet.

"All right. Let me tell Michael where to find me." Ronnie jabbed at her phone, dropped it in her purse, and looked at Irdu. "Lead the way."

An hour and a half later, the cocktail tasting was well underway as Irdu, Ronnie, and Tia sat at a table near the bar, laughing.

Ronnie grimaced as she downed her latest drink. "Definitely not." She coughed. "Lemon, mint, and chocolate aren't meant to go together. Eww."

"Acquired taste." Tia plucked the cherry from her appletini, and sucked it from the stem. Her laughter faded, and she kicked Irdu under the table. She nodded behind him and Ronnie.

He glanced over his shoulder at the same time Ronnie twisted in her seat.

Michael stood near the entrance, scanning the room.

That light clench of jealousy was back. Irdu tried to push it aside, but it was persistent. He was okay with this, it would just take some time to convince his heart.

Michael's gaze landed on them, and he headed in their direction with a smile.

Irdu turned away to see Tia's screwed up face.

"Isn't he super boring?" she whispered. "I hear he's all pious and shit."

Irdu couldn't see Ronnie putting up with that.

"I promise, he's not." Ronnie was fighting a smile. "Maybe a little. But not a lot."

"Not a lot of what?" Michael stopped next to the table.

"Nothing." Tia stood.

Irdu tossed a few bills on the table and slid from the bench. He bent at the waist, knotted his fingers in Ronnie's hair, and claimed her mouth. Lemon and chocolate still lingered on her lips when he traced his tongue along the seam.

He broke away. "Call me."

Okay, so there was nothing subtle about that. He didn't care. Michael needed to know Irdu wasn't going anywhere.

*

Ronnie slouched back in her seat as Irdu and Tia walked out the front door. His kiss still lingered on her lips and tingled along her skin. She was lucky to have him.

"I didn't mean to scare your... friends off." Instead of sitting, Michael drummed his fingers on his leg. In the faded jeans and thermal shirt, he looked more at home here than Ronnie in her black pencil skirt and matching jacket.

She wanted to change. The thought almost dragged a laugh from her. There was something deeper in that sentence, but she wasn't in the mood to examine it. "They had places to be." She stood and straightened her skirt. "We don't have to stay if you don't want. Though, wherever we go, I'd like to slip into something more comfortable first."

He raised his brows, and the corners of his mouth tugged up in an almost-smile.

"Not like that." She added her money to the stack on the table and nodded toward the front door. "More like what you're wearing. I came straight from the office."

"Do you still live around here? We can stop at your place, and then figure out where to go from there."

Answering his question meant admitting she hadn't moved out of his condo, and asking him to wait here, she'd be back soon, felt rude. "Or I could wear this. Do you have a destination? Paris?"

"It's two a.m. in Paris." He studied her. "I was thinking The Factory. I'm not in a rush, though. You have time to change. And I'd love to see your new place."

"I—" If he didn't already know, he'd find out sooner or later, and she wanted to get out of this suit. "That's probably a good idea." She reached for his hand and hesitated. In their circles, it didn't mean anything. It was how two agents traveled together. Suddenly, the familiarity and intimacy of the gesture settled deep and made her question herself. She shoved doubt aside and nestled her palm against Michael's. She wasn't that timid, lost little demon anymore.

In a blink, they stood in the living room. She dropped his hand the moment they were solid, and he looked around.

"I didn't expect that." Was that amusement in his voice? "I like what you've done with the place."

She hadn't done anything. "Sarcasm doesn't suit you." She strolled toward the bedroom.

"I'm being sincere. It looked good before. It's perfect now."

She couldn't help a small laugh, as she bent to grab something more casual from one of the suitcases on the floor. Unpacking never happened. Every time she thought about it, she decided she'd find her own place next weekend. Until then, it felt wrong to shift his things aside for hers. "I guess I never got around to moving out."

"I told you it was yours for as long as you needed." His voice sounded closer than she expected. She jumped and whirled, heart hammering an awkward beat against her ribs.

He stood in the doorway, leaned against the frame, and *fuck* if he didn't look incredible. Dark hair, pale eyes, and a few days' stubble on his chin.

She wasn't going to swoon. "Technically, you told Lucifer to tell me. And either turn around or wait in the living room."

He spun but didn't leave. She watched his back as she changed, feeling a sliver of hope he might sneak a peek. How childish was that? "Done," she said as she pulled a tank top over her head and smoothed it out. She rolled her back, breathing a sigh of relief that her shoulder blades had more room to breathe now.

"Perfect." The way he trailed his gaze over her, the appreciation in his tone, and his soft smile heated her skin faster than a rave filled with gyrating bodies and ecstasy.

God. She hated that he could do that to her with a look. At the same time, she never wanted it to stop.

*

Michael strolled next to Ronnie through the once-a-factory building that had been restored into a series of quaint shops and restaurants. The conversation stayed neutral. Light, meaningless—a bunch of chatter about the weather and politics. Not the celestial kind. She wanted to talk about world rulers.

He expected spending time with her again to be awkward, but not for these reasons. Conflict and confusion churned inside him as he glanced at Ronnie. He was done trying to fight the attraction. It was there, and he was going to enjoy it. He needed to understand who she was, though.

Before he left Uriel she'd been struggling to contain two entities in the same body. Either Metatron was trying to push Uriel aside, or Uriel was fighting to find a life she'd barely tasted. She'd reconciled the two entities. The two parts merged into one, and it wasn't the first time he'd seen it. But he wasn't prepared to witness Uriel and Metatron, two unique and distinct personalities, squashed into one set of flawless mannerisms and words.

In addition, she looked anything but comfortable here. The moment she started to relax, she'd look at him and switch gears, slamming back into bland conversation and walking stiffly.

This was ridiculous. "Stop." He spun her to face him. People milled around them like waves parting for a rock, some grumbling that Michael and Ronnie needed to move, but most continuing as if nothing happened. "Why are we here?" That wasn't quite a fair question. He couldn't say for himself, but he still expected her to?

"Always straight to the point with you." She studied her feet. "Going out with you seemed like the thing to do at the time."

"Would you rather call it a night?" Would he?

"No. I'd rather shove this awkward tension aside, pretend for a little while we don't have a bizarre kind of unfinished past together, and k— Bounce some ideas off you."

"That sounds like a good starting point." He refused to let himself read into the unfinished sentence. Idea bouncing sounded better than stilted conversation, especially since he didn't know where his own thoughts were going. "Do you want to stop somewhere? You pick." If she was Uriel, he'd suggest something sweet and baked again. That worked earlier today. If she was Metatron, it might be more of a wine and fresh fruit kind of evening. He wasn't in the mood to guess.

She nodded at a nearby bench, next to an island of plastic trees and an electric fountain. "Can we sit there for now?"

"Of course." He'd have guessed wrong either way.

She kept more than a foot between them, twisting her fingers together then apart as she stared at her knees. "I know you said *it's a date* and all, but can we not do that?"

"I meant it more as a general statement than a romantic commitment." Was that true? It felt true. "We can split the dinner bill if it helps you feel better."

Her shoulders seemed to loosen a bit at that. "Don't get carried away." She glanced at him and winked. "But probably. Yes. I can't owe you any more than I already do. Especially with what I need to ask."

"What is it?"

"I told you we were better off without you at Ubiquity, and you without us." She leaned back and turned her gaze to the windows that made up the ceiling. "There's more to it than that, and I can't believe I'm about to tell you. Someone would have a fit, I'm sure—proprietary information and all that bullshit. Besides, I don't like that you're *eliminating* agents. I can't make sense of all this in my head, though. I need your experience."

"You have it." He itched to reach out and cover her hand, or tuck her hair behind one ear so he could see her better. That seemed like a bad idea. The kind of thing she'd take wrong.

She sighed and shifted on the bench to face him, tucking one foot under the other knee. The sight was like the first time he saw in her in Izrafel's chapel, but instead of an aura of chaos, she radiated a kind of defeated uncertainty that ached through him. Her light flowed, but with wavers and breaks, like a film projector missing frames.

"You've heard about the SEC investigation, I assume," she said.

He nodded.

"Sa…omeone thinks we were turned in."

That sounded odd. "As in, there may be someone in the company you can't trust?" He tried to sound sympathetic, but trust was scarce at Ubiquity anyway.

She stuck her tongue out. "That's not helpful. I'm part of the machine, not blind to its flaws."

"You're right." He risked scooting closer, and was relieved when she didn't fold in on herself. "Do you think it's likely?"

"I don't want to, but I have a hard time trusting anyone these days. At the same time turning over the whole company doesn't make sense. The whole stealing-cherubs thing? That gives an agent more power. Blowing stuff up? Not everyone is sane. But taking down Ubiquity? Whatever else it is, it allows more of us to stay on this plane and experience life. Even when heaven and hell fought openly, no one was trying to kill each other." She winced and ducked her head. It took a moment before she continued. "This is a different kind of bad, and I don't want to believe it, but I can't get the possibility out of my head."

"You said it yourself—not everyone is sane."

She slammed her fist into the bench, which rumbled more than a punch should be capable of. She dragged in a shaky breath. "I need you to take this seriously. To take *me* seriously."

"I am. I do." He measured his next words. "What is it about the idea that keeps you coming back to it?"

"Why now?" she asked. "The company has been fine for decades. Why is someone looking at us now, with the kind of details only Lucifer has and at the same time these not-so-natural disasters risk exposing everything we are to the public?"

That was a good question.

Chapter Eighteen

"Can we get out of here?" Ronnie asked. As foot traffic thinned and the time crept past eight, she realized she didn't want to be this close to home. Something about the proximity made her uneasy and fidgety.

"Of course. Did you have somewhere in mind?"

She was tempted to grab a location from her event-finder app but wasn't sure she wanted Michael to know how she spent her free time. Unfortunately, that left her without an answer. "I guess not specifically."

"Really? Once upon a time you couldn't wait to see more of the world."

He remembered. The notion warmed her. Was she really that naïve as Uriel? "I guess I've already had the chance."

"You've ridden the waterways of Venice? Toured the Louvre? Stood atop a snow-capped mountain so tall you couldn't see the valley below?"

"Well, no. No one's done all that stuff."

He smiled and shrugged. "You'll find time. Where have you been? We'll build from there."

"A lot of convention centers. And Tokyo. I've been there." *God.* She sounded pathetic. In her head, it was impressive. Admitting out loud? *Not so much.*

He stood and offered his hand. "If you don't have a destination in mind, may I?"

"Sure." As long as it took the focus off her. Was Irdu right? Had she let her appreciation for crowds become an addiction? A fetish? No. She just liked people.

Instead of phasing, he led her toward a souvenir cart a few yards away. She bit her tongue, to hold back a snide comment about a T-shirt being as poor a substitute for seeing the world as the inside of a convention center.

"One of the zipper sweatshirts, small, in red." He let go of Ronnie's hand to pay, and handed her the top when he was done. "You might want this."

"Thanks?" It was in the mid-seventies outside. Even a little bit of a cool air in another country would be a nice change on her heated skin. Still, she draped it over her arm, and—

When the scenery shifted, Ronnie noticed several things at once. It was mid-afternoon and gray, rather than clear and almost sunset. And it was chilly. She rubbed her arms. "Where are we?"

"Wellington."

She shrugged the hoodie on, grateful both for it and that she'd kept her sarcasm to herself earlier. "As in Florida? Shouldn't it be nighttime? And warm?"

"Wellington, New Zealand." He nudged Ronnie, prompting her to turn, and awe spilled through her.

There were rows of cars, both old and new models, but all well-loved, and painted a gorgeous array of colors. It was like a metal-flower garden, with a faint grease perfume.

"Neat."

"Good word for it. I know it's not exotic food or a stunning landscape, but I like it."

There was so much about him she didn't know. As they wandered toward a row of vehicles, she kept her hand nestled in his. The contact was pleasant, and he didn't seem to mind.

"Any idea why someone would be screwing with Ubiquity now, and not—say—a year ago?" he asked.

She didn't expect him to jump back to the work conversation, but the question haunted her, too, so she didn't mind. Talking to him was nice, regardless of the topic. The realization hit her out of nowhere. "They're bored? I don't know why anyone would do it to begin with, so time and place doesn't change my opinion." She was grateful he didn't shrug the notion off, though.

"Does it have something to do with you?"

Her laugh was bitter, and she choked it off. "I know a lot of people think the world revolves around them. Pretty sure Gabe is on that list. But no, I can't see why it would be about me."

He stopped in front of a black pickup truck with stark chrome trim. Even given the cloudy day, its polish shone and glinted. She had no idea what any of the terminology was for the parts of the car, beyond basic names. The way he hovered his hand inches from the hood, gliding without touching, was reverent, and she didn't dare interrupt the admiration. She was afraid saying something like *it's pretty* wouldn't have the same impact as whatever Michael was thinking.

After a few moments, he moved away. "I don't mean you directly, but everything surrounding when you…came back? Were named? I'm not certain what to call it."

"*Was tossed into a raging inferno of confusion, woefully unequipped to handle what the world was about to throw at me?*" That sounded bitter. "It wasn't that bad." She met Michael, after all. And she got this life out of it, which had more ups than downs. Like coffee, good music, and sex. "How about *started working for Ubiquity?*"

"I suppose that will have to do."

She shivered and rubbed her arms when a gust of wind blew in around her. Shorts seemed like a good idea when she changed, but now she was wishing for jeans. "I suppose the timing coincides, but if anything, the impetuous seems more centered around Gabe and his special development staff. What happened with Ari… The others. I may have been a catalyst for her wanting something more powerful, cluing other agents into the possibility of growing through non-organic means, but I wasn't more."

"So maybe that's what it was. Ariel drew scrutiny to everything."

"Maybe." Ronnie turned the idea around. "That doesn't seem like a good reason to bring Ubiquity into the public eye. Anyone doing what Ari did, like Vine and Cassiel, would want it to stay secret. There are repercussions to such actions."

"It's another piece of the puzzle. Ariel proved some of us are in this for themselves. Given that, would they really mind what kind of consequences there were, as long as they got the power they wanted?"

"I guess not, though it feels a little cliché-villain for me. The whole *I want power, and I'll kill whoever gets in my way* thing. And if that's the case, it doesn't give me a direction or a solution."

"No, but it's a starting point, and if it's a new perspective—even if it's not the right one—it may point you in a revealing direction."

She couldn't argue with that. She was willing to dismiss the idea outright, but it did give her an angle she didn't have before. They wandered in silence for several minutes, stopping at certain cars. She tried to figure out why some and not others drew his attention. She asked, "Why are we here? Not that I'm complaining. I'm curious."

"They take these things that were never meant for more than utilitarian purposes—intended simply to move people from one place to another—and they give them new life and beauty."

"Is there some kind of hidden meaning in that?"

He shook his head. "I suppose there are all sorts of hidden meanings in it, but I never looked at it that way. I do this in my spare time. Restore cars. It's not a way to dive deep into the nature of how everything old can be new again. It gives me a chance to work with my hands. To escape the world for a few hours at a time and think. It's relaxing."

"You do *this?*" So much to discover. "A lot? Do you have a garage full of gorgeous cars somewhere?"

"No. And I don't go to this extent. The people who work on these love their cars almost as an extension of themselves." He stopped next to a cherry-red car with a convertible top and a Ford logo. "Like this one. This Thunderbird might as well be the owner's baby."

Was that why he paid more attention to some than others as they walked? "How can you tell?"

"Can't you?"

She bristled at the implication it should be obvious, but her ire faded when she took another look. The cars that seemed to shine without direct sunlight actually had a faint glow. Whispers of the same kind of passion she felt when she went to a convention or rave. Now that she knew what she was looking for, it was as evident as the stunning paint jobs. "Yeah. I guess I can. So what do you do with yours, then?"

"I finish it, I give it to someone, and I go find another one. The joy for me is in the work. Once it's completed, I need something else to work on."

A new thought occurred to her, and it sank heavy in her gut before she could put words to it. The funeral this morning was for— "You were there, with the flash fire at the garage."

He clenched his jaw and nodded.

"I'm sorry. I shouldn't have brought it up." Way to ruin a pleasant evening. Afternoon?

"It's all right. I'm coping, and I don't mind you asking."

"In that case, may I ask what happened?" Which was rude of her. He was mourning the loss of friends, and she wanted gruesome details so she could solve a work problem. Telling herself it was bigger than *making things better at the office* didn't help absolve her of guilt for wanting to know. It did keep her from taking it back, though.

He led her out of the main flow, toward rows of food carts. Her stomach grumbled at the sharp smells. Grilling sausages, ice cream… even the fizz of soda mixed in with it all. He leaned against a nearby fence and laid out the story of what happened when he was hunting Azazel. The destruction in the hotel the first time and the demon getting away. His rage the second time.

Ronnie listened and watched, fascinated and horrified, as Michael's posture and expressions shifted through grief, fury, and regret. The only thing she managed when he was done was, "I'm so sorry."

He dragged in a noisy breath, forced it out slowly, and fixed a smile on. It didn't reach his eyes. "So what do you do in your free time?"

A change of subject had never been more obvious, but if he didn't want to drag his emotions through the mud, she wouldn't force him to. Especially since she didn't want to answer his question, either. "Working. There's a lot of extra hours in management, but you know how that goes. Other stuff."

*

Michael was relieved Ronnie didn't call him out on the change of subject, and in return he didn't push for information she seemed unwilling to give. It was odd. He spent the last several months struggling with who she was, now that two wholes had become one, and telling himself to move on. With her here, the impulse changed. When she was Uriel, he wanted to protect the demon caught in the system but loving the world around her. When she was Metatron, the fire between them burned so hot and fast it left scars. This Ronnie was neither, and both. And she was holding something back that muted her in a way which made him want to uncover more. Or the desire to discover what she hid was because they'd never spent a lot of time getting to know each other.

"Do you want cotton candy?" He nodded toward one of the tents.

"No. But thanks."

He gave her a concerned glance. "Suit yourself." He stepped up and ordered one large cotton candy from guy working the stall. The kid grabbed a paper cone from the stack and lowered it into a machine that looked like it was spinning vivid, sugar-scented smoke. Seconds later, he handed Michael the results.

Michael nudged Ronnie back toward the crowds. "We can keep looking if you'd like."

She glanced at him, and a laugh escaped her throat—a gorgeous, playful sound.

"What?" he asked. This was better than lingering on the darker places the conversation threatened to take them. *Death. Destruction.* He shoved that all aside.

"I don't know. You look a little silly—a grown man plucking spun sugar from a stick."

The comment wasn't insulting. As long as Ronnie was having fun, he didn't care what anyone else thought. "You're jealous you didn't get any."

"Maybe I'll have some of yours." She reached out, and he held the cone away. She crossed her arms and stuck her bottom lip out so far, the pout had to be intentional. "Meanie." The corners of her mouth threatened to turn up.

It was nice to see her light and playful side. He tore off a piece of candy for her. A pleasant shudder ran through him when she sucked one of his fingers into her mouth and licked the pad clean. He expected a pang to accompany the sensation, but this was all appreciation for her rough tongue gliding along his fingertip.

They shared the rest of the snack as they roamed and looked at more cars, sometimes feeding each other, and sometimes snatching wisps of sugar for themselves. Afternoon melted away and crept up on evening. Five local time meant it was eleven at night back home.

Ronnie yawned for the second time in as many minutes. She rubbed her eyes. "I know it's boring to be tired so early on a Friday, but it's been a long day."

Funerals and all that. He understood. "It's not boring. I'll take you home."

It felt odd to land in front of the door instead of inside, but also appropriate.

She unlocked the condo. "Do you want to come in for a while? I mean, I guess you could come in anyway, it's your place."

"It's just a building. And I'd love to stay a little longer." That wasn't a completely accurate statement; it was more than a building.

They stepped into the living room. Though she hadn't changed the furnishings, her essence lingered on most of the things in the room—the couch, the coffee table, and he knew from earlier, the bed in the master suite. From the room to her, everything was so familiar, and at the same time, foreign. He felt out of sorts and wasn't sure what to do with the sensation.

Not suffering from the same hesitation, she tugged him to the couch and settled next to him when he sat.

"You never got a TV." He wasn't sure why he said that, but he couldn't sort out the rest of his other thoughts enough for something better.

"Why would I? You've got a kickass stereo system, and I stare at a screen enough at work all day. I was surprised by your music collection, though."

"Not modern enough for you?"

"Eh…" She fiddled with the frayed edges of her cutoffs. "Nirvana. Hendrix. Lennon. Joplin. Richie Valens. You notice there's a theme there?"

He had. They all died at the height of realizing their potential. A bittersweet notion that felt right but so wrong at the same time. "What would you prefer?"

"It's not a matter of preference. I expected you to have a wider assortment of classical, or something like that. Chinese opera? I don't know."

"There's Mozart in there."

"That's one guy."

"My tastes have grown and changed with time. It doesn't do to be stuck in the past." As he spoke, he watched her expression shift into something pained and sad. She smiled, but it didn't wash away the ache in her gaze. Did she think he meant her? The evening with her wasn't what he expected, but it was better—comfortable, friendly, and mostly angst-free. He wanted her smile to be genuine, though. "Would you replace it with something loud? A pounding beat?"

"Some days. Most of the time, I plug in my phone, pull up a random station, and let it play what it wants. I like it all."

He held out his hand. "So let's do that now."

She gave him her phone, and he crossed the room to hook it up to the stereo. "What do I choose?"

"Little blue button on the home screen, telltale *U* on the logo. Let it shuffle."

He did as instructed and returned to the couch. When he was seated, she scooted closer and rested her head on his shoulder. In the background, the music faded from country to rap to R&B, with a sprinkling of metal and some gorgeous orchestration mixed in.

They talked long into the night, and yet somehow managed to avoid sharing how they spent the last few months of their lives. Somewhere along the way, a nagging voice reminded Michael why he left the first time and asked if his reasons were still valid.

He didn't have an answer for that, especially with her distaste regarding how he eliminated the threat. If it came down to picking between keeping her in his life or continuing to do what was needed, would he be able to walk away again?

Chapter Nineteen

Ronnie was aware of two specific things, and had no interest in figuring anything else out at the moment. Falling asleep with Michael was as comforting as she remembered, but waking up with him still next to her was better. She didn't remember drifting off. Now the sun glared through the balcony window, and she was distinctly aware of lying with him on the couch, his arm draped over her hip.

And someone upstairs was moving furniture around or something. "Your neighbors are loud," she mumbled.

"*Your* neighbors. And that's someone at the door. Want me to get it?"

She never had visitors. Lucifer preferred to call and meet in a neutral location, and she didn't think anyone else knew where she lived except every delivery place in the city. The realization tugged at sadness in her chest, but she didn't linger on the feeling. "Probably not the best idea if it's for me." She forced enough consciousness into her brain to be able to stand, and made her way to the door.

Irdu stood on the other side, drumming his fingers on his leg, gaze shooting up and down the hallway. He looked at Ronnie, and the concern in his gaze gnawed at her. "I didn't know how late a nigh you had, but this is important. And you're not answering your phone."

"What is it?" Ronnie let him in.

Irdu stalled when he saw Michael. "I should have considered you'd still have company."

Ronnie didn't need to deal with Michael and Irdu glaring at each other on top of whatever this was. "What's going on?"

Why didn't she hear her phone ring? She wandered over to check the device for messages. Michael hadn't plugged it into a power source when he hooked it up to the stereo. Of course. It was dead now. She set it to charge and turned back around.

Michael sat on the couch now, hair a little rumpled—God, that was sexy—but otherwise composed.

And Irdu still lingered near the door.

"Irdu?" Ronnie prompted.

"This is about the stuff we've been dealing with. That Tia's been tracking?" Irdu darted gaze to Michael, before he focused on Ronnie again.

Ronnie hesitated. Not because she was worried about Michael hearing—the odds were in the high nineties she'd tell him anyway. But did she want to filter the information first?

She was tired of secrets, and if this was so urgent it had Irdu on edge, it would come out soon enough anyway. "No. We'll talk here."

Irdu let out a long breath through clenched teeth. "There is a series of explosions. Separately, they don't look big, and the details on the news don't make them seem significant. But there have been twenty, all identical, and all uploaded to U-View in the last two hours."

Shit. "Where are they happening?"

"Everywhere. Australia, Egypt, Hong Kong, Tokyo… The list goes on." Irdu's phone chimed, and he fished it from his pocket. "We're up to twenty-two."

Every profanity Ronnie knew, in every language she spoke, crashed into her thoughts in a burst. "We need to get to the office so we have access to locations, data, and anything else we need." She glanced at Michael. His help would be valuable, but the moment he walked into the Ubiquity building, cameras would know. Lucifer would find out. It might come out sooner rather than later, but something made Ronnie want to keep this quiet. "I have to cut the morning short."

"Don't worry about it." He was already on his feet. "Call me if you want to continue our conversation."

Ronnie was grateful he left the request vague.

"We can do it from here," Irdu said. "You've got a laptop, right?"

Even better. She crossed the room, stood on tip-toe, and brushed her lips over Irdu's. "Thank you."

She turned to see Michael giving her a questioning look, and she said, "Stay?" She wasn't sure how to define what was going on between them, but having him around would make it easier to figure out. She was tired of him walking out the door.

He nodded.

She turned back to Irdu and pointed to the desk near the back of the room, where her laptop sat. "I don't have the VPN installed."

Irdu made a *pft* noise. "Log in. I'll do the rest." He made a couple swipes on his phone. "You there?"

"Yup." Tia's voice drifted from the speaker. "You in?"

"Two minutes. Tops." Irdu slid into the seat as soon as Ronnie let him, and his fingers flew over the keys.

Ronnie crossed her arms, tapping her tow as she watched. How were they going to track something like this? How would they stop it? "Do we know if it's the same person causing them every time?"

"No. Every shot is a few seconds of calm before the destruction, but no people—agents, whatever."

Michael rested a hand on her shoulder. The simple touch was nice, but it didn't help untangle the knot in her gut.

"And they're not streaming?" Ronnie asked.

Irdu pulled up a remote connection to another computer. "No. Tia's nabbing them as fast as she finds them. They're not hidden, so that part is easy."

"They're not trying to mask their location." Tia's words mingled with the clack of keys.

"Who else knows?" Ronnie's questions weren't helping, but she had to do something.

Irdu spared her a glance. "No one. Well, anyone who saw the videos, but I didn't trust anyone else to deal with it."

A warm spark spread in Ronnie's chest, despite the stress. She sifted through her cluttered thoughts and forced them into some sort of order. "If we assume this is a demon or an angel, having the location where the video was shot or uploaded from won't matter. They'll be gone before we get there."

"You think?" Sarcasm filled Tia's retort.

Ronnie raised an eyebrow at the out of character retort. Not that she blamed Tia. "Give me the complete list of cities we've seen so far."

"None of them have anything in common," Tia said. "We've got single floors in the middle of downtown metropolitan areas. Rural farms."

Irdu pointed to a list on the screen. "There's one connection. They've all been abandoned within the past six months, as far as I can tell. Though I'm still checking. A warehouse in Beijing that collapsed in on itself two months ago. A grain silo in Uruguay that hasn't been used since its contents caught fire. A hotel in the middle of Nevada, condemned after lightning tore through it."

With each item she ticked off the list, Michael's grip tightened on Ronnie's shoulder. When Irdu reached the hotel in Nevada, Ronnie knew why. She reached up to lace her fingers with Michael's and try to get him to relax. That had to be where he encountered Azazel the first time. "Where are they going next?"

"If we knew that, we would have told you." Tia's frustration was clear.

"Not you," Ronnie said as kindly as she could. She turned to Michael. "And how many are there?" The question summoned a surge of nausea. If she was right, if each of these was a place Michael had taken out a rogue agent, then he'd eliminated more than twenty. Would it be better or worse if he gave her an exact answer?

"They're not in the order I executed them." He winced. "Poor word choice. I'm sorry. There are only twenty-seven total."

Only. The qualifier dug deep.

"And we just hit twenty-four," Irdu said.

Ronnie's gaze never left Michael. "Explosions in every single place you've hunted someone down and eliminated them. A message for you?"

He frowned. "With videos of someone destroying those spots now? I'm not a big U-View guy, so they've missed their target audience."

"But Ronnie is," Tia said. "Her obsession with tracking incidents like this is the reason we found them while they're hot."

Ronnie didn't like that implication. If none of this held a deeper meaning unless the perpetrator knew she and Michael were together as it happened, then it was either random after all—the locations a coincidence—or scarily calculated.

"You know I don't believe in coincidence." Michael seemed to be thinking the same thing.

Ronnie nodded at the list of locations on her computer. "Where are the last three? We'll divide. You and I will restrain one each, and Tia and Irdu will get the last one." She didn't want to do that to them. Irdu had never been trained to fight—Lucifer didn't want that—and if this was anything like Vine, Tia demon was no match for her elder. "You only have to be there long enough to call me, and we'll join you, if you find whoever this is first."

Irdu shook his head. "And what if they hit more than one spot at a time?"

"So far, it's been single locations." Ronnie didn't believe her own reassurance. If she had more time… If she trusted anyone besides the people in this room… "I don't know what else to do."

"It's okay. I'll be okay." Tia's confidence wavered over the speaker.

"No." Irdu's voice was hard. "You're not going."

"I am, and I'm going alone. You need to be online to monitor, and I can hold my own for two seconds."

Ronnie didn't like this, but she didn't have an argument.

Irdu looked between her and the phone. "All right. I've got your back. Be safe." He focused on Ronnie. "If anything happens to her…"

"I know, you'll never forgive me."

Irdu shook his head. "I won't blame you. I will make what Ariel did look like child's play, until I find whomever is responsible. Just like I would for you."

"Then we'd better not fall that far." Ronnie let out a shaky breath. "Where are we going?" She asked Michael.

"I can't give you anything like GPS coordinates, but I can take each of you to a spot."

Ronnie grabbed her phone. "We need to keep in touch. If you both ring me, I'll open a group text, and we'll go voice activated." And she'd hope the fifteen percent battery her phone had picked up in the last few minutes held out until they were all back in the same place.

Michael vanished to get Tia, and seconds later, he returned for Ronnie. "She's in L.A. I'm hoping that's not where they hit next, because there's a lot of nearby traffic."

Ronnie gave him a grateful smile, not sure what she could say. In a blink, green and mountains replaced the condo. "Do I dare guess where we are?" she asked.

"Toronto." He placed a finger under her chin, and a shock of heat raced through her, in contrast to the chilly morning. He pressed his lips to hers, and then stepped back. "Good luck."

Where did that come from? It wasn't fair leaving her with that when she didn't have time to linger on how such a simple gesture could fill her with giddiness. Her tension chased the flutters away, the muscles in her neck tightening as seconds and then minutes ticked away. Irdu used their phones to share everyone's locations. She hated this entire setup, but knowing he was watching was as comforting as anything could be right now.

According to Tia, there had been a new video every five minutes, and Irdu said local news supported that timing. Ten minutes passed, and then thirty. Ronnie's phone beeped with another low-battery warning.

Why hadn't anything happened? Did Michael miscount? Remember the locations wrong? It was twenty-seven spots. What were the odds he knew every single one? Ronnie would remember. She'd be haunted by all of them. He probably recalled them too.

Do we call it a day? Tia asked.

Not yet. Ronnie reminded herself not to fidget. The cabin Michael set her near was isolated. Trees for as far as she could see in every direction. The sun crept higher—that was pleasant. Her phone gave one more pathetic chirp and blinked off.

"*Fuck.*" Her curse echoed off the landscape. What was she supposed to do now? Tia had Michael on the line, and if Ronnie went to either of them, she left this place unguarded. Damage would be minimal, but it would still be caused by her inability to wait things out. In a flicker of desperation, she held her thumb to the charger slot and pushed the tiniest pulse of electricity through. She had no idea how much was too much, or if she was using the right voltage.

Her screen flickered on and connected to the network, and she allowed herself a second to breathe a sigh of relief.

Then Tia's message arrived. *He's here.*

Ronnie's phone shattered in her hand as too much juice flowed through her, pieces flying everywhere. She relocated to Tia without another thought. The sign out front read *El Camino High School*. She didn't want details about what happened here the first time. The sizzle of water meeting flame caused her to spin. Everything seemed to move in slow motion, but at the same time too quickly to process.

Vine blasted Tia with a rush of flame, and she slammed into the wall behind her. How the hell was he here? He would need interference from someone near the top of the ladder in hell to be allowed a physical form again. And he was flying toward Tia, not blinking in and out—that was something.

Ronnie's swords appeared in her hands, and she blinked out of sight to close the distance.

Michael was there first, glowing as bright as the mid-morning sun, wings spread and hand grasping Vine's throat.

"*No.*" Michael's command shook the ground and the nearby building.

Ronnie felt it more than saw it. Vine's essence didn't flow into Michael and then out again; it simply vanished, and so did his body. So that was what it looked like.

She was going to be sick. She respected Vine. Learned from him when she was a cherub. He was gone now, because he'd been willing to take others' lives to further his own. She saw it with Cassiel, and Tia almost suffered the same fate.

"Owie." Tia's complaint cut through Ronnie's haze.

Michael helped Tia stand. "Are you all right?"

"He ruined my shirt."

Ronnie didn't know if she wanted to laugh or sob that Tia didn't seem to comprehend Michael had killed Vine. Or didn't care. This was all wrong. The timing was too perfect, the string of events too much to be a coincidence.

It wasn't only that someone knew she was probably with Michael. Vine just happened to show up where they were weakest, breaking his timing pattern to do so moments after Ronnie's battery died?

"Irdu set us up." Michael's words jarred her.

No. Not in a million years.

"He didn't." Tia slid into a defensive stance. "Someone did."

Ronnie clenched her jaw. "It wasn't him. Why the fuck would you think that?"

Tia stalked forward until she was toe to toe with Michael. "I know you're some big might original angel, and I don't fucking care. Irdu didn't do this. I'd stake everything I have and could ever be on that."

"Ronnie." Michael looked at her.

She didn't try to hide the fury that raced through her. "I agree with Tia. He didn't. And he would't. He has *always* had my back."

"You would have said the same thing about Ariel twelve hours before she tried to destroy you," Michael shot back.

Hurt bled through Ronnie. "You're the one who knew every location. Seems like the odds are far better it was you." She snapped her jaw shut, but she could't take the words back. Might as well finish the thought.

"Is this your way of proving what you're doing is right?" Tia asked. So she did know Michael had killed Vine. "You know what? I don't care. You can go fuck yourself." She looked at Ronnie. "Don't become one of them. Please." She vanished before Ronnie could retort.

Ronnie stared at the spot where Vine stood moments earlier.

"I had to do it," Michael said. He kept his distance. "You know what would have happened otherwise, and every time I don't stop one of them, the repercussions are worse."

Ronnie knew that was true. She didn't like it, but if Vine couldn't be kept in hell, what other choice was there? "Irdu wasn't involved in this any more than you were."

"Are you certain?"

She whirled, letting her rage flare in licks of red and gold. "I'm positive. There are days I still question who I am and what my own motives are, but Irdu? I never question him. This isn't…" It couldn't be. Jealousy? "Because he and I are together."

"No, it's not. Someone did this," Michael's voice was infuriatingly calm. "They set us up, and they knew too much about the situation. If you trust him, so do I. And I want to help you get to the bottom of things."

Ronnie scrubbed her face. This was crumbling in so many ways. She wanted to tell Michael to fuck off. She didn't need his help if he was going to cast doubt on anyone on their side. His concession to back off would have to do for now.

Chapter Twenty

Ronnie couldn't sit still. Several hours after the incident in California, nervous energy compelled her to pace the living room. Michael was listening, and that helped. If she had to keep this all in her head, it might drive her insane. Again. She wasn't okay with Vine being gone, or with Michael's accusations, or that none of the pieces she had fit in the puzzle.

"It's circumstantial evidence"—she forced herself to stop, if for no other reason than to prevent wearing a hole in the carpet—"and it's no more likely than if Tia did it."

"How do you know it wasn't her?"

She glared at Michael. Why was he still here? Because he had knowledge. And even when he was being an asshole, he was an honest one.

Michael sat on the couch, looking as tense as Ronnie felt. "I believe you. I already said I did." His voice was strained. "You know Ubiquity as well as I do at this point. Who else is on the possible suspect list?"

He's trying to help. He's trying to help. He's not helping. "I don't know."

"No guesses at all?"

"Tia saved Izzy. And you heard Irdu this morning. He meant what he said about burning the world to the ground." She itched to tell him who Tia and Irdu really were. That she didn't know a single other agent who had less of a stake in the matters of heaven and hell. But that wasn't her secret to share.

"She may have put him in danger in the first place."

Ronnie growled. "And what do you know about it?" She couldn't keep the irritation from her voice.

Michael furrowed his brows. "Izrafel told me."

The reminder of Izzy, and that he wasn't talking to Ronnie, added another layer of stress to the heavy ball sitting in her gut.

"I'm simply playing devil's advocate." Michael sounded sympathetic.

It didn't help. "Don't. It doesn't suit you." How did her world go from car shows and cotton candy and rediscovering each other, to this, in less than a day?

"All right." He stood, closed the distance between them, and searched her face. "I'm trying to get you to look at this from a different perspective. That's why I'm here, isn't it?"

It was. "Neither Irdu or Tia is behind this. If you're going to keep pushing it, you can go."

"I believe you." He sounded sincere. And unlike with Lucifer, it was pretty easy to tell when Michael was lying. "I'm looking at this from the outside, and they're the only variables I see that I'm not familiar with. I meant it earlier. If you trust them, so do I." He took her hand. "Come sit down."

The contact, familiar and safe, soothed her more than she wanted. "I'm good here." She didn't pull away.

He squeezed her fingers. "I don't have a motivation for why Vine did this today. Or Ariel, or any of them. It could be a drive for power. That's almost what Gabriel did."

Back to motivation for destroying buildings—the conversation she preferred to have. "Maybe they lost their sanity. Too many voices in their heads." As she said it, something hovered just out of her grasp. What was it? "I know from personal experience, having that extra personality up there can wreak havoc on a mind."

"How close did you come to wiping out a city block?"

That was a fair point. "I almost cut down Raphael because he pissed me off in the office. I tried to kill you twice."

"You pulled your swords. It's not the same, and that wasn't you."

"If cherubs are driving them out of their minds, they're not themselves either. Why are you fighting me on this?"

"I want answers as much as you do." He raised his free hand, but dropped it again without making contact. "But I want them to be the right answers. I'm not sure you're looking at this objectively."

A tiny part of her argued he had a good point, but she wasn't in the mood to listen. "It was me who drew the swords." She struggled to keep the petulance from her voice. Michael of all people should understand she wasn't some faker in this role.

"I never pull my weapons unless I intend to use them."

"That's not you. That's Metatron."

"*Fuck.* You know how this works. You've helped others through it. I *am* Metatron. Why don't you get that?"

"You're not."

"Yes. I'm Metatron. I'm Uriel. I have their memories. I lived their lives. I have their power." She didn't know what else to say to make herself clear.

*

"And yet, you talk about them in third person." Michael almost felt Ronnie's frustration. It blasted out in waves every time she spoke. He didn't want to aggravate her, but some things couldn't be left to temper and chance. "You're Ronnie." The true impact of those words clicked in his head. He struggled last night—and in Moscow, and in the months leading up to this—to figure out whom he was distancing himself from. Now it made sense.

"Ronnie is both of them," she said.

He'd avoided reaching out, to prevent her from feeling he patronized her, but seeing the frustration and anguish on her face, he couldn't help himself. He cradled the back of her neck, to look her in the eye, and kept his tone calm. "I know. And yes, you are both, but you're also more than the sum of their parts. You didn't stay stagnant after they became one. You've learned and grown and changed since. You're like a complex compound."

She rolled her eyes, but the tense cords of muscle beneath his palm relaxed. "No fair throwing sciency terms into the intangible." She sounded frustrated, but her voice stayed steady.

"Am I making sense?" He stroked his thumb along her skin where jaw met neck.

"Fucking asshole. Yes. I still want a motivation for why Vine—or any of them—did this."

He was about to tell her they'd find the answers to both, when someone knocked.

An irritated grumble rose from Ronnie's throat.

"You might as well answer it," Michael said.

She squeezed his hand, then pulled away.

"Why aren't you answering your phone?" Lucifer's familiar voice reached Michael's ears before he saw his colleague.

Ronnie stepped aside and opened the door wider. "It blew up."

"That must be one hell of a story…" Lucifer trailed off when his gaze met Michael's. "I didn't realize you had company."

There was a bit of that going around. "You didn't ask." Ronnie kicked the door shut behind him and crossed her arms.

"Because you weren't answering your phone. Is this getting repetitive? Not only the conversation, but also him"—Lucifer nodded at Michael—"being back. Again. What about Irdu? And I thought you and Michael were doing the whole *I never want to see you again, for the greater good* thing."

Was that jealousy in his voice?

Michael had said that. So much had changed, but he hadn't. Or had he? If Ronnie was different, maybe he was learning to accept some things too. It was odd to think he could make that kind of shift after millennia. Could he allow himself to love someone—her—and not be tempted to fall?

"You're here for a reason?" All of Ronnie's frustration from earlier spilled back into her voice.

Lucifer raised his brows. "You need to turn on the news and— You don't have a TV. How did I forget that?"

"I don't know. Too busy keeping secrets to remember reality?"

This was getting awkward. Michael should leave.

"You're going to want to stay." Lucifer looked at him.

Was Michael that predictable?

"What news?" Ronnie's voice rose in volume.

"Any of it. Samael is freaking out. Raphael has been calling me all afternoon. Would you like me to keep going down the list of upper management who are bothered by this?"

Was Lucifer was getting some kind of perverse kick out of stretching out this conversation? At least *that* would be predictable. Except it meant Lucifer wanted Ronnie on edge, and that made no sense.

"I want you to tell me what *this* is." Ronnie spoke through clenched teeth.

Lucifer handed her his phone.

She scanned the screen, eyes darting back and forth. "Oh shit." The fire vanished from her voice in a whisper.

It seemed the day could still go downhill.

"Yeah." Lucifer took his phone back and pocketed it. "You on this?"

"What am I supposed to do?" Ronnie asked.

"Make something up. Tell the best fucking story you've ever told. Lie."

Arm at her side, Ronnie clenched her fist so tight her hand shook. "How do you know I won't be telling the truth when the press release says, *This is a coincidence. We can't cover everything*?"

"Is it?"

"Fuck." Ronnie rolled her head. "I'm on it."

"You're having marketing write you a press release. Art-film it and release it?"

Michael felt like he was watching a tennis match.

"No. I'm doing it myself," Ronnie said.

"Of course. *Now* you want to keep secrets." Lucifer's tone stayed pleasant, despite the tension in the exchange.

What did that mean?

Ronnie turned away and headed toward her laptop. "Are you done?"

"For now." Lucifer vanished.

"Fill me in." Michael wasn't sure now was a good time to ask, but with the stress thrumming through Ronnie, he had to do something. If this got them closer to answers at the same time, that was an added bonus.

She clicked through her computer as she talked. "Some local news program in Nevada ran a story about the explosions this morning, asking why Ubiquity didn't have any record of these seemingly unrelated events. Why they don't show up in our search engines, what with all the explosions being identical and happening around the world. Why, in this age of instant information and internet streaming, weren't we returning any information at all?"

That sounded suspicious. "You had it *all* pulled?"

"Irdu put something in place for me. Fuck." She drummed her fingers on the desk while something loaded on the screen. "How did someone put this all together? How did anyone else know about this?"

Michael was searching for an answer, when her speakers crackled to life. The audio was filled with static, and poor quality, but the words were clear. "*...already in the midst of a federal investigation, Ubiquity is not only withholding information from their investors, but also filtering what the rest of the world sees. It's clear this behemoth of a corporation is hiding something from the general public. But what is it?*"

That explained the shift in her mood. "Technically, Ubiquity is hiding almost everything from the general public." Michael wished he could take the words back as soon as they were out. There were more tactful ways to put this. "It's not as if people are going to believe angels and demons sit behind desks all day, keeping tabs on the world through a massive data center."

Leaving the news running in the background, Ronnie turned to face him and rested her weight against the desk. "Wouldn't that be one hell of a motivation for whoever's behind this?"

"Exposing our existence to the world?" The idea left a bad taste in Michael's mouth.

"It doesn't make any more sense to me than destroying things does." Ronnie spun her chair and dropped into it. "I have to write a press release, apparently. But I'm not going on camera. Being the boss has some perks—I get to make that call myself."

Michael knelt in front of her and grasped her hands. "Is there anything I can do?"

"Keep me company so I don't crawl into my own head and drive myself insane with questions that don't have answers?"

"Absolutely." He stood and turned the chair and her toward the computer. "Get writing." He settled his hands on her shoulders and kneaded his thumbs into her neck, loosening the knots running underneath her skin.

Her groan of satisfaction flowed through him, kicking his pulse up a notch, and turning tension into something more intense and passionate. She leaned her head back. "As much as I appreciate the thought, I won't get any work done if you keep doing this."

"Fair enough." With monumental reluctance, he broke away. He resisted the desire to kiss her neck. If he started, he wouldn't want to stop. To help keep temptation at bay, he settled on the couch.

For the next couple of hours, Ronnie did a lot of mumbling, a bit of bouncing sentences off him for a second opinion, and a fair share of typing. Finally, she declared it done and wheeled away from the desk.

When she stood and stretched her hands above her head, elongating every inch of her body, Michael couldn't pull his gaze from her curves.

"What?" She dropped her arms, and a flush rushed onto her face.

He rose and moved toward her. "I thought I remembered how gorgeous you are. It haunted me for months. The memory? Pales in comparison to the reality."

"Flatterer." The pink on her skin darkened.

He cupped her cheeks. "I'm being sincere." Some temptations couldn't be ignored forever. Like the scent of caramelized sugar that crackled around her, spiking each time her mood shifted. He kissed her, and sweetness flowed through him, carried on the softness of her lips and made more delicious by the whimper that escaped her throat.

She rested her palms flat against his chest, and the heat seared through. She broke the kiss and met his gaze. "This has yet to end well for us."

"I know." He didn't want to have this conversation. He wanted to press her against the wall, strip off her clothes, and feel her wrapped around him. "I can't begin to guess how things will go this time. I can't make any promises."

She gripped his shirt. "And the only reason you're watching me like I'm a lollipop for you to unwrap, is because the last day or so has been stressful, and this is an outlet."

"It's not the only reason. It does add to the intensity."

"As long as we're on the same page." She relaxed her arms, though not her grip, rose on her toes, and kissed him.

When she draped her arms around his neck and pressed into him, he lost any hope of backing out of whatever came next.

Chapter Twenty-One

In her time with Irdu, Ronnie had experienced *a lot* when it came to sex. He never left her wanting. But he also wasn't Michael. Being with either of them was equally incredible, but very different. She had yet to find something that could fill the void Michael created when he left.

It was why she surrounded herself with people who radiated happiness and lust; she could never recreate for herself the intensity that spilled from a human when they *desired.*

Michael knotted his fingers in her hair and crushed his mouth to hers. Something in her chest snapped, and that missing *something* flooded her skin. Her nerve endings. Her every thought. The scents of fresh pine and sunshine filled her nostrils. She could sink into this and be happy never emerging.

He yanked her hair and deepened the kiss. A whimper tore from her throat. She had memories of the night they spent together a few short months ago, but they were diluted by the perspective of two different minds. This was all her, and the uncut contact was new and intoxicating. She dragged her nails down his back and under his shirt, drawing him closer, needing to feel more.

When she dragged her fingers along his bare skin, memorizing each contour and reflex at her touch, he growled against her mouth. He broke away to strip off his shirt, before pulling her in again. He lowered his mouth to her neck, kissing and then sucking on the tender skin. "A lollipop, is it?" His words hummed through her.

"Or something else sweet and lickable." More of her bold wit evaporated each time he touched her.

He alternated licks and kisses along her collarbone, as he glided his hands under her shirt and up her sides. "You paint delicious pictures with metaphor."

Everything felt and tasted and smelled distinct, as if a filter had been removed from her senses. As clothes came off, and he guided her toward the bedroom, anticipation built inside.

She hesitated at the foot of the bed, and he propelled her forward, urging her to lie on her back. He crawled toward her, his gaze tracing every curve and nuance of her body as he moved. He kissed her navel and followed a path up her chest, until he claimed her mouth. He tasted like candy and smelled of pine and felt like satin sliding against her.

His fingers slid easily between her folds, and she groaned. Teasing and foreplay were fun, but she wanted to be part of him.

"I wanted to see the expression on your face as you enjoy yourself." His growl slid through her. He rolled onto his back and tugged her on top of him.

She smirked and hovered, keeping enough distance to feel him without making contact. Maybe a little teasing was okay.

He reached between their legs and grabbed his shaft. A guttural cry tore from her chest. when he thrust up with a grunt. "I missed you, angel." She liked the way the endearment rolled off his tongue.

She rose up almost to the tip, then dropped down against him again. The slow build-up raised the friction between them. She wanted to memorize every touch. Every groan that drifted from his throat. He gripped her thighs, digging in his fingers, and increased the speed. When she closed her eyes and leaned back, driving him deeper inside, he hit deep inside her.

He drove one hand up her chest, pinched a nipple, and rolled it between his fingers. She gasped and pushed harder against him.

He dug his fingers into her thigh as their pace grew more frantic. Her lips parted, gasps blurring together. He found her clit, swollen and peeking from its hood, and drew tight circles around it.

She leaned back with a cry, and she raked his legs with her nails. She clenched around him, milking him. Breaking down his resistance. God, he was incredible. He spilled inside her, hot and frantic, thrusting until he was spent.

They both struggled to catch their breath as they slowed to a stop. She shuddered, smile never leaving her face, when he pulled out of her. He tugged her forward so her head rested on his chest and trailed his fingers up her spine.

He rolled to the side, and she curled up and settled her head against his shoulder.

He brushed a loose strand of hair off her forehead and kissed her. His thumb traced tiny circles over her spine. "I'm glad I stayed." The hunger was gone from his voice, but the commanding power remained.

She smiled and rested more of her weight against him.

The glow radiated through her was more intense than any second-hand high she got in Las Vegas. The conversation with Irdu from the day before, that she didn't need to lose herself in someone else, drifted back to her.

"You're quiet. Are you all right?" Michael drew his finger along her arm, light enough to tease but not tickle.

"Enjoying the moment." Which would end by morning. He'd go back to what he was doing, and she'd have to deal with work.

Like that, her rambling thoughts dampened the mood. She grasped for the amazing sensations of a few minutes ago. Any relationship with Michael besides a professional one was temporary. She'd known that since he left. There was no reason to lose herself in that past or wallow in pity about things she couldn't change. She had the memory of tonight, and she'd face the rest as it happened.

Why couldn't the reality be as easy as thinking it into existence?

* * * *

"I wondered if I'd hear from you today." Abaddon sounded better than last time Michael spoke with her, but her tone held traces of exhaustion. "Actually I thought it would be yesterday. I'm wounded you kept me waiting."

The expectation cranked Michael's suspicion another notch. "Why would I call?"

"Because you miss me, silly." The teasing sounded forced.

"What's your schedule like today?" He couldn't summon the flirting they'd fallen into before, even knowing it was an act. He expected her to push back with a line like, *what makes you think I'll drop everything to see you?*

She sighed. "I have time now if you do. You name the location."

"There's a local little bakery. Can you meet me there?" he asked.

"By local, I assume you mean that place around the corner from corporate?"

He knew what she meant by *corporate* without clarification. When did Ubiquity become so much a part of every angel's existence, whether they worked there or not, that it could be referred to in such a generic term? "I do. I'll grab us a table."

"I'll be there in ten." She disconnected.

Michael already stood outside the building, which was wedged between a tanning salon and vitamin store. He wasn't surprised the bakery was the only one of the three that did steady business.

When he stepped inside, the scent of baking bread mixed with a hint of sweetness greeted him. It was just after ten, so most of the Ubiquity agents were done grabbing last-minute breakfast, and were now counting the minutes until lunch, which left the place almost empty. That was perfect for this conversation. Easier to sense if anyone besides Abaddon was nearby.

He didn't like having to be so alert around old friends, but apparently this was a different world. He ordered one of the house specials for Abaddon, and two coffees. Something about the idea of a giant cinnamon roll drenched in cream-cheese frosting and caramel sauce didn't sound like the right kind of sweet. Ronnie, on the other hand… sharp, sugary, and tantalizing described her perfectly. That wasn't the place he needed his mind right now.

Abaddon joined him a few moments later and settled into a chair on the other side of the battered wooden table. She raised her brows when he slid the plate toward her. "I'd heard rumors. I didn't believe them." She twirled the fork between her fingers, before sectioning off a bite. "And it really is heavenly."

The levity was nice, despite feeling strained. "As I understand it, one of the demons from marketing requested it one day, and once word got out they offered such a thing, it became their top seller."

"Go figure." Abaddon dumped a large quantity of sugar in her coffee before taking a sip. "I thought you weren't back at Ubiquity."

The statement amplified his concern. She might figure he was from his choice of a meeting location, but there was more to his suspicion than that; she'd also expected his call. "What gives you the impression I am?"

"I'm not here to play games, regardless of what you think." She met his gaze. "They seem to have the inside track on those explosions from over the weekend. The ones the news says they're covering up. I gave you half those locations that were attacked. Don't tell me you've forgotten already. It's the only reason you call me these days."

He wouldn't get sucked into a simple jab and feel guilty. "We didn't speak for more than two hundred years, and the only reason you reached out was because you wanted information on Ronnie." During his brief stint at Ubiquity, Abaddon tracked him down. She said she wanted a job, but her questions at the time all focused on Ronnie.

"How long have you known that's why I was there?"

"Since that first day." When he'd watched her fumble through excuses for contacting him, he realized why everyone said he couldn't lie. She suffered the same ailment. Funny. Once upon a time he'd considered it an asset.

She nibbled on her food. "But you kept in contact despite that."

"I enjoy the company." With a heavy supply of backstabbing running rampant through the ranks, it was nice to talk to someone who—while she kept secrets—couldn't hide much when he asked a direct question.

"And you wanted your own information."

"And that."

She smiled and shook her head. "Since Ubiquity is covering up the attacks, and they have something to do with you, maybe you stashed your ethics for more information. You're not above it."

He really didn't like the double-talk, even in small doses. "I'm not back there. I know people on the inside. Like we all do."

"Since you're pumping me for information, can I get some in return?" she asked.

"Probably not."

"How's that fair?"

He had a list of reasons. She sent him into Moscow. She kept a cherub when she shouldn't have. He could start ticking things off, but she already knew his concerns. "It depends on what you want to know," he said.

"Are you talking to *her* again?"

"I'm not sure how that's relevant to you, but she goes by Ronnie."

"Which I'll take to mean *yes*."

Lucifer had told him about the name preference, but Michael saying anything besides *no* implied *yes*.

Abaddon pushed her empty plate aside. "I don't plan to use the information for anything nefarious." She chewed on her bottom lip and furrowed her brow. "The thing is, I've been doing a lot of thinking since Boston, and more after Moscow. I didn't expect things to go down this way. I'm not in this for the destruction. I'll tell you everything I know."

It was almost too easy, but that was no reason to not hear her out. Even if she fed him snippets of the truth or an entire story woven in bullshit, he could suss it out. He wanted to think the best of the offer, though. She did help Izrafel and Tiamet. She'd been giving Michael names. And she tended to fiddle with her jacket when she was hiding something.

"I'm listening."

"He wants the three of you out of the way. He doesn't like the way you do things."

"Gabriel." That was old news to Michael. Gabriel told Ronnie himself he wanted to be the only original left standing.

"He's picking and choosing from the ranks of agents, both heaven and hell, those who he believes have the same goals he does. The cherub thing—access to extra power—is a bit of extra incentive."

A year ago, Michael wouldn't have believed a motive like that. Now it sounded all too plausible. "If you're in enough to have one of your own, to have achieved the gold star so to speak, why have you been giving the others up to me?"

"Getting the power-up isn't the gold-star reward. Gabriel's far more liberal with that information than he should be. As in, everyone knows how to do it, and he makes no effort to keep it under wraps. Which is biting him in the ass. He gave me names. Those he felt might become a threat, or who were too hard to control, like Ariel. It was to keep me in your good graces."

Michael couldn't hide his scowl. Apparently he didn't have as great a handle on the situation as he thought.

"But when I saw what Azazel did, both times." She shuddered. "And Vine. I don't like that. I want order. Gabriel promised submission, and chaos isn't the way to get there."

"Were you supposed to give me Vine?" Michael asked.

"No. Cassiel. Vine was supposed to behave. Be rational. Prove I wasn't the only one who could be talked down. Give you another point of contact and a little more reason to hesitate before killing. I don't know why he went the violence route instead. Gabriel didn't expect you to be so efficient, and Vine should have been a way to make you question your actions."

"I see." Michael let the information roll around in his thoughts, working to process everything it meant.

Abaddon leaned closer, voice low. "I don't want to be a part of that anymore. I wish I could give you more information. If what Vine did in Moscow was his idea or someone else's…"

"Who let him out of hell?"

"I—what? You killed him. That's what you do. Seek and destroy." Her surprise looked genuine.

He shouldn't tell her the next bit, but if she was feeding him a story, she already knew, and if her surprise was genuine, this would cement her decision. "I did, but not until Saturday. Ronnie got to him before me the first time. Sent him back home. He was behind the explosions over the weekend."

She scrubbed her face. "Fuck. I don't know who did it. Vine was the highest-ranking demon I was aware of working for Gabriel."

He hoped this meeting would clear things up for him, but it only left him with more questions. "If you're telling me this, you must be out now."

"Yes. So, I can't feed you names anymore."

Any names he didn't get from Abaddon were luck on his part—right place, right time, tracking patterns. But those opportunities were few and far between, and if Gabriel was… what? Building an army? Well, then, he had a lot more than a couple dozen agents answering to him. This meeting was one bit of bad news after another.

For the first time in his existence, Michael understood why people hated Mondays.

Chapter Twenty-Two

Irdu paused in Ronnie's office doorway. Michael's accusation hadn't stopped grinding under his skin. Arrogant fucking asshole.

Ronnie was looking at her phone, a tiny smile on her face.

"Good news?" Irdu tried to keep his tone neutral.

She looked up, startled. She worked her jaw up and down. "Dinner invite from Michael."

And she was happy about that? "Do you have ten minutes?"

"I have a meeting at eleven."

"That would be a *yes*." He closed the door behind him, but didn't bother locking it. Apparently that didn't matter here. "You know what Tia adores about you?" He was going down that path, because his list was too long.

"I have good taste in ice cream?"

The reply might be cute any other day. Right now, it felt like she was shrugging off a serious conversation. He was angry with Michael, but it dug deep that she wasn't just still talking to the bastard, she was getting goofy smiles over him. "Unlike all the other originals, you're here, slinging shit with the rest of us."

"I… thanks?"

"And Michael's not. The few months he was here, he didn't do anything. He poked into my HR records. He was in the office a total of what, five times? He doesn't know us. He doesn't know how things function here. He's arrogant and presumptuous and how the fuck are you flirting with him still after what he accused me of?"

"He's sorry."

"And I deserve to hear that from him." Irdu snapped the words off. "I gave you Tia's location. I would have been by her side if it was an option. Does he have any idea how much it would destroy me if either of you got taken out?" Frustration leaked into his words, and he swallowed it. He hated that he wasn't a fighter.

Ronnie crossed the room to him, and paused less than a foot away. "You do deserve to hear it from him. I can tell you all day he's sincere. He was trying to be logical. He doesn't know you. I know you both. I want us all on the same page. I want you to be able to trust each other. You're all I've got."

"So, this is selfish on your part?" He wasn't forgiving Michael so easily, but he was tired of arguing with Ronnie.

"Yes. But there's more to it than that. No one else has our backs on this."

He tugged her closer. "I give him a chance because you trust him. I'm only asking for the same consideration."

"That's fair. And if I didn't think he was sincere about being sorry, I'd cut him out of my life. I promise you." She rested her hands on his chest.

Irdu believed that. He kissed her lightly. "So, did you get laid?"

"It was just sex."

"Bullshit." He trailed his fingers along her neck and down her chest, stopping at the first button on her blouse. "It's not *just* anything with him. Besides, if I have to share you on a long-term basis, as least it's with someone honest and sexy."

Ronnie smirked and pressed closer, molding her body to his. "Sexy, huh? You know when you say *share*… That's got a lot of possibility."

He undid the top button on her blouse, and then the next couple, drawing his fingers along her skin as he moved down. "It does." He kissed along her collarbone. "But can you really imagine a guy like that fucking you while I'm in the room." He worked one breast free from her bra, and flicked his tongue over the nipple. "Sliding inside you, filling you up, while I roam my hands all over your body?"

"I don't know." Her response was breathy. "I'm having a hard time with the visuals. You might have to help me out."

He kneaded one breast while he sucked and nibbled the other. With the slightest mental flick, he sent similar sensations racing over her body. Her groan and the arch of her back said he'd hit several right spots.

"I don't know if I'd rather watch or join in." Irdu continued to lavish attention on her nipples while he dropped his other hand to inch her skirt up.

"I bet the two of you are one hell of an aural light show. Especially when he's pounding you hard."

He traced his fingers along the outside of her panties, and thrust her hips into his touch.

"I've never been focused on the lights. But he's not really anything hellish." Her chuckle was strained.

"That's a shame." Irdu moved kissed up her chest to suck on her neck. "Everyone needs a bit of devil inside them." He slid the crotch of her underwear aside and teased along her slit.

"That's something I'd watch."

Irdu fucking Michael? That was a tantalizing thought. "We probably have to work up to that. But I don't think I could keep my hands to myself with you." With another flick of magic, he could make her feel the sensation of being penetrated.

She gasped and dug her fingers into his back.

"I'd have to feel how much he was turning you on." Irdu slipped up to her clit. "Stroke you while he was buried in you." He traced circles around the button.

Her breath came in short gasps, and her hips thrust in time to his attention. His cock was so hard it hurt. He wanted to actually be fucking her, instead of using an ethereal dildo. But the expression on her face and the glow of pleasure were worth the attention he focused on her.

He crushed his mouth to hers and slid two fingers on either side of her clit. He increased his pressure and pace. Her whimpers were frantic, and she ground into his touch.

Desire spilled from her in waves, spiking and encasing him. He swallowed her cries when she came, and didn't let up until she shuddered away from his touch.

"So," Irdu said breathlessly against her lips. Why did she have to have a meeting now? "You get him to grovel for forgiveness, and we can make the fantasy real."

She bit her bottom lip. "Just like that?"

"Absolutely." He kissed her more lightly this time, then pulled her close. He held her, listening to her breathing return to normal.

Someone knocked. He didn't think anyone in this place did that anymore. "I think your eleven o'clock is here," he murmured against her hair. "I'll leave you to it."

He was reluctant to let go of her, but he forced himself to step back. He waited until she had her clothes straightened. It was tempting to help, but he'd probably take them off rather than put them back on.

She gave him one last playful look, then opened the door.

"Is now a bad time?" Samael asked, looking Irdu over as he stepped in the room.

"Now's fine. You're on my calendar." Ronnie's tone was professional, but she didn't try to hide the pink dotting her cheeks.

Irdu didn't like the needles that crawled over his skin when he brushed Samael's shoulder. He didn't care that Ronnie had a past with the guy, or was friends with him now. Something about the other demon radiated deception.

Then again, he was a demon. And an accountant for a company cooking their books. So maybe that was to be expected.

Irdu had a feeling there was more to it than that.

* * * *

Michael stretched out his legs and leaned back, resting his weight on his arms and wrists. "You're a wonderful cook."

Ronnie flushed. "Irdu taught me. He makes these crepes…" She ducked her head. "That I'm sure you don't want to hear about."

He didn't know how to respond. He'd never heard her say anything unkind about the incubus, and it was impossible to miss how much Ronnie and Irdu cared for each other. Maybe Michael should get to know the guy. "I still own him an apology."

She blushed. "Yeah. You do."

Michael hadn't been surprised when Ronnie asked if she could pick their dinner location, but he didn't expect it to be a picnic on the roof. The condo complex didn't have standard access up here, so he'd never thought to visit. From the large, cleared spot of concrete near the edge, he could tell she spent a lot of time up here. She always did love watching the stars.

She tucked her legs under her and fiddled with a pebble. "We're spinning our wheels." They were discussing how to keep something like the Vine incidents from happening again. "We know what we want but have no idea how to find it. Where are you getting your tips?"

"Some are luck. The rest came from Abaddon."

Ronnie clenched her jaw. "You realize she was involved in Boston, right?"

"She didn't cause the damage, but yes." He wasn't in the mood for an argument. The evening was going so well. "It doesn't matter. She can't give me any more."

"Can't or won't?"

He couldn't ignore the edge of suspicion in her question. "Can't," he said. "She doesn't want to work with Gabriel any longer."

Ronnie sat up straighter, hand on her stomach. Her aura flared, and the faint scent of burning pepper filled the night—a smell he associated with Metatron.

Michael should have known the name would have that effect on her. "Are you all right?"

"I'll be fine. Bad memories and all that. It's not as if I thought he was gone, and Irdu reminded me Gabe's still got influence. I just… I wanted to pretend he might not have anything to do with this."

"Would it be better if all these events were random and unrelated?"

"Of course not," she snapped. "Sorry. What else did she tell you?"

He related the morning's conversation as best he could, hating the pain that flashed across Ronnie's face every time Gabriel's name or motivations came up.

"I see." The emotion vanished from her voice. "How long have you been talking to her?"

"To Abaddon? Most of her life." He smiled, to lighten the mood and let Ronnie know he was joking.

Her weak laugh implied she didn't appreciate the humor. "For a few months," he said. He left out the details about why Abaddon came to him in the first place. This didn't seem like the time to drag up more demons from Ronnie's past.

Ronnie shook her head. "So, we're looking in the wrong place. We don't need a pattern or algorithm; we need to know who's loyal to Gabe."

"Who's going to tell us that?"

"We both know people." The frustration in her tone grew. "I mean, I've been out of the loop for a while, but you haven't. We can ask them?"

He grimaced. "Those of us who don't work for Ubiquity tend to exist in silos."

"Especially you. *Fuck.* Not that I blame you. I keep pissing people off left and right."

"Aren't you on good terms with Samael?"

She hesitated, casting her gaze to the ground. "Not exactly. Lucifer probably knows who's loyal to Gabe, right? And he's on our side."

What started off as a lovely picnic under the stars was rapidly deteriorating into one awkward topic after another. Michael wanted the calm back. "Lucifer is on his own side."

"He—"

"Gave you this chance. I realize that. And the two of you have a bond literally older than humanity." Michael tried to keep his tone kind and sympathetic. "But remember how much he kept from you along the way. And how many lies do you tell for him?" The cryptic conversation from Saturday night rolled into his memory.

"Not as many as I used to."

Had things really fallen this far among their ranks? "Whom do you trust?" he asked.

"You." She managed a smile, but it didn't reach her eyes. "Irdu. Tia…"

"Who else?"

"That's it. It's a short, pathetic list."

"It's not pathetic." It was longer than his list.

Ronnie furrowed her brow, as if diving into an intense thought, and the red and gold around her flickered and danced in the darkness. "What about Abaddon? If she was on the inside, she knows who else is."

"If Gabriel doesn't already realize she's turned her back on him, he will soon."

"We don't know five people between us who we can trust." Some of the sorrow vanished from her words, replaced with fire. "You killed twenty-seven of his, and that didn't make a dent in his numbers. He can't cut them off and replace them all overnight, just because he thinks someone close to him might sell him out. I guarantee he's got a backup plan for someone betraying him—he lied for three-thousand years about why he tried to kill me—and it's not to obliterate everyone who hasn't and start from scratch."

Michael couldn't help a smile.

"What?" Ronnie asked.

"I like hearing your determination." He stood and moved to sit next to her. When he intertwined their fingers on the rough concrete, she leaned into his shoulder. The contact felt right, especially accompanied by the brush of sugar and spice she radiated. "What if his contingency is moving everyone else into hiding?"

"They're already there, as far as we're concerned. And if his order is to lie low, it means fewer exploding buildings, right? Win-win. A list of who's been with him in the past, regardless of if it's complete, would be more than we have now. Irdu said"—she sighed and rubbed her face with her free hand—"most of us don't hop from place to place on a regular basis. Agents prefer to settle down. Whether or not you're not keeping up on your contact list, you've heard rumors about where some of them are."

It was a shot in the dark, depending on what Abaddon gave him. And that was only if she agreed to. There were thousands of agents scattered around the world, depending on what their jobs were, each going about things in their own way. Ronnie was right, though. It was more than they had now. A direction to look in next. "I'll get leads from Abaddon. Can you do the same with someone at work?"

Again, she hesitated. Her grip tightened around him, and her knee bounced. "Irdu is the only person I know who might consider helping me, and he's not too happy with you."

"He's not doing it for me."

"True. And he'll see it the same way." She rested more weight against Michael's arm. "When did heaven and hell shift from helping the world to this complicated cup and ball scam?"

"You should be used to the deception. You trained in the intricacies of lying, right?"

Seconds ticked by, and she didn't answer.

"I don't say it to insult," he said. "It's a part of the training everyone from hell receives."

"It is. It's the same thing that makes me second-guess almost everyone."

"I think we're all reaching that point." Michael hated it. He shouldn't have to scrutinize a list of agents he knew, wondering which planned to turn on him and which simply didn't care. When did this all become infighting and near-war?

"What happened to angels and demons?" Ronnie's question echoed Michael's thoughts.

"Nothing. Everything. Ever since …" He couldn't finish the thought, given how much Gabriel's name seemed to bother her.

"Gabe tried to kill me. The first time. You can say it."

He'd rather not. The words devoured him, though Gabriel hadn't succeeded. "We'll figure this out. I'll talk to Abaddon."

"Why do I feel like we're woefully under-equipped to handle this?"

"Because out of the four originals, only half of us aren't in it for ourselves." He shifted on the ground to sit behind her.

"But that's the problem, isn't it?" She leaned back, resting her head against his chest. "This isn't about the four of us. It's about every agent. All celestial beings."

"And the whole of humanity."

"Yes. Them too."

Michael wrapped his arms around hers and gave her a light squeeze. "We'll figure it out. We have a next step now."

"If we don't manage to decide on a few more steps, and quickly, it won't matter."

"I know." That was one thing he didn't question.

Chapter Twenty-Three

Ronnie did as she had on so many mornings before work really started—she stopped in at Irdu's office.

Her gut sank. It was empty. *What the fuck?* Every other thought she had evaporated. The only things left in the room were the desk and a couple of push pins in a paper tray. Correction—there was also a power cable hanging limply off the desk edge.

Did he move to a new location? Odd thing to do first thing on a Monday, but he'd been assigned to different departments on a whim before, and her mind refused to consider any other option.

She forced herself to run through a list of possible reasons the office was empty. There was… *No, not that. Maybe… Not likely.*

Tia would know.

Ronnie rounded the corner in the section of cubicles where Tia sat, and her feet stuck to the floor. Another empty desk, as forlorn looking as Irdu's. Ronnie had a place she could go for answers on this one. She found Tia's manager—an angel Lucifer brought on after he promoted Raphael.

"Where's Tiamet? Did she transfer?" she asked.

"Laid off. Fired. Whatever you want to call it."

Ronnie's shock grew. "Why?"

"Don't know. Came in this morning, found the note in my email from Human Resources, and she was already gone."

No. Nonononono. Ronnie didn't want to think that was the case. Only one person had that authority besides her. Lucifer wouldn't, though. Hadn't. She made her way back to her computer, and with a couple keystrokes, accessed Tia's and then Irdu's employee records. Both said the same thing. *Terminating Manager: Lucifer.*

Why? Best way to find out was to ask, but where was he most likely to be? Here? Back in hell? Other side of the world, having steak and wine for dinner?

Her email chimed, drawing her attention, and she stared in wide-eyed disbelief at the meeting request. From Lucifer. For five minutes from now. *Asshole.* The presumptuous invitation didn't make it any easier to sit still as the seconds ticked away. At two minutes to the top of the hour, Ronnie relocated to outside his Ubiquity door. And waited for another five minutes.

When Lucifer greeted her, with a pleasant, "I'm sorry to keep you waiting," she had to bite back a scream of frustration.

"I'm sure." She brushed past him and took a seat. "What's on the agenda for this morning?"

When he sat, he leaned back, arms behind his head and one knee crossed over the other leg. "I figured we'd play things by ear. We haven't had a chance to talk in a while. This is a good chance to catch up.”

God, she hated these games. On another day she might ease into the conversation, but they both knew why she was there. “You can’t fire my people on a whim.”

“It wasn’t a *whim*, and technically, I can.”

“Is this your thing now?” She didn’t like arguing with Lucifer, but it seemed to be status quo for them lately. “Every six months or so, you lay a few people off, to keep the rest of the company on their toes and terrified of your wrath?”

He maintained the casual posture. “I discovered they were subverting records. Tiamet was responsible for the debacle on Saturday; she had a habit of deleting U-View videos. Irdu was deleting Tracker App records.”

This was a game to him or something. Ronnie didn’t like the arrogant dismissal. Then again, that was probably to keep her off-guard. “Tia was deleting videos of agents with cherubs destroying things. Buildings. Blocks. She was keeping *us* out of the public eye.”

“Do you know what one of the amazing aspects of humanity is?” Lucifer leaned forward and rested his clasped hands on the desk.

“They figured out how to make baked Alaska?”

His smile was flat. “That too. I was thinking, they can see something as clear as day—magic, the unexplainable, any number of fantastic acts, right in front of their eyes—but they’ll be so busy looking for the strings and mirrors making the illusion possible, they’ll miss how incredible the reality is.”

"I don't—"

"You did but shouldn't have. If you'd let the videos stay, no one outside of conspiracy theorists would have thought twice about them. Instead, you made things vanish and left a trail of nothingness. Now people want to know what we're hiding and why."

That wasn't true. *Was it?* "Even if that's the case, it was my decision, not theirs. They did what I asked them to."

"Keep that in mind next time you consider giving a misguided order to an underling. You'll have this example to help you remember to think things through."

This wasn't right. An object lesson where someone else suffered to teach her? No. Lucifer was a lot of types of manipulative, but that wasn't in his wheelhouse. "Since when is this you? Subversion—fine. I get that. But whatever you're doing, the fluctuating between walking a hard line on the rules and the liberties you asked me to take with Samael and the SEC is inconsistent."

"And your point is…?"

"My point is I don't believe your reasons." It hurt to say the words more than she expected—to accept Lucifer's lies might be more than a way of looking out for her.

"In that case, what's the truth?"

"I don't know."

"Then how do you know I'm lying about my motives?"

"Because everything out of your mouth contradicts all you've stood for in the past. I'm giving Irdu and Tia their jobs back."

"No."

How much more direct could she be? "What's going on? You keep talking about the big picture. That there's something more important than any of us comprehend. Why do you have to make this about lies and complications? Why do you have to keep so many secrets?"

His smug mask wavered, his brows furrowing, before his smirk slithered back in. "I do what I must. I'm looking at the bigger picture, not just Ubiquity, but the entire world, the way we all should be. Sometimes that means I have to keep secrets to get things done."

"*No.* That's not an answer. This *prince of lies* bullshit? That's dogma. Stories people tell to scare their children and anyone else they want to control. It's not you, and it never has been. Maybe you've changed over the past three thousand years—"

"I have."

"Stop fucking cutting me off." Losing her temper in this conversation was a bad idea, but chipping away at the stone wall in front of her wasn't proving effective. "You haven't changed like that. You left heaven, took celestials with you, and created hell, because you wanted more freedom than the angels believed you should have when it came to your job."

"It's true; that's what happened. I still work toward that goal. I'll let you in on a little secret. I'd ask you not to tell anyone, but that hasn't worked out so far."

Did he know she told Samael the details about the incomplete financial and employee records? Asking was the same as admitting guilt. "What's the secret?"

"It's not freedom if someone tells you to do it or suffer the consequences."

"I disagree. Punishment doesn't stop people from doing what they aren't supposed to. They always have the choice. Look at all of us, angels and demons. We *know* the truth. What the consequences are. That breaking some rules means surrendering immortality before we're ready. That ignoring others means death." Should she have said that? Did anyone else have any idea what Michael was doing? He and Lucifer talked, but did execution ever make the docket? Too late to take back what she said. "Even humans do it; they break their laws, knowing there's jail time."

Lucifer's smile turned genuine. "And that's another reason I love you."

Eons ago, the words meant something. In this context, they didn't. She was done being spun in circles. "Whatever your point is—distracting me from the conversation or something else—I'm hiring Irdu and Tia back."

"And I'll fire them again. You may hold a high-ranking title and position at Ubiquity, but I rule hell. I created them."

"And you'd steal their freedom, to spite me?"

His expression turned cold again, amusement fading from his eyes.

She wasn't going to win this argument. Backing down felt wrong, but she didn't like the alternative of throwing logic at an illogical surface for the rest of eternity. "Did you have another reason for calling this meeting?"

"No."

Despite her irritation, she kept calm on the surface. "I have other things to do." Such as finding out where Irdu and Tia were, and hoping it was just frustration that kept him from calling her when he was laid off.

The next question was where to look. She called their phones first and went directly to voice mail. Of course, it couldn't be that easy. If neither Tia nor Irdu were at home, she had no idea where she'd go.

She phased and landed at Tia's place in a blink. A knock yielded no response. No answer when she rang the bell, either. Unless Tia was hiding. Which left Irdu's place.

When Ronnie appeared in front of his door and knocked, footsteps and murmurs filtered out from inside. Someone was home. She waited for several seconds, but nothing. She was about to ring the bell, when the door flew open.

"Fuck that," Irdu said to someone behind him. "We're all in this together." A glance past him told Ronnie Tia was on the couch, arms crossed and a scowl on her face.

"Hey." Ronnie managed a week smile. "At least one of you is talking to me."

Irdu looked at her. "She'll come around."

They'd lost her jobs because of her. She deserved Tia's hostility. "I'm sorry." *That was a good starting point, right?*

"We made our own decisions." He hooked a finger with hers. It was as simple and small as a touch could get, but the contact sent waves of comfort through her.

"If you're going to be all kissy-facey, instead of yelling, let her in. The world doesn't want to hear it if it's not drama." Irritation lined Tia's words. That was unusual.

Ronnie's guilt grew.

Irdu squeezed, gave her a soft smile, and tugged her inside.

Ronnie didn't know what she would have done if they hadn't made things right. Having Irdu on her side was a billion times better than arguing with him. "I really do want to apologize. For everything. For your jobs—"

"Oh fuck me." Tia's exclamation mingled with the clatter of the TV remote as it struck the coffee table. "All's forgiven. Yada-yada, blah blah blah."

Ronnie raised her brows, and Irdu shrugged.

Tia grabbed the remote again and cranked the volume. Irdu and Ronnie crossed the room to see what was on screen, and her gut plummeted. *Fuck me* was an understatement. Ronnie was on screen with Tia, Michael, and Vine, in front of a high school in Los Angeles. The image was complete with swords, wings, lightning, and water. It was a poor-quality clip and only lasted a few seconds, but it was undeniably them.

Lucifer's logic rang fresh in her mind. People would be too busy looking for strings and mirrors to believe the rest.

He was wrong. What people were doing, according to the news anchor, was analyzing the video to see if that was the COO of Ubiquity, in the midst of chaos, on the other side of the country from where she was spotted less than an hour later.

She wanted to sink to the floor. Scream. Pass out. She settled for hugging herself. "What are we going to do?"

"If I were mean, I'd tell you there's no *we*." Irdu wrapped his arms around her. "That's not me, and they don't care who Tia is."

Ronnie hoped this was going somewhere good.

"But like I said, we're all in this together." He pulled her into him, so her back rested against his chest.

Tia stomped the ground as she stood. "This is so so bad."

Ronnie didn't have anything to add to the concisely accurate assessment. She spun lists of possible outcomes and consequences in her head. At best, this came out as a hoax. Would denying it go over well, or would it make things worse? What were her next steps?

Her phone chimed with a new text that vanished in a ring. She checked the screen. The message was from Michael. The call was Samael. That neither was Lucifer was something to be grateful for. She took the call. "Yeah." She didn't try to hide the stress pumping through her at high velocity.

"We have a problem," Samael said.

"I know. I'm watching the news now."

"What?" Panic bled into his words. "This shouldn't be public yet."

Or ever. "What problem are you talking about?"

"My office, five minutes?" Samael sounded as tired as she felt.

"On my way now." She glanced at the message from Michael.

Are you seeing this?

She couldn't believe she hoped he meant what she was watching. *Stepping into a meeting. I'll let you know as soon as I'm out.*

Irdu kissed her on the cheek. "Come back here as soon as you're done. Fuck anyone who tells you that you can't."

Ronnie nodded. At least that she could do.

Chapter Twenty-Four

Ronnie appeared in front of Samael's office in less time than it took to say his name. The door was open and he sat behind his desk. Lucifer was in another chair, which meant he was there when Samael called her. *Fantastic. Not.*

Lucifer met her gaze as she sat. "If you'd given me some warning you needed me in meetings all day, I could have cleared my calendar, rather than having to cancel everything." His tone was cool and even.

"Neither of them have been my meetings." Her ire rose several degrees past the scorching level it rested at.

"Are you certain?"

A growl rose in her throat, and she forced it back. Of all the places she could be, and the things she could be doing—like finding out why the video from the high school existed and how it made national news—putting up with Lucifer's shit was on a completely different list. Instead of sliding into whatever argument he hoped to provoke, she turned to Samael. "Are we waiting on anyone else?"

"No." Samael crossed the room and closed the door before returning to his desk. He rubbed his face, a sigh escaping through his fingers. "Where to start?"

"With the punchline, probably." Lucifer's posture remained casual, but when Ronnie took another look, she saw the tension in his neck and the set of his jaw.

"Right. I talked to the SEC representative this morning. They believe they have enough information to proceed with filing official charges."

"What?" The last of Ronnie's restraint evaporated. If someone asked her to describe her worst-possible workday, it wouldn't have been this bad. Mostly because, at this point, the building exploding would be less stressful. The occupants would survive that unscathed. "Discovery takes months or years. They've been here for a week."

"And you're suddenly an expert in legal proceedings?" Lucifer asked.

God. What was wrong with him today? "I am. I read all about it online." She let the sarcasm bleed into her voice.

"I hear rumors the Ubiquity search engine isn't the most reliable these days. I hope you used a different resource."

Samael cleared his throat. "Yes, discovery takes longer, and they're bringing in an independent prosecutor to confirm their findings… and let them move on to less clear-cut cases. What they have is damning enough to take before a judge. I thought you'd want to be looped in before the news went public."

An ache started behind her eyes and spread through her skull. When she woke up tomorrow, would her personal life be making the news as well? It was a selfish thought; this was bigger than her. Which didn't make the headache go away.

"So we settle," Lucifer said.

"It's a criminal charge, not a lawsuit." Ronnie regretted the words as soon as they passed her lips. She braced herself for another dig.

Samael gave her a dry smile. "It's more complicated than that. They're going to pick the charges most likely to stick. Their burden of proof isn't the same in a civil case, and someone here"—he looked at Lucifer—"is adept at finding loopholes."

Lucifer stood. "That's settled then. We'll pay a fine, we'll go on with life. No harm, no foul."

"That's it?" Ronnie struggled to understand which of her concerns about the situation was strongest. "No one goes to jail? There's no media circus? We pay a fine, and it's done?"

"Would you rather someone was arrested?" Lucifer's calm tone faded into irritation. He rested his hands on the back of the chair, the posture making him look imposing and tired at the same time.

She had to strain her neck to look up at him. "It doesn't sound like that was ever a threat. All this bullshit about us being in trouble, and keeping secrets, and not telling…"

"Not telling… Samael?" Lucifer finished for her.

"Telling me what?"

Ronnie already all but admitted her guilt, and she suspected Lucifer knew anyway. She might as well own it. "Exactly. The plausible-deniability thing. If you were never worried about the outcome, why all the secrecy?"

Lucifer narrowed his eyes. "I'm not sure I can answer that, since the secrecy didn't happen. Samael, I leave the rest to you. Grab someone from marketing to make a press release. Email me if you need anything else." He strode out of the room without a backward glance.

Annoyance raged inside Ronnie at the brush-off—at the casual approach to a serious conversation.

"Do you have a minute?" Samael's question cut into her thoughts.

Not really. She had to get back to the fact she made national news as an angel, rather than a Ubiquity executive. But his request polite and she needed kindness today. "Sure."

He flicked two fingers, and a gust of wind blew the door shut. The pressure in the room shifted, and Ronnie raised her brows. He was extending a shield, to keep power from getting out. Or the other way around. Instinct clenched in her gut.

"You and I have this history. As friends. As lovers. With a very close mutual connection." Despite the filter he set around them, he kept his words so quiet they barely reached her.

Her anxiety grew, and ribbons of energy slid through her. "All right?" Her phone buzzed, and she ignored it.

"I know all of us—angels, demons, born in heaven, created in hell—are unique. You and I, though… Foolish enough to love originals, despite the fact those men won't have us." He shook his head, as if to knock something loose. "My point is, it's presumptuous of me, but the connection makes me trust you. I can't tell this to anyone else." There was no threat in his voice or the way he kept his fingers intertwined. He stayed seated. None of that calmed Ronnie. "I don't want to start a witch hunt. That's the last thing heaven and hell need," he said.

It might be a little late for that. She couldn't bring herself to say the words. Concern and anxiety raged with reason in her thoughts, pointing out that being the only person at Ubiquity who was kind to her didn't mean he was sincere. But this was Samael. "I think that's smart. What are we talking about?"

"You've run into some of this—Gabe being gone doesn't mean those loyal to him are."

The same thing Irdu said. "All right…"

"I overheard a couple of them the other day. Two agents in Media, talking about how… It didn't make any sense."

Her tolerance level for drawn-out points had vanished over the last couple of hours. "Well? What was it?"

"I didn't hear it all. Something about how happy it made Gabriel that she was looking in all the wrong places for answers."

"She?" Ronnie's phone buzzed again. She hoped it wasn't Michael, waiting for her reply.

"Keep in mind I'm quoting. *That impostor in operations.*"

Ice bled into the irritation flooding her. "What else did they say?"

"Not a lot. Something about abandoning… hope? Abandoning someone? As I said, a lot of it didn't make sense. I caught snatches about planting an older agent close to your friends. How people you trusted would vouch for the real threat, and you'd never know."

Ronnie's inner circle wasn't exactly existent. The only person who met that description was Michael, and she didn't buy for a second that he was on Gabe's side. "Thanks for the heads-up."

She grabbed her phone as soon as she left his office.

The texts were from Lucifer. A string of repeated, *We need to talk.*

She turned in the appropriate direction, and then paused. No. He'd wait. She was tired of letting his whims and bizarre moods toss her around and interfere with her priorities. No reason to ignore him, though. *About what?*

I'll tell you when you get here.

Send a synopsis or schedule a meeting.

No.

I have other places to be. She wasn't playing his games anymore. If he couldn't give her a hint up front, it wasn't critical.

*

Michael forced his gaze from the video playing on his phone. He'd been watching one after another since his phone buzzed with the alerts nearly an hour ago. Clips and analysis of the fight with Vine in L.A.

Why wasn't Ronnie returning his call? He understood she was busy; her schedule had to be packed. This was urgent, and he needed her to be aware. Perhaps she was dealing with it. He wanted to be there, to help—to offer support.

"Is this a bad time?" Abaddon's question cut into his unsuccessful attempts to figure out a next step.

Yes. He'd called her though, before this news hit him. "It's fine."

"Are you certain? Because that was the third time I asked."

"Now is great." He set his phone aside, but within view, so he could see when Ronnie replied. "The news has part of my attention, but I appreciate you meeting me."

Abaddon settled into the wrought-iron seat across from him in the cafe. He'd picked a spot a few blocks from her house, both to keep things convenient for her, and because it was afternoon here. The sun warmed his back, and people passed by on the sidewalk inches from their table.

"I saw some of the reports online. How's Ronnie coping?" Abaddon asked.

"I don't know. That's not me being coy and evasive. I have no idea."

She slid an envelope across the table. "I'm sorry—not that it helps with your current concerns. Or it might. That's a list of everyone I know of whose loyalty lies with Gabriel."

"Do you mind if I take a look?" He was already sliding the flap open.

"Be my guest. Depending on how long you were at Ubiquity, you'll see a few familiar names on there." She waved over a waiter and ordered an espresso and a sparkling water.

Michael scanned the names. There were a lot. Three pages, two columns each. Too many for him to process at once, but someone was bound to stand out. He recognized several of the angels who, like Abaddon, had worked with Gabriel for millennia. Others he'd never heard of before.

And then one all but flashed bright neon, despite the fact it was typed like all the others on the list. *Samael.* "How current is this?"

"I've only been gone a week." Abaddon rose in her seat, to glance over the top of the page. "Oh. Yeah. Samael's as old as I am. You knew about him, though? The fallout with Lucifer, the jealousy… You didn't know."

He knew things had soured between Lucifer and Samael when Metatron refused to go to hell with them. He didn't realize that could still be impacting anyone so many millennia later. His phone chimed, and he grabbed for it.

Ronnie's note read, *Where are you?*

Italy. With Abaddon. He sent Ronnie details about the location.

The air shifted, pressure weighing on Michael for a second before lessening again, and Ronnie stood next to them. Her shorter sword was drawn and pressed against Abaddon's throat.

"Game's up." Ronnie's voice was a low growl. "I hope you had a good run."

"Ronnie," Michael warned. "Stop." Every inch of him hummed with barely repressed energy as he debated best courses of action.

Abaddon held her hands up, palms out in surrender. "I heard you weren't psycho anymore. What changed?"

"I should have guessed it was you, getting close to one of the people I trust more than anyone. Making him vouch for you." Ronnie didn't back away or push in.

Michael wanted details. To figure out where this came from and why so abruptly. The electric blue growing around Abaddon and clashing with Ronnie's ethereal blades told him that was a low priority. "I don't know what you've heard, but it's not Abaddon," he said.

"Really." Ronnie didn't look at him. "Who is it then?"

Abaddon laughed, but fear lay underneath. "Did it ever occur to you Gabriel doesn't want me here? That he had an idea this would happen? That he's got a backup plan?"

"Like feeding you more bullshit to spread?"

Michael would take Ronnie's side in any battle, but she wasn't facing an enemy. He didn't doubt Abaddon's growing terror was real. "Back down *now*."

"Like having Samael plant the idea in your head that I'm your enemy, not him," Abaddon said.

"No. His loyalties have always been clear. Samael would never side with Gabriel." Despite Ronnie's firm tone, her stance wavered.

Abaddon scooted her seat back, and Ronnie didn't close the distance. "Are you sure about that?" A quaver ran through Abaddon's question. "A broken heart makes people do funny things." She stood, taking herself further out of range. Around them the world passed by as if nothing were happening.

"You're lying." Ronnie's sword faded then sparkled into a pile of glitter at her feet, before vanishing.

Abaddon let out a shaky breath. "It doesn't matter what you believe; the list is a favor for Michael. And I was wrong about you."

"Oh?"

"You're not an original. You're a scared little demon, fumbling your way through more power than anyone should have, and you don't have the confidence to convince yourself you deserve it." Abaddon met Michael's gaze. "I consider us done. I won't take your calls again."

Ronnie's aura flared, but before she could say anything, Abaddon vanished.

"*What* was that?" Michael demanded.

Chapter Twenty-Five

It wasn't fair. Michael couldn't turn on her the way everyone else had.

The childish thought bothered Ronnie, but the day was crushing in on her and it was barely noon. She faced him but couldn't find enough resolve inside to keep her expression calm. "Why are you taking her side?"

"That's not what I'm doing." He raked his gaze over her face, sympathy hiding behind pale eyes.

She swallowed the frustration burning up her throat. "Are you sure?"

"We don't need to argue. Something pointed you toward her. What was it?"

"Samael overheard a conversation."

Creases deepened across his brow. "His name is on the list of people who are loyal to Gabriel."

"A list you got from *her*." Ronnie might ask how the day could get worse, but she was afraid of the universe's answer. "Everyone knows he works at Ubiquity. That he's got an inside track to Lucifer. How convenient that she puts him on a list of suspects."

"And no one except the people who work for Gabriel know she's been talking to me. Remind me, if you will, who trained Samael. Who taught him about deception?" Anger lined Michael's words. The sympathy had vanished.

She didn't want to admit that someone she had so much history with was the one stabbing her in the back. "So… what? He's hiding in plain sight?"

"*Yes.* That's what you people do." He snapped his jaw shut, a hiss escaping.

How did so few words dig so deep? "*You people.* You mean demons? Because everyone who wears the mantel of angel is a saint. They don't do things like burn down large portions of Nashville or explode city blocks in Russia." Her voice cracked, and she almost choked on tears of frustration.

"Ronnie…"

"*What*?"

"That's not what I meant. I need you to be rational about this."

A tiny whisper of reason said to listen to him. To back down and approach the situation with a cool head. The multiple weights of the day crushed it out of existence. "You need *me* to be rational? An unknown number of agents are working with Gabe, to bring down Ubiquity from the inside and expose all of us for whatever bizarre reason strokes his ego. They're blowing up buildings and trying to frame me in the public eye. But *I'm* the irrational one?"

"Gabriel doesn't have exclusivity on being a childish egomaniac." Michael's voice rose, drawing the attention of passersby.

The words hurt as much as Gabe driving his spear through her gut all those centuries ago. Neither she nor Michael was maintaining a shield, so people stared as their argument grew. Judgment, curiosity, and accusation radiating from those around them sank into Ronnie's skin, feeding her emotions. "I'm sorry I'm such an irritation. I kind of thought we were on the same side, but my mistake."

"And that's part of the problem. There shouldn't be any sides."

"But there *are*. Even you think there are. I know; it was a Freudian slip and all that bullshit."

"I don't want there to be. I'm not going to delude myself into thinking that makes it true." The anger in his words faded to a sigh. "This isn't getting us anywhere."

"Neither is anything else we've tried." She didn't want to back down. Frustration still burned through her, but she didn't have a direction for it.

"Maybe some of it will pay off in the long run."

She rolled her eyes. "Easy to be patient when you've been alive for four thousand years."

The corners of his mouth twitched in an almost smile, and more of the tension around them evaporated. Or his shielding them from the outside world, blocking off the emotions of the people around them, made it feel that way.

"Take me seriously," she said.

"I am. This isn't something that we have decades or even weeks to fix. What we're doing isn't a solution, though."

"But the yelling makes me feel better now, instead of later." She forced herself to relax—pushed aside the part of her that wanted her words to carry more venom and concentrated on calming down. "And don't you dare tell me I'm cute when I'm angry." She choked out a laugh to show she was teasing.

His smile grew. "You're terrifying when you're angry. You spark in red and black. But that's kind of sexy."

"No trying to distract me with compliments." She didn't know if she should be flattered or pissed off. She was too tired for more anger.

"If you don't trust Abaddon, I'll err with your judgment. I think you need to take a closer look at Samael, though."

She sank into a seat at the table, and the cool iron bit into her bare back. Now that he'd taken the bluster out of her fury, exhaustion spilled in. It was barely noon back home, but she felt like she'd lived another lifetime this morning. "I don't want to." The childish protest pinged through her with a heavy dose of reality. Sammy was kind. Sympathetic. Understanding. Then again, Gabe had been all of the above and tried to convince her he loved her, and he stabbed her in the back. Literally. "But I will. *Shit.*"

"What?"

"If it's him, the damage is done. The SEC is filing charges against Ubiquity. Those videos with my face are out there. We already have a public-image problem. There's no way to fix whatever Gabe is up to, because we don't know what that is." Frustration welled inside again, amplified by tiredness.

He covered her hand with his. "Quit."

"I'm *trying*." But the avalanche of problems was burying her.

"Not what I mean. Though take a few deep breaths. We'll figure out the rest."

She glared at him. "Vague statements followed by *not what I mean* aren't helping."

"Resign your position at Ubiquity."

"I— What?" She should be offended. Outraged and pissed off, the way she was every time someone referred to her as an impostor. So why did the notion soothe her fractured nerves? This was driving her insane. "I can't do that."

"I understand you're making a difference. Keeping up with the inside track. Gathering knowledge no one else has and making sure no innocent agents get caught in the crossfire." His tone was calm.

His words cut through her like the sharpest of accusations. She didn't know who she could trust, including her own judgment. She'd cost Irdu and Tia their jobs. *Damn it.* "I can't."

"Okay. I understand."

"Explain it to me?" She had no idea what she was doing. Fumbling in the dark. Reacting, instead of getting there first.

"Gabe's resignation hurt public opinion. They're starting to accept you. Losing a second executive within a few months won't look good for Ubiquity. Especially with the SEC— Did you say they're filing charges? How did they get there so quickly?" His rational words vanished in disbelief.

"That's what I wanted to know." At least someone agreed with her surprise. The rest of his logic bounced in her thoughts, sounding the same as her arguments, and each time she shot herself down. "I'm not helping anyone on the inside. Those videos from L.A. have me in them, and even those people who don't believe it's me have questions. If I step aside now, maybe it does something good for Ubiquity. Makes them look smart. Like they have a handle on things."

"I'm more worried about you. Do you like the job?"

"It doesn't matter. It's what I was assigned to do."

His brows knitted together, and he drew his lips into a thin line. "However, it isn't what you want to do, and that *does* matter."

She was about to snap at him for being vague and obtuse again, until the meaning of his words sank in. All demons and angels were created to help people and each other achieve their potential. Some preferred to sit behind a desk—Tia seemed to enjoy what she'd been doing, before Ronnie cost her that chance—but Ronnie didn't like watching and not interacting. It gnawed at her soul and devoured her sensibility.

"I don't know what to do." Her phone buzzed. Another message from Lucifer, identical to those before. "Whatever it is, I have to go back to the office to do it. If I'm resigning, I'm telling Lucifer to his face."

The conversation was a nice respite, but a to-do list ticked through her head the moment she considered heading back to work—figure out how to do damage control on the video of her, Tia, and

Michael; work with Marketing to smooth over the road bumps the SEC investigation caused… She wanted to curl up in a ball and sleep just thinking about it.

Michael stood when she did, studying her with concern. "Good luck. Be careful. Think about what I said." He placed a finger under her chin to lift her head, then pressed his lips to hers.

A shiver of comfort blanketed her, and a whimper tore from her throat. It was such a simple gesture. How did it hold so much power over her? Unsure she could find the right words to reply, she nodded and phased back to Ubiquity headquarters.

Instead of going to her office, she planted herself outside Lucifer's open door. She knocked on the frame.

He didn't look up. "The moment's passed. Email me, and we'll set up some time later."

"No." She stalked into the room and swung the door shut behind her. "You said it was urgent. Enough for multiple texts. I'm here. Let's talk."

"You can't storm into my office and demand I drop everything when it's convenient for you."

His tone and dismissal snapped loose the argument she reined in with Michael, but her annoyance had simmered long enough she could grasp a cold anger instead of an irrational rant. She wrapped the icy irritation around her, to keep her tone even. "Three times this morning—I won't waste our time by counting the number this week—you've asked me to drop everything and meet with you."

He opened his mouth, but she held up a finger. "I know. Sammy wasn't *your* meeting, and Irdu and

Tia were my fault. Technically, Sammy was too." If she was going to have things out with Lucifer, she was laying all her cards on the table, so he didn't have any claim to her keeping one up her sleeve. "So don't pull this bullshit. If you want to talk, we do it now, rather than you making me sit for five more minutes or hours, so you gain some sort of petty upper hand."

He raised his brows. "Are you done?"

"No, but it's a good pause point."

"Have a seat. My calendar just cleared."

"Thank you." It was too easy, but she wouldn't argue with having her demands met. She took the chair across from his desk. Not the one he gestured to, but rather the seat that was two inches taller, had even legs instead of one that was a hair off balance, and with no breaks or thin spots in the padding.

He leaned in, forearms on his desk, and held her gaze. "I like to think I have a gift for reading people. Having a good idea how they'll react to a situation. Predicting what will motivate them. But every time I think I've got you figured out, you surprise me."

"Thank you?" *Great.* Now she was a broken record.

"It's not necessarily a compliment. I keep expecting you to put the pieces together faster. To be smart about this."

If the insult was meant to ruffle her, he'd be surprised. She'd reached the point of pissed off where his words added to the fuel, but she was past the breaking point, so there was nothing for him to snap. "If you want me to have a piece of information, you know what works a lot better than hoping I'll decipher whatever cryptic mind games you want to play? *Telling me.* Send an email. Call. Text."

"That didn't work for me today."

"*Don't.* You can't derail this conversation by pointing out single variations instead of focusing on the norm."

He had a neutral gaze. Not a smile or a frown. No shift in facial muscles. Not that she was surprised at the mask of nothing staring back at her or the apparent shift in topic. "How many agents do you trust here at Ubiquity?" he asked.

The nature of the question squeezed her chest with a grip she didn't care for. "Irdu. Tia. Michael, when he was here."

"Not me, then."

How long since he'd been on her *trust* list? Since he asked her to lie to Sammy? *No.* Since he kept her origins secret from her. Or perhaps it had always been this way. "And you. I meant to include you."

"No you didn't."

She shook her head. "No. I didn't."

"And I didn't know if I could trust you." A thread of hurt wove into his words. Part of the act, or was he sincere? It would be nice if she didn't have to second-guess every gesture and nuance. "Metatron's ties were different back in the day. She—*you*—and Samael were always close. I was trying to figure out if you were in on the deception."

"Which once?"

He gave a snorting laugh but didn't look amused. "It's all the same, and it all leads back to Gabriel."

"You thought I might be working with *him*? He tried to kill me. Twice." She had to force out the disbelief, to ignore the way Gabe's name crushed in around her, trying to steal her thoughts and reason.

"You and he were the only ones there the second time. I couldn't be sure… I'm sorry." Lucifer turned his gaze to his clasped hands. "I didn't want to believe it, but things have been falling apart at the seams for decades, or longer. And you protested so much, demanding information when I asked you to keep everything quiet. You're not the only one doubting their colleagues."

Sympathy and hurt warred inside, and she wasn't sure which to give attention to. The first time Gabe tried to kill her it was intended to drive the four originals apart. Turn Lucifer against Michael, and leave Gabriel as the last power standing. He'd probably love to hear it was about to happen without anything drastic on his part—except making Ubiquity crumble from the inside out.

"Yes, I told Samael what you were keeping from him," she said. "Because I hated being left in the dark, and I didn't think he'd like it either. It wasn't an attempt to subvert you."

"Technically, that's exactly what it was. But I hoped you would."

Because if she had to tell Samael anything, it meant she believed he didn't already know. Which also meant… She frowned. "So he is part of this mess."

"Ninety-nine percent sure." Lucifer pinched the bridge of his nose. "I hoped it wasn't true, as much as I wanted to trust you. Gabriel has always known how the money flows here; he and I set it up. And before you go off on a tangent, I know we blurred lines. That's not the point."

She thought it was very much the point. If the evidence wasn't there, it would be a lot harder to make the charges stick. Or not. *Wow.* This corporate-finance stuff was screwed up. Mix in a handful of vengeful angels and demons, and it was a convoluted mess. She kept the thoughts to herself, rather than disrupt the answers she was finally getting.

"I figure it played out something like this," he said. "The SEC is tipped off by Samael or Gabriel, or it doesn't matter who. But a tip isn't the same as evidence, and they have processes to follow. If you were in on things, it would be easy enough for you to say as an executive you had inside knowledge of illegal happenings. That's the proof they need. As it was, Samael had to wait for you to confirm."

Something wasn't right about his logic. "But Samael is in charge of the books. Top of the ladder. Why couldn't that information come from him in the first place?"

"He didn't want to tip his hand too soon."

"But if I were complicit, I would have?" She'd be insulted at the implication she wasn't as clever as Samael, but this went deeper. Lucifer was covering more up.

He stood and walked to her side of the desk, then leaned against it, which brought him close enough to grasp her fingers. "The point is you didn't tell him until I told you. Even then, you hesitated. I'm sorry I doubted you. I'm glad I didn't need to."

"I wish I could say the same." She pulled from his grasp and stood, putting distance between them. He was still lying to her, hoping she wouldn't put the pieces together. Or hoping she would? He was dealing doubletalk with more of the same, and she was tired of guessing which words had a twist, or two, or none at all.

There was no one thing that gave him way, but everybody had tells. The twitch of his fingers, the way his gaze tugged toward the ceiling, and the too-smooth assurance in his voice all added up to a lie.

"Ronnie?" He had the gall to look wounded.

This was too much. Not only his deception. Maybe he'd been lying so long he didn't know any other way. "Don't." She took another step back as confusion snapped into a giant glob of confusion in her skull. "Everything you're doing at Ubiquity is a joke. Not the funny ha-ha kind, either. It's some sort of *who has the biggest celestial weapon* contest between you and Gabriel."

"Is that how you see this? You're missing so much." His tone was smooth and condescending.

"Stop. If I'm missing things, it's because I haven't been told. It's not reasonable to expect me to puzzle out every bizarre deception that tickles your fancy. Even if I could, the two of you are screwing with everyone. Agents want these jobs—they enjoy this chance to help—but you're pitting them against each other. And humanity? I don't think they factor into your equation. That's wrong on about every single level it can be."

"That's not what's going on." Lucifer's impassive mask returned. "I brought you in to help undo the damage Gabriel did here. To fix those exact things you're talking about."

"No. You brought me in hoping I'd be easy to manipulate. I haven't done any good here. I don't come into the office half the time. Irdu covered my ass because…" Because he loved her. But there was more. Because he saw what she refused to. The founders never meant for this to be a joint initiative. Ubiquity was never intended to make it easier for heaven and hell to work together, but she played it off like it was. She didn't know why it really existed, but Lucifer wouldn't tell her that. "I can't be a part of this."

"What's that supposed to mean?"

Michael was right. This place was devouring her and so many other agents. She wasn't helping from her position, because she resented everything about it. "I'm resigning, effective immediately."

"You can't do that." Orange flickered in his eyes—a flash of anger wrapped in power he normally hid. She suspected it was the first genuine emotion he'd shown since the meeting started

"What was it you told me this morning? *I absolutely can.*"

"You're an executive officer for a global corporation. You can't simply walk off the job because you don't like some of the company politics. Where the hell is your professionalism? What are we supposed to tell the press?"

She should feel disbelief at his priorities, but she'd lost more faith in him than she realized. "Is that what you care about? That's really the first thing that comes to mind, to talk me out of this? The company's image?" She couldn't keep the disgust from her voice. "When did the opinion of *anyone* become more important to you than doing what we were made for? You left heaven to make sure people got the attention you felt they deserved, and now you're going to screw over a building of agents and an entire civilization because of a dispute with Gabriel?" That wasn't what she meant to say. It was a bit melodramatic. The words bounced in her head, insisting she figure out where they came from.

"And how does your quitting make anything better?"

"I don't know. But if I'm not affecting change from the inside, I'm helping the two of you play your games."

"Don't do this. It's not what you think, and you can make a change."

She wanted to believe the apology in his tone. She was desperate to cling to the promise that this was anything but a giant clusterfuck. She couldn't. "You know how to reach me outside of the office. Goodbye."

Before he could say anything else, she phased from the room.

Chapter Twenty-Six

"I need your help. Please." Ronnie forced herself to sound contrite and braced herself for the backlash.

Raphael twisted in his desk chair, to look behind him and then around his office, before turning back to her. "I'm sorry. You're talking to me?"

Wonderful. He had a sense of humor after all. Now was the perfect time to find that out. *Not.* "Yes. I need help with something, and I don't trust anyone else here." She didn't care for Raphael. Would be happy if they never spoke again after today. But like Tia, he loved his job. He *believed* the company mission statement and was at U-View to make a difference.

"Okay. I'm going to pretend I'm whoever you think I am and play along." The corners of his mouth twitched. He thought he was being clever.

That was fine with her. "Fantastic. I need you to film something for me, and then make sure it's distributed to all the media outlets. Get it on the U-View front page. Make sure the world sees it."

"Ah. So this is one of those instances of you throwing your weight around for some whimsy that's caught your mood today." His amusement vanished.

She didn't have the strength for another argument. Or discussion. Or whatever would come out of engaging him in conversation. "No. I promise you on everything you hold holy and dear, this is something you'll want everyone to see. If I'm lying, you can strike me down."

"Tempting, but we both know that doesn't have a lot of impact on you. If I don't like what you say, I'm destroying the footage."

"Fair enough." She wondered if she sounded as exhausted as she felt. Giving into her need for sleep would have to wait a little longer. She needed to be sincere and apologetic.

Moments later, they were in a conference room on the far end of the floor where his office was. He'd grabbed some portable equipment, and swore up and down he didn't tell anyone what it was for. As he set up the tripod, she clipped the microphone into place.

"Ready?" he asked.

Last-second inspiration struck, and she turned off her company phone and set it on the table to her left. "Set."

"Rolling."

That single word tugged all of her doubt loose and sent it tumbling around her. Her mind froze. Why didn't she take a moment to script this out?

"We'll edit out the dead air." Impatience filled Raphael's words.

Right. She could do this. She wrapped herself in a mask of regret—not that it was hard; the stuff almost leaked from her pores—and looked into the camera. "For those of you who don't know me, six months ago I took on the role of the public face of Ubiquity. Since then, the company has faced its share of trials from all directions, culminating with the SEC investigations, rumors of suppressed search results and deleted content, and recent video footage showing an individual rumored to be me." She didn't want this to be lengthy, but it was important she take as much focus off other angels or demons as possible.

"In light of recent events, I've resigned my position, effective immediately. The things I did or didn't do were my choice, and meant to give people direction, not take it away. Ubiquity does not support and is not responsible for any of my actions, and I don't wish for them to be affiliated with my mistakes. Thank you." She looked at Raphael, who stared back, wide eyed. She made a slicing motion in front of her neck, to signal he should cut filming, but there was no response.

"That's it. I'm done," she said.

He shook his head, as if to clear away a fog, and pressed a series of buttons on the camera. "Of course. Or not. Are you serious?

"Told you you'd like it." She felt lighter, having taken this step. At the same time, the backlash would hurt more than her. Her gut clenched at possibilities of the immediate fallout.

"I hate it. But you're doing the right thing."

A knock on the conference-room door kept her from asking him to explain.

"Yeah?" Raphael called.

A demon Ronnie recognized but couldn't name and stuck his head in. "Sorry to interrupt." His tone was terse. "The FBI is in the lobby, and they're looking to ask her"—he nodded at Ronnie—"a few questions."

So much for controlling the video of the L.A. incident going public.

"How did they know you were here?" Raphael asked. Ubiquity and U-View were two separate buildings, several miles apart, and she'd phased into Raph's office.

For all she knew, Lucifer told them. "The walls have ears."

Raphael turned to the demon in the doorway. "Tell them I'll be right there."

The demon nodded at Ronnie. "And her?"

"I'll be right there," Raphael said again.

"Got it." The guy closed the door behind him.

Ronnie might have wondered about Raphael's defense of her on any other day. Now there wasn't time. She needed to be other places and couldn't express enough how much his help meant. "Can you trust him?" she asked.

"Yes. Do you still want this video distributed?"

"Absolutely."

Raph smirked. "Well, if the public finds out the FBI has a hold of it, portions will go viral real quick. Especially if we get it uploaded before the FBI gets their hands on it. They'll need to do damage control. Do what you have to do. I'll take care of them. You've drawn the blame to yourself, so as long as we cooperate, we'll be fine."

"I know you hate me—"

"I don't. But you do irritate the fuck out of me."

That made her smile. "I can be a bit of a prima donna sometimes."

"What's going on? You're deleting data. Lucifer's firing people who kiss your ass. The SEC investigation. The FBI. Things have really gone to hell since you started working here."

"Hell. Because I was a demon. I get it." She might have been offended by the sentiment, but he was right. "I don't know what's going on. I have a couple theories and a bunch of pieces that don't make a whole picture, but no real answers."

"How can I help?"

The offer caught her off guard, but as she processed, it made sense. A conversation they had so many months ago rushed back to taunt her. "I think you're one of the few doing what we were meant for—looking out for humanity and helping agents."

"Except you, but I'll make an exception today." He winked.

"I appreciate that. I'll probably call the favor in before it expires, if I'm actually a fugitive. That is, if I have a way to get back to you. I'm starting to get a bit paranoid about who's watching."

"Is Tia with you?" he asked. "I know that's her in the clip."

If she forgives me. "I hope so."

Someone knocked, and he glanced at the door then back at her. "She has my secure email. Encrypted. Private. All that good stuff. When you know what I can do, have her reach out to me."

For the first time since talking to Michael, Ronnie felt like something might be going in her favor. "Thanks. I mean that a lot." The pounding on the door cut her off from saying anything else.

"Good luck." He gave her a dry smile.

She nodded and phased away.

* * * *

"Is Ronnie all right?" Izrafel asked.

Michael raised his brows at the bizarre greeting. He'd been in the fallen angel's apartment less than thirty seconds. "She's under a bit of stress, but otherwise all right, the last time I checked. Why would you ask me that?"

"You're in the video too, so I figure you've got the inside scoop." Izrafel pointed at the television, which was running a cable news channel. Clips from the fight in L.A. played out, and then the camera split to show two faces. The sound was turned down, but the ticker at the bottom said the FBI wanted Ronnie for questioning.

"What else have you heard?" Michael didn't like the new surge of tension boiling inside. After the conversation with Abaddon and talking Ronnie down, he'd forgotten what kind of havoc the high school footage could wreak.

"This is their top story. They repeat the highlights every ten minutes. The FBI are also looking to identify the other people in the footage. Where they previously believed the explosion wasn't related to similar ones in other locales, they're taking a second look at all of it. The four of you are wanted for questioning, and speculation is that you're working for some militant or terrorist organization."

Did Tia know that? Michael didn't have a way to get a hold of her. If they wanted Ronnie, they only had to go to Ubiquity. A nudge drew his attention back to the TV and an employee-badge photo of him, along with his name.

"Looks like you've been identified," Izrafel said.

"I only left her an hour ago. How did we go from *maybe that's one of those Ubiquity executives* to *wanted for questioning and possible terrorist connections* that quickly?"

"A better question is, how did you let them take that horrible photo of you? No wonder you left the company."

Michael glared.

Izrafel shrugged and gave him a half smile. "I understand this is critical, but I'm trying to lighten the mood. If you blow a fuse now, you won't make it through whatever's going on." He turned up the sound, as a new shot of Ronnie appeared over the news anchor's right shoulder.

"The FBI has released this clip and asked the Nashville, Tennessee region to be on the lookout for the fugitive." The video expanded to fill the screen, and Ronnie's voice filtered through the speakers. "In light of recent events, I've resigned my position, effective immediately. Ubiquity does not support and is not responsible for any of my actions…"

The camera zoomed back to the anchor desk. "At this time, officials are asking anyone who has information on the case to please call the tip line, rather than approaching the suspects."

"And now it's a full-on manhunt?" Izrafel sank onto the edge of the couch. "What did you do to get instant upgrades?"

That was a good question. The answer tumbled into Michael's head and he frowned at how much sense it made. "It has to be coming from someone at Ubiquity or who's working with Gabriel. That's how they got the photo. If the tips come in and they match the evidence…" Which they would. Tension cranked through him, dialing up another notch when Tiamet's photo appeared on screen as well. "And now we've all be identified." Where did he need to focus first? Finding Ronnie? Figuring out where the others were?

Izrafel studied him, concern in his gaze. "Who did you piss off?"

"The usual suspects." Which didn't explain why Gabriel was doing this. "Whom do you keep touch with? Fallen, celestial, cherubs with human hosts."

"It's a long list. Do you want every name?" Izrafel grabbed his phone from the coffee table and swiped the screen.

"No. I want you to vanish, and get a hold of as many of them as you can and tell them to do the same."

"Why?"

"I don't know"—Michael was skipping through a list of *what next* in his head— "but it seems like the smart thing to do, until we figure out what Gabriel's plan is." His phone chimed, and he grabbed it in a flash. Relief mingled with stress when he saw Ronnie's name. "Are you all right?" he asked her.

"Depends on what you know, and if it's something I don't." Her sarcasm was a relief.

He related what Izrafel told him and what they were watching on TV.

Her sigh echoed in his ear. "Well, fuck me."

"Check on Tiamet and Irdu. Tell them to drop off the radar. Then meet me in half an hour," he said. There was no time for niceties if this had escalated so quickly.

"Meet you where, and what are you up to?"

"To check on a friend. I'll be in our favorite spot."

Would she know what he meant?

"Got it." Her words were clipped.

"And be careful." Until they knew what they were dealing with—beyond a group of angels and demons with the power to blow up entire cities and use the media to turn the world against Ronnie—caution was the only answer.

He hung up with her and cautioned Izrafel again to be careful, before phasing to Italy. When he saw Abaddon's place—or rather, the crater where her cottage used to sit—concern tightened through every one of his muscles, until his neck ached and his jaw protested being clenched. He'd hoped he was being paranoid, but he might have understated the danger.

Chapter Twenty-Seven

We're in your favorite place.

Irdu's text made a lot more sense to Ronnie after she talked to Michael. Almost the same phrasing as Michael, but with a very different meaning. Ronnie spilled through fragments of thought, forcing order into the chaos that was her brain, and pulled out which places she'd been to the most while using the Ubiquity Tracker app.

Las Vegas. Without question. Except that left a huge territory for her to cover, even if she stuck to the tourist spots. She phased to the south end of the strip. Despite assuming her physical form, she kept a tiny shield around herself, to distract people and motivate them to look anywhere but at her.

She scanned the faces of the crowds. The swatch of people and emotions threatened to distract and overwhelm her. There was no way she could pick two angels out of this. And then she saw the giant banner on the side of a pyramid-shaped building. *Criss Angel. Believe.*

She cut a straight path toward the Luxor, and paused inside the main entrance to figure out which way the restaurants were. Moments later, she found the food court, and two familiar glows sitting at a table near the frozen-yogurt shop. Tia wore a Luxor hat pulled low over her eyes and kept her gaze focused on a half-melted cup of fro-yo. Apparently Ronnie wasn't the only person hiding.

Irdu looked up as she approached, and met her halfway. "I'm glad you found us." He crushed his mouth to hers.

The kiss settled her thoughts for the few seconds it lasted. When he broke away, he tangled his fingers with hers.

She didn't want to be abrupt, but given how quickly things were escalating, she didn't see an alternative. "I'm more sorry than you know, and you don't have to forgive me, but I need to know now if we have the same goals or if we're going our separate ways."

"Why would we leave you?" Irdu asked.

"I cost you your jobs and made you fugitives. I can't guarantee it, but I'm pretty sure if you went back to hell right now and told Lucifer it was a mistake to trust me, he'd take care of you."

Tia looked up, lips pursed. "He's the one who fired us."

"For working for me," Ronnie said. She drifted her attention around the food court and landed on a group of five people, pointing and chatting with their heads bent together. When she made eye-contact with one of them, he jerked his gaze away, said something to his friends, and they all left. Weird. She was all over the news, but the shield she radiated should keep anyone from caring Ronnie was there. The situation must be screwing with her focus. She poured a little more effort into diluting their presence.

Irdu pulled her closer, and drew his nose along her jaw to kiss her cheek. "We never did anything we didn't want to. We saw your resignation video, though. The entire world has seen it at this point. You were right to do that, whatever your reasons. And we're all on the same page. You have to already know I'm not walking away from you."

"Me neither." Tia nodded. "I'm in for whatever. I always have been."

She wanted to sob with relief. She settled for pulling up a seat at their table. "Thank you." Something flashed out of the corner of her eye, and she turned in time to see someone dropping a camera in her purse and trying not to make eye contact with her. "I'm glad the two of you got out before SWAT or whatever kicked in your doors."

Ronnie glanced around them. Every third or fourth pocket of people seemed to be staring at them. Pointing. Grabbing cameras. Whispering. She looked behind her, to locate an attraction she might have missed on her way in. Nope. Just more food court. The crowds couldn't be looking at her, Irdu, and Tia. Her shields should convince them the three were the most bland, non-interesting things in existence. Not worth a glance, let alone a murmur and a photo.

"We need to go." Maybe Ronnie was just being paranoid, but adrenaline coursed through her, amplified by a series of off-the-cuff actions that had driven her all morning, and she couldn't ignore the hum of anxiety. When she stood and made her way toward the main hotel, Irdu and Tia followed, falling into step beside her. They needed to meet Michael, so it wasn't as if she was running. They were on a schedule.

For the first time since she could remember, she searched for a remote place, out of the public eye, to phase from. It shouldn't matter if they stood in the middle of a stadium full of people; no one should see them come and go. Another couple turned and watched them walk past, and Ronnie clenched her fist by her side. She found a quiet corner in the lobby, tucked away from view of anyone, and took Tia's and Irdu's hands.

"Where are we going?" Irdu asked.

In the time it took her to register his question, their surroundings vanished and were replaced with sand and a crumbling temple.

"Israel," she said.

"You were right." A familiar voice she couldn't place made Ronnie whirl.

Michael stood a few feet away, next to a man in a black jacket, matching slacks, and a white button-down shirt, topped with a *kippah* and *tallit*—skullcap and prayer shawl. A rabbi. He wore a faint glow. Ronnie met him once, many months ago, when she was trying to figure out who she was, and why Metatron lived in her head. Relief flooded her at the friendly faces, and she crossed the distance to Michael in a few short steps.

When she threw her arms around his neck, he squeezed back. "I'm glad you're all safe." His words echoed her thoughts.

She wished it were that easy. That this were the last stage of an exhausting journey. Too bad that wasn't the case.

* * * *

Michael sat next to Ronnie, who was half in Irdu's lap, on the couch in the rabbi's apartment. It felt natural to have her heat here, mingling with his aura, despite the fact she was flashing like emergency lights on a snowy night. Tiamet took a chair at the kitchen table, which was only a few feet away.

"Thank you for your hospitality," Ronnie said.

"For you, anything." The rabbi gave a nodding bow, then went to the fridge. "Can I get any of you drinks? New identities?"

Ronnie chuckled. "We're okay for now. Thank you." She leaned forward and rested her elbows on her knees. "You seem to know me. We've met before, but we weren't introduced."

"Of course. I'm Sandalphon." He extended his hand, and she shook it. "Del, if you prefer."

Sandalphon was another fallen angel who had acquired a cherub and used the bond to extend his life. Michael had helped him through the transition, and Sandalphon helped people far more as a rabbi than he was able to as an angel.

"I do. And it's nice to finally meet you. Izzy talks about you all the time." Despite Ronnie's pleasant tone, red and black continued to intertwine around her.

The demons she brought with her fared far worse, surrounded by a fractured array of peach and

305

blue. Their auras seemed to feed each other. When Tiamet's clashed, Irdu's would flare as well. When his smoothed out, so did hers.

Michael had never seen such a thing. A curiosity for another time. "I wish we had time for catching up and getting to know each other, but a few of us have gone from nobodies to terrorist suspects in a matter of hours. We need to get to a point, information-wise, where we can act instead of reacting. What do we know?"

"Cable news made us famous." Tiamet smirked, and sarcasm peppered her response.

It was as good a starting point as any. "Why?" He left the question vague on purpose. None of them knew, but if enough different views were tossed out, they'd get somewhere.

"Because of me."

Despite Ronnie being right next to him, Michael had to strain to hear her response.

Irdu shook his head. "Because of assholes who aren't in this room."

Since the fight in Moscow and Ronnie's reaction to being called an impostor, Michael had watched her slide further into a pit of defensive self-pity. He'd hoped their conversation this morning knocked her out of whatever brought this on, but that didn't seem to be the case. He turned and put enough distance between them that he could look at her and not feel the pulse of her energy. "Do you know what one of Gabriel's biggest flaws is?"

"He's a megalomaniacal asshole?" Ronnie said.

"Well, yes." Michael couldn't have summed it up better, but it also didn't make his point. "But to look at it more in depth, he thinks he deserves something because he's an original. He's always held the belief that being created first entitles him to more. The problem is, so many of us believe it's true—about him—he gets away with the attitude."

Ronnie twisted her mouth in irritation. "Lucky bastard. Maybe I can learn something from him after all."

"Or perhaps you shouldn't think that way. None of us is owed any sort of special privilege. We don't get an award for being one of the first four. Yes, we have responsibilities and skills that are unique—naming cherubs and ruling our own corners of the kingdoms. But every agent, from heaven or hell, has something. We're not owed worship or followers."

The way her lips drew into a thin line and her brow knit together told him this wasn't the right way to approach the situation. He grasped for something else. "Why did Samael follow Lucifer to hell?"

"Because of love." Frustration filled Ronnie's words. "And thousands of years down the line, look where that's gotten all of us. I think we're off-topic."

"Because of adoration. Respect. Everybody who left with him did it out of respect. I still don't know why *you* stayed in heaven."

The furrow of her brows deepened, as if she was considering the statement. "Same reason I resigned this morning—I've never agreed with his tactics. But things weren't like this when I was Metatron. We weren't focused on amassing armies of followers, to undercut each other. Or ..." She sighed.

"What?" Michael prompted.

"Maybe Gabriel and Lucifer have always believed that was the only way, and the two of you are the only things keeping them in check." Irdu's sharp words reminded Michael there were others in the room.

Michael's first instinct was to deny that was the answer. He couldn't. "It seems that way, but I don't think we were meant to be divided like this."

"That's where you're looking at it wrong," Tiamet said. "Honestly, it's like you higher-ups never listen to yourselves. There's no *meant to be* in this world. We get to live our lives the way we choose, and every decision ripples out into the world, collides with other ripples, and changes everything. That's the point."

Michael had never heard it phrased quite like that. "Perhaps we shouldn't have been given that."

"Free will?" Irdu narrowed his eyes. "Fuck you. I wouldn't surrender that despite all the mistakes ever made at any time, by me or anyone else."

Tiamet waved. "Hi. Off-topic police here. You asked what we know? We don't know anything. Compared to whoever is doing this—Gabe, or I don't know—we're stupid lost. Information is power. If you have information about the whole planet, you have power over the whole planet. He's got that; we don't."

"Now the whole planet has information about *us*." Michael was trying to be rational about this, but he was running out of straws to grasp.

"Holy shit." Ronnie's quiet exclamation shut everyone up. "I know what Gabe's doing."

Irdu twisted his mouth. "Throwing a tantrum of epic proportions because he's not king of the playground?"

"Yes. Lucifer knows it, too," Ronnie said.

"We all know that." Tia didn't sound impressed.

Ronnie looked at Michael. "The rules change if someone tells you to do what you want, versus *do it or suffer the consequences.* Faith versus knowledge."

A light clicked on in Michael's head. "Gabriel wants order. For people to do what he says, because he knows best."

"Exactly." Despite the enthusiasm in her voice, Ronnie frowned. "Best way to get them to do that? Expose us. Not just those of us in this room, but all of heaven and hell. He's going to prove to humanity we exist and take away any doubt of whether or not they should fall in line."

"Sounds a bit misguided, don't you think?" Tiamet asked.

Kids these days… No appreciation for the simpler things in life. "So does our entire existence, if you take that stance. Gabriel likes order. He doesn't believe people know what's best for them. This way, he believes he'll be able to make them grow."

"You assume." Irdu added.

"It's a safe assumption. And it sounds like you don't have better." Sandalphon spoke for the first time since the discussion started. "Even if that's not the goal, what he's doing puts us all at risk. Those of us who are fallen don't have the big corporate machine behind us, and I'd hate for someone to start digging and figure out I've been here for almost two-hundred years and not aged a day. You can stay here until you regroup. Anything you need, I'll get you."

"Thank you." Michael gave him grateful smile. "So how do we stop it from happening?"

"Kill Gabriel." The edge and formality in Ronnie's tone caught him off guard.

Irdu coughed, and Tiamet's eyes grew wide.

Michael focused on Ronnie. "Just like that?"

"*Now* you have a problem with it?" Disbelieve filled her question

"I've always had a problem with it."

"*Whoa*. Back up. I thought she was being facetious, you know? Tossing out random ideas." Tiamet's words all ran together. "You don't mean actually *kill*. We can't do that. We're immortal. The body dies; the soul lives on. The punishment is we're removed from earth. Death isn't an option. Is it?" She finished her question with a squeak.

Michael felt a familiar surge of regret that he'd taken on this mantel. "It's not something anyone else knows how to do. It's not something *I* want to know."

"But he does it anyway." Ronnie crossed her arms and sank back into the couch.

"Gabriel's one of us." Michael regretted the words as soon as they were out.

Ronnie growled. "What did you tell me not fifteen minutes ago? *We* don't get special privileges for being originals. And—oh yeah—he's tried to destroy me twice. The agents you're killing? Most of them just wanted a little extra power."

"*Just*? This isn't cold-blooded murder." The irritation snapped out before Michael could stop it, and he clenched his jaw to bring his temper under control. "I agree it's the only option."

"So why are you hesitating?" Ronnie asked.

"I'm not. Not for me. A week ago, you refused to talk to me when you found out about this. Your friends look freaked out. I don't need the weight of this decision to infect all of you."

She uncurled from her defensive position and slid her hand under his. "You're not in this alone. The fact we've been so isolated is part of what's making this difficult. Don't push away the only allies you have."

"This isn't the kind of burden someone shares."

"Maybe you'd stop hating immortality so much if you let more of us in."

He snapped his head to the side and stared at her, trying to make sense of her suddenly flat tone. "I don't—"

"You do." Ronnie pursed her lips. "You can have whatever reasons you want for considering falling, but wouldn't it be nice if it was because you learned all immortality could teach you? Consider what it would be like to not be so burned out on life that you're running away instead of looking to add to the experience."

Chapter Twenty-Eight

Irdu and Tia set up a network tunnel to bypass regional restrictions, so U.S. news played in the background.

"Officials now have information linking the incident in Los Angeles to other incidents around the country."

"Ubiquity stock closed at an all-time low, following a day of disaster, including the resignation of their Chief Operations Officer, her alleged involvement in terrorist activities, and the announcement that the SEC is pursuing their investigation against the information giant."

"Law enforcement believes the identification used by all three suspects to gain employment was falsified."

With each passing hour the bad news compounded, but Ronnie couldn't look away. It might be nice if their ability to cloud minds extended to something more severe. Mind control or mind reading. Not that it would matter. It was the same as a magician's illusion, the trick only worked if someone was looking the other way. With the world focused on them, with so many people *wanting* to know what was going on, a simple distraction like clouding their minds wouldn't work. The realization sank into her bones. It was why people had stared at them in Las Vegas, despite her shields. Humanity was looking for them, rather than away.

The TV clicked off, and a hollow hum filled her head, driving anxiety through her.

She whirled to see what happened and found Michael holding the remote. "That's hurting more than helping," he said. Sympathy shone in his eyes.

Ronnie opened her mouth to protest.

"Turn it back on." Tia's shrill demand interrupted. "They're dissecting my life."

Ronnie felt the despair. It echoed her own.

"It doesn't matter." Michael dropped the remote on the table. Plastic clattered against wood, jarring without the television to muffle it.

Tia was on her feet in a blink and standing toe to toe with Michael. "It doesn't *matter*?" Her voice stayed an octave high. "I don't know if time has made you a callous asshole, or you were gifted with the ability to not care, but they're destroying our lives. I *like* my life."

Tia's words and frustration burrowed deep into Ronnie's chest, squeezing with a pain she didn't expect. But what Michael said made sense. She rested a hand on Tia's arm. "I know this sucks."

"No, you don't." Tia turned on her. "You've spent the last several months hiding from your life. I helped you, not just because of what you meant to Irdu, but I looked up to you. An original who understood the rest of us are important too. But you're kind of pathetic. More power than anyone—certainly more than the great and mighty Michael—and you spend your time whining that no one respects you and hiding from the fact you got a third chance at life."

Ronnie wanted to protest, but the words wouldn't come.

Tia went on. "Irdu knows it. Michael knows it. Fuck, the guy at the convenience store probably knows it. So don't stand here and give me some bullshit line about how you know how this feels. I understand this will pass. That in five years or ten, I'll be doing something else anyway. I *know* that. I look forward to that. But if I'm going to live this life now, it should mean something, and right now it hurts like fuck to watch that being torn away, and don't you dare try to take that from me with pretty words and hollow reassurances."

Ronnie didn't have a retort. She'd spent months resenting Michael for running away from life, when she'd done the same. "I'm sorry." That hardly covered it.

"That's nice." Tia's shoulders slumped.

Irdu stepped up next to her and wrapped an arm around her, and she leaned into him. "You should get some sleep," he said quietly. He looked at Ronnie. "You know where to find me. All the way in the other room."

Ronnie nodded, unable to summon more. She couldn't look up. Didn't want to see Michael's face, whether his expression was one of pity or resentment. Couldn't stand to gaze around the small room. She wandered to the window and gazed out over the desert. It was her favorite place. Vivid memories of her first life and death were attached to those sands. And now of her humility as well. She didn't know how long she stood staring into the night, letting the accusations pummel her until her soul was battered and bruised.

A warm palm settled against her back, and Michael's familiar energy mingled with hers, soothing and clashing at the same time. "I have no desire to fall." His statement wove into the stillness rather than shattering it.

"Oh?" Ronnie couldn't find a better response. Her thoughts were too jumbled, and her heart ached with the reality of the day.

"Mm hmm. Once upon a time, I did. Before you came back, I was running on autopilot. I did because I had always done. When I met you and saw how much you appreciated the simple things, it occurred to me I'd surrendered my appreciation for life."

This was the last conversation she wanted to have right now. "Which was why you left. I know. We've had this talk."

"I was wrong to do so. Or rather, my reasons for leaving were wrong. You saw that, and I couldn't grasp it. I don't have to give everything up and intentionally shorten my life, to re-learn how to appreciate what I have."

"Neat trick. Can you teach me that?" What she meant to sound like a joke ended in a sigh.

"We can figure out it out togeth—"

Something shifted in the air, like a piece of steel wool wrapped her body and was then yanked free. Michael's fingers tightened against her spine.

"What is that?" She barely dared breathe. The air felt wrong in a way she couldn't put words to.

He moved away and nodded toward the two bedrooms at the back of the apartment. "Someone's here."

The feeling evaporated as quickly as it appeared, and she blinked several times in surprise, struggling to process the shifts in energy. With a shared glance, she and Michael dashed to Del's room. Tia and Irdu stood in the doorway but didn't enter.

Del lay in bed, looking like he slept peacefully, but there was no telltale glow. Ronnie swallowed the lump in her throat. This was like what happened to Izzy; someone took the cherub that granted him immortality. At least they hadn't injured him in the process.

The thought stalled in her head, and she realized no one was moving. She forced her feet one in front of the other, until she stood next to Del's bed. She checked for a pulse. For a hint of emotion. For anything radiating from him, to indicate he was still here.

Nothing.

"He's dead," she whispered.

Stomping sounded from the stairwell, and seconds later, a loud *crash-bang* tore through the apartment, like the front door was forced from its jam and rocketed into the wall. She met Michael's gaze. "I know a place," she said and grabbed Tia's hand.

"*Freeze.*" The command was in Hebrew. Several people in body armor filled the hallway, leveling guns at them.

Irdu took Michael's hand and then Ronnie's, and she phased them from the room, the explosion of gunfire echoing in her ears as a street in Omaha, outside a diner, replaced Del's apartment.

* * * *

"If your quarry goes to ground, leave no ground to go to." Irdu settled his chin in his palm, his fingers over his mouth muffling his words.

Michael pinched the bridge of his nose, knowing without looking—thanks to the flare of aura next to him—this conversation could in fact head further south. Fortunately, the diner was relatively empty this time of night

"I would give anything to be watching *Serenity* right now." Ronnie's voice was quiet. She sat next to Michael, but her arms rested on the table, so she could tangle her fingers with Irdu's.

Michael tried to block out the surge of grief and anger trying to burst from him. He grasped in vain for the numb calm that had been his consistent companion for centuries.

So many years of work. They all taunted Michael. Stepping outside the structure of heaven and hell to keep people safe. To make sure the individual got attention instead of being lost in the machine that eventually became Ubiquity. For what? He'd cost half a dozen lives this week. Close friends… He had no idea where Abaddon was.

Michael couldn't stop the hiss that pushed through his teeth. "This isn't helping."

"They really are destroying all our options, aren't they?" Tia sank lower in her seat, picked up her coffee, then set it down again without taking a drink.

"Shit." Ronnie sounded panicked. "What about Izzy? If they went after Del…"

Irdu clenched his jaw. "Izzy has to be all right."

"I don't know. I wish I could guarantee he's fine." Michael hated this. He'd rather see empires crumble than watch good lives end prematurely. "Tracking him down to ask is the worst thing we can do to him. I warned him. I should have done the same for Sandalphon." *Why* did he bring everyone to Israel? Did he think location didn't matter?

Their pictures flashed across the news channel playing in the diner. Nothing new. They were fifteen-minutes-of-fame celebrities. Between him and Ronnie, they kept a steady bubble of distraction around them, so no one would look twice at the group. The staff here thought nothing interesting ever happened in Omaha, and with any luck, that included suspecting the group of four were the faces on TV. "*Fuck*," he whispered when he read the closed captions.

Ronnie glanced up, muttering along with the words as they scrolled by. "The terrorist suspects were spotted in Israel, and are wanted by local authorities in association with the death of a local man."

The news flashed back to the anchor, who wanted to know how this was possible.

"Hey. Can we get some sound over here?" A woman in the corner waved a waitress over.

"Sure, hon." Seconds later, TV voices filled the dining room. The woman with the remote glanced between Michael's table and the TV several times, before focusing on the news again.

"We need to go." Ronnie's voice was low.

"In related news, this clip from the Luxor in Las Vegas was released to media outlets just moments ago." Every muscle in Michael's body coiled as he watched Ronnie, Tiamet, and Irdu wander into an isolated corner of the hotel and vanish.

"Ubiquity officials have confirmed at least one of the suspects was in Nashville moments earlier, which hardly seems possible." TV woman laughed, showing too many teeth.

Her colleague looked familiar, and Michael frowned, trying to place the face. "You know what they say, Glenda. If you eliminate the impossible, you might be surprised at what you find."

"I'm sure that's not how the saying goes, Craig. Besides, these people didn't vanish into thin air and teleport around the world."

"Why not?" Craig asked.

Tiamet said, "I can't believe the cameras caught us. How did we not think about the fact that entire fucking city is lined with cameras?"

Remote-control waitress called over a coworker and pointed at their table.

Realization struck Michael. The wards only worked if people didn't want to see. His group had just become the most fascinating thing on the planet, and everyone wanted to see. He tossed some money on the table and stood. "Ronnie's right. We need to go *now*." He kept his tone quiet and pleasant, in contrast to the jumbled mess in his head. "Outside. No witnesses when we leave."

"Excuse me." One of the employees called after them. "I need you to wait, please."

"I don't think discretion is a choice anymore. Where are we going?" Irdu took Tiamet's hand.

"Your place?" Ronnie asked Michael.

He nodded. "Yes."

"Meet you there," Irdu said before he vanished with Tiamet.

Seconds later, Michael let them into the condo.

"How is this better?" Tia didn't let go of Irdu's hand. Her aura spun like a whirlpool, mingling with her counterpart's.

Irdu nodded toward the door at the far end of the room. "Doorway to heaven. Which… if Gabe wants to find us, puts us directly in his path. No?"

"He doesn't. That's not the point." Ronnie sank onto the couch and dropped her head in her hands, muffling her words.

Realization spread through Michael. So help him, if this kept up, he'd start to see this insane double-thought everywhere. "He already knew where we were in Nashville and Israel. The point isn't to find us; it's to keep us hopping so we don't have time to react."

"Which means we can't stay in the condo long. I'm sure he'd love to have it blown up with us in it, to distract us." The exhaustion had faded from Ronnie's tone, and she sounded determined and angry. "We don't stay in any one point longer than we have to."

Michael nodded. "We have Abaddon's list. We pick out any names we have a last known location for." This was good. It was a plan. If Gabriel expected them to keep running, they could act before his people knew what was going on. "We split up the list, we seek, and—"

"Not destroy," Tiamet said with disgust. "I'm not killing anyone."

Michael could appreciate that. "Eliminate. I was going to say eliminate. If they have a cherub, they've broken the rules. Take the cherub. Send it and the demon back home."

"Why are you assuming they'll all be demons?" Irdu sounded defensive.

"I'm not. But only Ronnie and I can send angels home, so as we divide the list, we keep that in mind."

Tiamet raised her hand then dropped it back into her lap again, as if she realized what she was doing. "Irdu and I can't send anyone anywhere. We're grunts, named to work at Ubiquity. Not taught anything else. If Lucifer decided he wanted to call us home at any time, he could."

"He wouldn't, though. Would he?" The mask Irdu had worn since he arrived in Israel faltered.

"Probably not." Ronnie's reassurance sounded anything but. "He's a pretty textbook definition of a wild card, though. He knows this is all going on, and he's not stopping it, either because he wants it to happen, or because he thinks it looks worse if he steps in. I wish I could tell you that letting you stay here was in his best interests, but I can't guess with him."

Michael snarled at himself. Why hadn't he thought of any of this?

Chapter Twenty-Nine

"I can change that." Ronnie hadn't called on the knowledge since she was just Metatron. She hadn't named any cherubs since her return. But in the early days, before there were tens of thousands of angels and demons, it was common for one of the originals to name someone and have that agent serve their purpose and then move on. Back when being an original was more than a numbers game. God, how much things deteriorated after she died.

Michael studied her. "One foot in heaven, one in hell. Good point."

Hesitation worked its way through Ronnie. What they were talking about wasn't a big deal.

This wasn't the same, for so many reasons. Lucifer had always been the only original in hell, so this didn't happen with demons. Which, Irdu and Tia weren't the typical demon. And there was how she felt about Irdu. This changed their relationship. If she did this, in a way she'd own him.

Then again, he owned her heart, but that wasn't a literal magic bond. She met his gaze. "Can I talk to you? I'll give Tia the details too, but I need to speak with you first."

"Sure." Irdu shrugged.

Michael gave her a nod of understanding and agreement. She grasped Irdu's hand and tugged him into the kitchen, letting the door swing shut behind them.

He dropped onto a stool. "You got so serious. What's wrong?"

"Nothing's wrong." She paced as she searched for the right words. "We don't have much time, but I have to do this right with you."

He swung her to a stop, and cupped her face between his palms. "I know things are rough right now. Something tells me it's going to be that way for a while. And sometimes you and I clash. That goes with the passion, I think. But I love you, and I can't imagine not loving you. Whatever this is, you can tell me."

His words smoothed over her tattered nerves, and calmed her racing thoughts. She didn't know any way to say this other than just spit it out. "You know that when a cherub is named, that agent serves the original who did the naming. But there's a way to change that affiliation. For instance, an angel that Michael named, if they wanted, could *serve* me instead. I can do the same for you and Tia. I can make it so you belong"—she didn't like that word—"to me instead of Lucifer."

"You're binding me to you." He didn't look upset.

"It's not that simple. When it comes to you and me, I feel like it changes the meaning."

"This would mean I'm not Lucifer's anymore?"

She nodded. "He can't steal you back. He'd need your permission, just like I do."

Irdu kissed her hard, stealing her breath and lingering while her heart soared. "Of course I want that," he said.

"It doesn't bother you that in a way, I'll own you?" Relief spilled inside.

"You already do. I understand why you're hesitating, but we already belong to each other. If you can take Tia and me out from under Lucifer's thumb… I mean, I guess you have to ask her too, but there are few things I want more in this life than to be free of him." Irdu rested his forehead against hers. "Make it happen."

"I wish we had more time." To ensure this was the right thing. To physically seal the commitment—

"We'll get out of this, and then we'll have time," he said. "We're free of Ubiquity. You're in charge. We'll go see the world when this is over."

"We just have to get out of this."

"And we will."

His confidence and affection helped boost her mood. She nodded toward the living room. "I need to ask Tia, too. And then we can do this."

They rejoined Michael and Tia. Ronnie explained again what she was planning to do, if Tia agreed.

"If I do this, can I call you Mommy?" Tia asked.

Ronnie stalled. "Uh… Awkward."

Tia laughed. "I'm joking. Completely. But, sister?"

"I like the sound of that." Ronnie summoned a mental image of a ledger. Not because she needed to, but visualizing always helped her think through things, and adjusted their report-to paths. "Done."

"Just like that?" Irdu patted himself. "Are you sure you did it right? I feel the same."

"I'm certain. This will be a little more jarring." She took Irdu's hand first and summoned the knowledge she had about how to bind a demon to hell, so they couldn't be released without her authority. Sparks of black flowed between them in her mind's eye, crackling through her veins and passing into his mind, sizzling with the impact of shared knowledge. He tugged, but she didn't loosen her grasp.

When she let go of his hand, he jerked away. "*Holy fuck.* I usually want sex to go with pain like that."

Ronnie laughed. So was so glad he was making this easier.

"My turn?" Tia held out her hand with hesitation. When the transfer ended, she shook her head several times, as if trying to rattle something loose. "No wonder they usually do that while we're cherubs. Ow, my brain."

"I apologize if this doesn't make any sense, but what did I just see?" Michael asked.

Ronnie looked at him, surprised. "Same thing that always happens when we do something like this."

"No. These two, they're different from other demons. Their auras are linked, and what you did just now… Something flared." Michael was studying Irdu.

"They're—" Ronnie stalled. She looked at Irdu and Tia. "This isn't my secret to tell."

"Were siblings," Tia said. "And we used to be human, and Lucifer made us swear to never tell anyone, but now that we don't belong to him, fuck that guy."

Irdu filled in more details about what had happened, and Michael listened, shock on his face.

"Do the two of you share power? Draw it from Lucifer? Something else?" Michael asked.

Irdu shrugged. "Don't know. We've never thought to explore it, but as far as I know, we're enough like any other demons that no one's called us on it before you."

"All right. Cool." Michael didn't have anything else to add. It was fascinating, and he'd love to explore the concept, but now wasn't the time.

Ronnie turned to Michael. "Now that we have that out of the way, how about that list?"

They worked through names, separating them into angels, demons, and unknowns, and adding last known locations whenever possible. The TV ran in the background. Michael protested, but Ronnie argued that, if a media war was launched against them, they needed to either counter attack or avoid public notice.

"Ubiquity is offering its full cooperation to law enforcement, having denounced any knowledge of or affiliation with the suspects." The voice drilled into Ronnie's thoughts, like a familiar nagging she couldn't grasp—a sound she swore she never wanted

to hear again, and not only because the woman was delivering news Ronnie didn't like.

They each took their first assignments. The objective was simple. Four hours to survey the area, find the angel or demon in question, and determine if they had a cherub. If so, extraction and deportation. If not, leave them alone.

"We can't do that," Michael said. "If the names are on this list, they have to be detained until you or I can confirm where their loyalties lie."

Ronnie wanted to agree. Every inch of her said to listen, except that teeny tiny bit reminding her of the flaws in his logic. "We haven't vetted the list. Some of these agents are doing good things. Besides, Abbie told you Gabe is careless with the knowledge. Odds are high we won't encounter anyone without."

"If we do? If we see a trend of angels without?" Michael asked.

"Then we reevaluate."

The news never stopped. Every time they touched base, they absorbed more media attention. *"The individuals in question are terrorists; there's no doubt. We don't know where they come from, and they've made a campaign of destroying lives, directly and otherwise."* Ronnie stared at the man on screen, trying to figure out why he looked familiar. Sure, she'd seen him on the station, but there was more to it. Something she couldn't place.

* * * *

Two days later, with no sleep and forty-eight unsuccessful searches between them, Ronnie fought the urge to scream. "How are we at zero percent? Law of averages says… I don't know. But even if there wasn't an agent of Gabriel's in any of those spots, one of us should have seen someone. A friendly demon. An unknown angel. *Someone*."

"What now?" Tia scrubbed her face, but exhaustion hung in her eyes. For as much phasing as they were doing, spending little time in their mortal forms, they didn't technically need sleep, but the process was mentally draining. Their spirits sank more with each failure.

Michael straightened, his face becoming a stony mask. "We go again."

"Because that's doing us so much good?" Ronnie wanted to slam her head into a brick wall. It would be more effective than this.

"It's doing something. You said it. None of us have seen anyone with an aura, and the odds of that happening naturally, given how many of us are out there, are almost zero. That means we're close. If we can grasp *something*. Keep your eyes open," Michael said.

A sinking feeling formed in Ronnie's gut, but she didn't have an argument for his logic. "All right. We'll go again."

"Video footage willingly surrendered by U-View shows more evidence of both former executives involved in numerous attacks. Far more than originally suspected. Panic is growing in several parts of the world, after the implication that the terrorists seem to be capable of being multiple places at once. Past phone records and satellite tracking corroborate eye-witness reports." Ronnie wanted to

punch the annoyingly familiar on-the-scene reporter in the face to shut him up. Not that it was the poor guy's fault, but it would give her anger focus.

"The FBI and CIA are working with authorities worldwide, comparing incidents previously thought unrelated. One disturbing development all the incidents have in common is the lack of forensic evidence. There's no proof of explosives or other primer needed to cause this type of damage."

Ronnie grabbed the next name from the list, and they all agreed they'd be back in four hours. She phased into a remote corner of Chicago. It was five in the morning, so it was easy to avoid eye witnesses. If she was lucky, the cameras would miss her too. Irdu had tried to pinpoint the least likely places they'd be spotted phasing, but there was no guarantee. She pulled up the hood on her sweatshirt, kept her head ducked low, and strolled onto the street.

Daniel had a public face for a long time, serving as a campaign manager for several locals running for public office in less publicized positions. Michael had heard he was working on a campaign for the head of city council. Daniel always kept ridiculously early hours, so Ronnie hoped to find him in the office with no one else around.

A chill blew down the street, and she hunched her shoulders against the wind. She didn't like covering her wings, but at least she didn't have to wear the bulky clothing in the middle of summer. A cat darted across her path, bolting between her legs and almost tripping her before it vanished into the pre-dawn. Ronnie kept her attention focused on the building across the street. A storefront in the middle of a block of faded awnings and worn signs had a poster in the window, requesting that people *Vote Zeke*.

The lights were on, but she didn't see any movement through the expanse of glass. If Daniel was in there, he was in a back office. She'd wanted to phase inside the building, but suspected it had security cameras.

Another blast of wind bore down on her, and something in the air sparked over her skin. It vanished in a flash, but not before she identified the sensation. Excitement and nausea surged in her gut, and she extended her senses for the source. *Finally*, something other than a dead-end lead.

"It's true, then." Daniel stepped in her path. He looked like the same as the picture on his website. Brown hair cut short. A sharp suit without a flake of dust or hair on it. He radiated wealth and affluence. Literally. The uncomfortable aura slid around Ronnie, clashing with hers and making her want to go home and take a shower. But he didn't share the glow with a second source of power. He wasn't hosting a cherub.

"Lots of things are true." She kept her tone casual. "Caramel lattes are one of the best inventions of the modern day."

He smiled, uncrossed his arms, and approached her, hand extended. "That's an opinion, not a fact. I'm glad to see the rumors of your demise were exaggerated."

"Me too. Possibly more than you are." She laughed and shook his hand. The slimy power radiating from him set her nerves on edge, but she could keep her outward appearance friendly.

"Wow. Three thousand years. A lot of us missed you. It's really great to see you're back."

She wanted to fall into the pleasantries. It was nice to run into an old colleague who didn't call her names like *impostor* on sight. Her ego didn't need that reassurance, though. The realization felt good. Something foreign danced across her, muted in the midst of his slippery power, but distinct. Did she misread him? Did he have a cherub after all?

"I'm loving it. Whoever figured out roasting and crushing coffee beans, and filtering hot water through them is a genius. I hope one of you inspired that," she said.

"Maybe."

The crackle burrowed deeper, making the hairs on her arm stand on end. Instinct flashed through her before she named the source, and she shifted to quasi-mortal milliseconds before a ball of fire hit the sidewalk beneath her feet. Concrete shattered, shrapnel flying up to strike the buildings and nearby cars.

Fuck. Ronnie whirled and stepped to the side at the same time so she could see whoever was behind her. *Maalik.* Like Vine, one of hell's oldest.

"You've still got it. Seeing you move never fails to impress." Daniel's smile vanished into a sneer. The crater in the ground grew, rocks and gravel continuing to pelt their surroundings, leaving dents, smashing windows, and breaking streetlights. It was Daniel who shattered the sidewalk.

Maalik sent another ball of flame hurtling at her, but she was only half there. As the fire flew through her and exploded against a food truck behind her, she realized she wasn't the target. Discretion didn't matter anymore. The world knew she was out here, and these two were about to destroy the landscape and who knew what else. She blinked out of sight, appeared next to Maalik, and whispered the command needed to send him back to hell. She whirled on Daniel and grasped his wrist. As she met his gaze, knowledge snaked through her. How to do what Michael did. The information she needed to destroy.

"Gabriel read you ever step of the way," Daniel said.

The command hovered on her lips, fueled by anger and the conformation they'd been manipulated this entire time. She tried to force out the words. To rip Daniel's essence from him, destroy what he was or ever could be, and then incinerate his empty shell. When she met his gaze, fear stared back, as if he knew what was about to happen.

She couldn't do it. Instead she issued the command to send him back to heaven, then vanished from the city street as sirens sang in the early morning.

Doubt and a million questions assaulted her as she appeared in Michael's condo.

Why did she hesitate?

Because I'm not an executioner.

But he was blowing things up.

I didn't know his motivation.

The arguments raged back and forth in her head until she wanted to scream.

When Michael appeared in the room seconds later, she grasped the excuse to ignore her mind. If he was back early, he found more than *nothing*. "Well?" She wasn't sure she wanted to ask.

"He was waiting." Anger and frustration filled Michael's voice. "Flooded downtown Santa Fe in a flash. I nailed him, but the damage is done."

"Anonymous tips and uploaded footage are spilling into our website—supposedly just taken—of the terrorists at it again."

Why did they leave the news on?

"Irdu and Tia." Concern clawed through Ronnie's chest.

"Here." Irdu sank to the couch the moment he appeared, looking battered, scorches marring his face and arms. "Where is she?"

"Alive." Tia dropped in next to him, looking just as bad.

They should have both recovered and healed when they phased. That they didn't meant they were too distracted to make it happen.

"The station urges everyone submitting information to us to please contact law enforcement instead. What we can tell you now is that we're getting early reports of explosions in Santa Fe, Chicago, Detroit, and Evanston. Death tolls are unknown at this time. However, the terrorists have been identified at all places, and a new name has been added to the list. A former Ubiquity developer."

Irdu's picture flashed on the screen, and Ronnie clenched her jaw. "How did they get his name so fast?"

"They had it. They just needed an excuse to use it." Michael raked his fingers through his hair. "Even when we think we're a step ahead, they're stomping us. What are we supposed to do? We're the only ones who don't know what's actually happening."

Ronnie didn't have an answer or even a witty comeback. They were so fucked and out of their element, she was drowning in deception and conspiracy.

Chapter Thirty

"That's Asmodeus." Tia's soft exclamation forced Ronnie's attention back to the TV. That was why the bastard on the news looked familiar. He was a demon.

Ronnie scrolled through her memory. "Fuck me. Half of the reporters attached to this story are from heaven or hell."

"It's you. You're doing this." Tia sounded exhausted.

"Excuse me?" She struggled to keep the edge from her voice, but the accusation was ill timed at best. "I'm framing myself? Making my life and everyone else's miserable? What would possibly be the point in that?"

Irdu closed his eyes, flickered to transparent and then back, and his injuries vanished. "She's right, but it's all of us. How did we pick every single name we've investigated so far?"

"They're some of the oldest and most powerful," Michael said. "The most dangerous if they're really a threat and continue to roam free."

Realization spread over Ronnie. "Which makes them the most obvious names on the list. Those who have been around for centuries? Everyone knows their names. Everyone knows we'd know them. Of course we'd go after them first." Which didn't help as much as she hoped. It meant Gabe was a step ahead of them.

"The names aren't a plant. Abaddon didn't set us up." Michael sounded certain.

Ronnie would argue his logic later. "At least some are probably real."

"So we need to go after the people none of us know." Tia sat up a little straighter.

"Unless that's what they're expecting us to do," Irdu said.

"No. It's a list of hundreds." Ronnie sifted the information around, trying to merge and link it with what they knew. "It's easy for them to identify the powerful from the list, and watch and wait to discover our patterns for going after them, so they can ambush us. It's a lot harder to guess how we'll pick the lesser known. He can't cover every single base. He doesn't trust them all that much." She hoped. The logic felt sound, but she'd been wrong too much lately to believe it completely.

"Despite toppling Ubiquity stock value, the information giant continues to be the best source of information for law enforcement to hunt down these criminals."

"It's funny." Irdu's chuckle sounded anything but amused. "They're getting the majority of their information from anonymous tips and Ubiquity software. I never realized before how much we drive the world."

Michael's eyes grew wide. "We have to shut down the flow of information. They're using it to track us. To spread evidence of our existence, which is what Gabriel wants. We need to bring it to a halt."

"Now you sound as bad-movie as him. Dude, you can't stop the flow of information." Tia pursed her lips.

"No. But we can bring it to a halt. Shut down Ubiquity. Take them offline." Determination shone in Michael's eyes.

On another day, Ronnie might ask if this was a dream come true for him. She'd save that argument for later, though. "It's not that simple. You're talking about a site that can never be down. That's how many fingers they have in the world's pie. They have redundancies everywhere."

"No they don't," Irdu said. There was no hesitation in his counter.

She stared at him in disbelief. "Of course they do. They control the majority of the world's data. There's the hive-mind project they implemented with other companies. The underwater data centers. The open-source hardwa—"

"None of it exists." Irdu perched on the edge of the couch, concern and excitement warring in his expression. "Projects on paper that never happened."

Had Ronnie really missed that much? She couldn't have. "That's not possible. People would have noticed. That puts everything Ubiquity's built at risk. Just because you don't know where the centers are doesn't mean they aren't out there."

"People did notice. The SEC is filing charges, and it's not only because of forged employee records. Money was allocated that never got spent. And I do have that information." Irdu gave her a dry smile. "I spent months scrubbing your activity from the public record. I couldn't have done that unless I had access to every mirror and backup. I made an efficient worm, but it wouldn't work without network permissions."

"This can't be true," Michael said. "That would make the entire thing, all of Ubiquity, too easy to physically destroy."

Ronnie's gut performed a somersault. "Shit."

Michael met her gaze. "That's what they want. Isn't it?" He pinched the bridge of his nose. "They're pointing us toward destroying Ubiquity. They use it to propagate the information they want and then cut off the main source." Everything he said lined up with her thoughts. "Gabriel has a team of developers who wrote large amounts of that code. If Ubiquity doesn't own those things Ronnie mentioned, he might. He shuts down the news feeds, and he's the only one who has a replacement."

"That's terrifying," Ronnie muttered.

"Of course it is."

She gave him a weak smile. "I didn't just mean that, though it's horrific and—Tia's right—a bit evil-villainy. What scares me is that you figured all that out. We'll make a liar out of you yet." She tried to keep the teasing in her voice.

"Don't count on it."

"So we have a solution, right?" Tia asked. "We stop them from bringing it all down. Except, there's no way we can save every single data center."

"We don't have to." Irdu looked more alert than he had in days. "As long as some of the mirrors and backups survive, a couple of losses don't matter. That's the point of the system redundancy."

Michael frowned. "But how do we guarantee that?"

Ronnie dug through everything she ever learned, in either incarnation, clipping and rearranging data, discarding first thoughts, questioning second and third ones. Looking for something none of them ever did. "We put up wards on every location we know about. It will be tedious; they'll need to be reinforced regularly."

"We can't all do that for the rest of eternity," Irdu said.

"No. The two of you need to do that." Ronnie pointed and Irdu and Tia. "Keep on a rotation. If Gabe's plan is to have us destroy them, you're watching and waiting. If he's got something else planned, in case we don't act as expected, you'll find agents at those locations and banish them before it's too late. You'll need Raphael's help too. You won't split up. We don't know who Gabe's assigned this to, but the three of you are powerful, especially together."

"And you'll be doing?" Tia let the question hang in the air.

"We're going to the source. Samael. If someone is pulling the metaphorical trigger, it's him or Gabe, and we don't know where Gabe is."

Irdu hopped to his feet. "Right. So when do we get started?"

"As soon as Tia gets Raphael here and I teach the three of you how to cast the wards. No reason to wait." Ronnie didn't want to throw them into this, but didn't see another option. Besides, if she hesitated any longer, she'd second-guess herself out of any action at all. And for all she knew, that was Gabe's back-up plan.

* * * *

Ronnie's bravado vanished the moment she and Michael appeared in Samael's office. She stashed her doubt and apprehension behind the mask of a timid smile she needed for this to work.

"Ronnie." Samael was on his feet in an instant, and came around the desk to give her a hug. "I've been so worried about you. Not the kind of famous most people want, right?"

She squeezed back, forcing everything friendly to the surface, despite wanting to choke on the pleasantries. "I just want it to be over."

"I don't blame you. The media is shredding all of you. I wish there was some way to stop it."

If she could keep him chatting, it'd buy her time to figure out what to do next. She was playing this more loose-and-improv than she'd like. "You're so sweet. Thank you. I swear it feels like everyone else is against us."

Through the exchange, Michael was quiet. She was grateful for that.

Samael stepped back, to look her in the eye. "Did you stop Abaddon before she made things worse?"

"Who?" Ronnie wanted to yell *gotcha*.

He frowned. "We talked about it before you left. The conversation I overheard."

"Oh. *Oh.* I didn't know that's who they were talking about. I thought you didn't either."

Samael rolled his eyes and leaned his weight against the desk. "How much longer do you want to do this?"

"Until you get tired of it." She'd rather not do it at all.

"That was eons ago, Ronnie. I've been tired of this for centuries. Lucifer promised change, but that wasn't supposed to include idleness. Letting people destroy themselves."

"Excuse me." Michael stepped forward. "I'm wondering how you envision this going. Could we skip the bullshit and cut to the point?"

The chuckle that rolled from Samael's chest sent shivers down Ronnie's spine. "I hate to bore you, but we can't do that," Samael said. "There's protocol to follow, and your darling demon is all about appearances. She worries about whether others think she's strong enough. An original. Keeping her shit together while her world crumbles... You're a little harder to read, keeping private and such, but she tends to draw you out. Twice now. Being able to watch the two of you— I'm getting ahead of myself. You wanted a fight, right?"

"We were hoping you'd stop all of this, whatever it is, if we asked nicely." Ronnie didn't know if Samael was trying to provoke her into acting out of hand, or hoping she'd hesitate. Either way, she'd missed her window of opportunity. Frustration built inside, fueled by indecision.

"No can do. Sorry. For me, this ends with a big flash bang that destroys the building and causes enough destruction it makes news around the world."

Out of the corner of her eye, she saw Michael vanish, then reappear next to Samael before she could blink. Sammy had already phased to the other side of the room. As Samael reappeared, a loud roar and a gust tore through the room and echoed from the hallway. The windows shattered, and pebble-sized shards of glass flew through the air, impacting with walls, furniture, and bodies.

The tiny slices cut into her skin, and Ronnie devoted enough attention to the tens of thousands of wounds to heal them. Her feet froze to the floor, despite the voice in her head chanting for her to do something. Was she supposed to fight? Walk away? Try to keep Samael talking? What was he expecting, so she could do something else?

"Ronnie. I need you here." Michael's quiet but firm voice cut through the cloud of indecision but didn't disperse it.

"She's torn." Taunting filled Samael's words. "Doesn't know what to do next. Tell you what—you two stay here and talk. Coax her out of this haze. I'm going to the roof, because if I'm going to blow this place up, I want an audience, and I want to take my time."

The threat mobilized Ronnie. She vanished when Samael did, appeared above Ubiquity in a blink, and wrapped Michael, Samael, and herself in a bubble as the demon summoned his next attack. "It's the middle of the day." She struggled to keep her voice even. The impact of his attack hit her harder than she expected. "The building is full."

Samael shrugged. "Of agents. This won't kill them." He lobbed a fireball at Ronnie like he was tossing a softball. The speed it flew at her contradicted the ease of the motion, and it singed her skin as she ducked. The distraction made her drop her shield, and he sent a much larger projectile toward the building.

Michael blocked the impact, and Ronnie phased closer to Samael. When she reappeared, she collided with Michael, who'd done the same thing, and tumbled to the roof. Samael's next attack slammed into her chest, and agony rocketed through her soul, despite her being ethereal when he hit. How long did it take him to learn that trick? She shook off the pain and launched back toward him. For the next several minutes, her frustration mounted, as he dodged every move she made, or she landed in Michael's way.

On the ground, agents had spilled from the building. Most watched, some left. She wanted to scream at them to do something. At the same time, inexperienced bodies would make this worse.

It was the attention from the main roads that concerned her more. She didn't have to waste any time looking. Every turn of her head revealed another person with a phone out, filming the entire event.

"The longer this takes, the happier I am." Samael lobbed another stream of fire at the building, like slicing off a piece of cake. The concrete slid to the ground, shaking the earth and sending dust flying.

She pushed past her inability to quickly bring this to an end. "The only thing you're doing is causing a spectacle."

"She has a point." Michael joined in. "This could be a publicity stunt, to draw attention from the company's issues. It's not as though you can bring the entire infrastructure down from here."

"Technically, I can. The explosives planted in every single data center around the world are remote activated. We have an app for it." Samael smirked and sent another attack hurtling toward the freeway. Ronnie blocked it, and Samael countered with another burst toward the ground, but Michael was there waiting.

Something slammed into her from behind, knocking her off balance and sending her rolling across the fractured rooftop. Her ethereal form was battered and bruised, and the newest hit made it difficult to stand.

"Thought you might want some help." Asmodeus joined Samael. He was still in the suit he wore on air, tie loose but everything else polished and shined. "You're getting brilliant coverage, by the way."

Ronnie tried to stand, but her right leg wobbled and gave out. She collapsed to one knee. From this vantage point, it looked like Michael wasn't doing much better. She didn't know what to try next. Samael seemed to have an intimate knowledge of her skills and tactics, and she was out of ideas. If he had a second demon by his side, she and Michael were fucked. Even if they managed to take these two out, if the Ubiquity hardware was destroyed, Gabe won.

Damn it.

Chapter Thirty-One

This was why Michael worked alone. Ronnie's hesitation kept planting her in his way. She was holding back. He didn't dare do what he needed with her obstructing him.

He dodged another attack, mind churning with anger. Every inch of him throbbed with pain. They weren't doing anyone any good like this. Irritation surged inside until it threatened to tear out in yell. He forced it back, and an icy calm nudged his center, whispering for attention.

He and Ronnie had brilliant moments when they were in sync. Too bad it was once upon a time, in another life.

No. They'd found it recently, too. Not while fighting, but in other things. He'd just been doing this alone for so long, and she was filled with doubt.

He phased as a spear of lightning sliced through the air, but appeared next to Ronnie instead of Asmodeus. He stayed close. "Do you remember the first time I took Uriel to heaven?"

The Ubiquity corporate offices crumbled bit by bit. Samael and Asmodeus didn't seem to care what

Michael and Ronnie were doing, as long as it didn't interfere with the destruction.

"I'm Ur—" She frowned. Did she understand why he phrased the question that way?

The moment was seared in his memory. In his little corner of heaven, in a dojo he created to remove himself from the world, they struck a brilliant synchronicity for a few seconds, where they felt each other without looking.

Shrapnel exploded around them. There wasn't much left of the rooftop to stand on.

Ronnie tossed out another attack. "I remember, but I don't have that kind of focus right now."

"You need to find it." Michael dodged, and knocked her aside from the next incoming explosion.

"What you did to Vine. Was it hard?" she asked.

The question caught him off guard, but he knew she meant destroying the demon. "It's never gotten easier. I don't regret any of them, though."

She nodded and closed her eyes. Her chest rose and fell as she breathed deep, and he felt her—the shifts in her aura, her emotion through her energy. He focused on it, until it was the only thing flowing around him, and said, "*Now*."

He knew without looking that she summoned her swords at the same time he did his. He cut a straight light for Samael, confident Asmodeus was her target.

"Those might hurt, but they won't kill us." Asmodeus's taunt wavered.

Michael blocked it all out. The weapons were a distraction. He drove his blade through Samael's gut, and grabbed the demon's wrist when Samael doubled over in pain. Ronnie was doing the same with her foe. Her unseen actions swirled around Michael. He issued the command to destroy Samael's essence and incinerate his form, then stepped back from the abruptly empty space.

Ronnie landed next to him on the rubble, and their weapons vanished into piles of glitter that blew away with the debris and smoke. The rest of the world swam into focus again. Screams and sirens. The whir of helicopter rotors and the roar of fire. It was a simple act to extinguish the flames. The rest couldn't be wiped away with a mere thought.

"Damage control?" Ronnie sounded tired, but the surrender was gone from her voice.

"Not much to do here. See if Samael pulled the trigger, or if there's anything left of the Ubiquity data?"

She nodded.

Without exchanging more than a glance, they phased to one of the data centers. The place lay in smoldering ruins and was being swarmed by local fire and police, and no sign of Tiamet, Irdu, or Raphael.

"*Shit.*" Ronnie's curse echoed his thoughts. They traveled to the next, and then to several more. The scene was the same each time—annihilation. All the hardware was buried under rubble, and if Michael had to guess, in useless slags of metal.

His phone rang as they watched their seventh stop from afar. "Hello?"

"Hi. Um… sorry. I know this your phone, but hers isn't working, and I need to talk to her, and— Is Ronnie there?"

"It's Tiamet." He handed the device over.

Ronnie gave a tiny smile of relief. "Hey… I know. We saw— You are? You're fucking brilliant. We'll be there in less than two." She gave Michael back his phone. "They're back at your condo. They found the explosives in two of the data centers and reset the wards, but they didn't make it to the rest in time. It didn't all crumble, after all."

The news was more reassuring than he expected. For all the issues he had with Ubiquity, it had its role. It gave agents a way to acclimate to the world. It linked heaven and hell with humanity in a way not possible before. He intertwined his fingers with Ronnie's. "Should we head back?"

She nodded.

* * * *

Ronnie sat at the back of the coffee shop, hunched over her coffee, hood pulled over her head. As long as she looked inconspicuous—faded into the background, like the majority of mortals—no one looked at her twice. Colored contacts and a new hairstyle helped, too. It had been two weeks since Ubiquity almost crumbled. They were recovering. Her life in this world wouldn't be the same for a long time. She was on every most-wanted list she ever heard of and didn't dare phase from one place to the next unless she could guarantee no one saw her come and go.

Someone took in the seat across from her. A familiar orange aura and the faint scent of spice radiating from Lucifer. "I know why you did what you did"—his tone was pleasant and conversational—"but if you'd listened to me and backed off, this all would have faded into the woodwork."

She met his gaze with a glare. "No, it wouldn't have. I was a convenient scapegoat, but they would have done this either way."

"You wouldn't have been implicated. Blonde is a good look for you, by the way."

"This way, everything that happened to me was my choice. My world didn't change because I let someone else call the shots for me." She refused to respond to the hair comment. Whether he was sincere or not, she wasn't pleased about having to bleach the hell out of her locks. Irdu wasn't happy either about giving up the Kool-Aid red hair.

He shrugged. "Call it what you will. The rules have changed. You're on your own."

The rules *had* changed. It wasn't just having to keep a low profile as an individual. Even though most of the world still argued over what they saw, every day more people agreed the incidents were more than smoke and mirrors. The destruction had stopped, but other pieces of information were emerging. Gabriel's people performing *miracles* around the world to correct the destruction. It was a subtle move, meant to build trust in his direction now that Ubiquity had killed the world's faith.

She hated watching it, but it meant she, Irdu, and Michael had time to plan next steps. "Except I'm not on my own. I'm just not doing this with you."

"Like old times, huh?" His smile stayed in place, but it had faded from his eyes.

"I'm sorry about Samael," she said.

"I expected it. Water under the bridge and all that." He was lying about being over it. She wasn't used to being able to read him that well.

There was no reason to call him on it. "Of course."

"I'm glad I brought you back, even if you are a headache and a half."

"Are you ever going to tell me how you pulled that off?"

He shook his head and stood. "I haven't decided yet. I don't know when we'll speak again."

"Tomorrow. Next decade. Whenever our choices bring us back together." She rose and gave him a hug.

She let go, and he captured her neck with his hand, holding her in place. He searched her eyes with an unreadable expression. "Samael never mattered. Not the way he wanted to. I can't apologize for that. But you…" He leaned closer, his breath teasing her skin. "I've waited millennia for you, and I'm not surrendering now." He brushed his lips over hers so lightly she felt his power more than his touch. "Take that as you will."

She didn't get to respond before he vanished. It hurt watching him leave, and the kiss deepened the ache. Mentor. Friend. Former lover. She didn't like there being a rift between her and Lucifer, but something told her it was for the best.

Ronnie started at the table after Lucifer left, studying the scratches, letting the background noise filter through and around her. The ambient emotion she usually loved so much gnawed at her calm.

The air shifted. It was subtle and soft, but it screamed out over everything else. *Michael*. Since the fight, she was trying to make feeling him second nature. To keep her senses extended enough to detect anyone with an aura get close, but especially to fall in tune with Michael.

She made her way to the exit, with a quick detour to the cash register to grab two brownies. When she stepped outside, she didn't have to search him out to know he stood on the other side of the street. His nearness drew tiny smile.

They hadn't defined their relationship beyond *let's not rule anything out*, and her reinforcing that Irdu was in her life to stay. She was okay with taking their time and seeing where things went. Even having to live on the downlow, they had as close to eternity ahead of them as mattered.

She reached Michael and handed over a parchment-paper wrapped pastry, then bit into her own.

"Well?" He hooked an arm around her waist.

"He's out. We're on our own. I don't suppose that's new to you."

He steered her toward the apartment complex a couple of blocks down. "It is, and we're not. If it's more than me, I'm not on my own."

The warmth in his voice drew a smile, and she leaned into him as they walked. "Good point."

They reached the place they were renting while they regrouped, and he unlocked the door. She was grateful he was able to secure the place. Her accounts were frozen—as good as gone—and Tia and Irdu weren't doing any better.

Michael had lived long enough he not only had spare resources, but kept accounts under multiple names and trusts, to keep from drawing attention to the fact he'd been around for thousands of years.

Tia and Irdu looked up from their spot at the kitchen table, when Michael and Ronnie stepped into the room. The bond with Irdu was different now too. She didn't feel Tia any more than she did any other host, but the connection with Irdu tugged at her whenever he was nearby. It hummed under her skin and made her heart sing.

The next few months would be hard, adjusting, finding work, and staying off the radar, while they looked for Gabe. But at least they had a path forward, and enough access to what was left of Ubiquity to bring it back online.

THE END